'Powerful . . . Statovci is a tremendous talent'

Library Journal (starred review)

'Compelling . . . [an] important exploration of the aftershocks of war'

Publishers Weekly

'Beguiling, intelligent and tender . . . a masterclass in defining the soft spots which mark human vulnerability'

Big Issue

'A thrillingly unique exploration of exile'

AnOther Magazine

'A startlingly original tale . . . This novel's singular ingredients combine to make a strange but thoroughly intoxicating brew'

The National

PAJTIM STATOVCI (b. 1990) is a Finnish-Kosovan novelist. He moved from Kosovo to Finland with his family when he was two years old. He is currently a PhD candidate at the University of Helsinki. His first novel, *My Cat Yugoslavia*, won the prestigious Helsingin Sanomat Literature Prize. His second novel, *Crossing*, also published by Pushkin Press, won the Toisinkoinen Literature Prize in 2016. Statovci was awarded the 2018 Helsinki Writer of the Year Award.

This book should be returned/renewed by the latest date shown above. Overdue items incur charges which prevent self-service renewals. Please contact the library.

Wandsworth Libraries
24 hour Renewal Hotline
01159 293388
www.wandsworth.gov.uk

Wandsworth

Jeff VanderMeer, author of *Borne*

'A writer of brilliant originality and power, and his debut novel conveys as few books can what life feels like now'

ngs to You

My Cat Yugoslavia

Pajtim Statovci

Translated from
the Finnish by
David Hackston

PUSHKIN PRESS

Pushkin Press
71–75 Shelton Street
London WC2H 9JQ

First published in the UK by Pushkin Press in 2017
This edition first published in 2018

This work has been published with the financial assistance of
FILI– Finnish Literature Exchange

FINNISH
LITERATURE
EXCHANGE

9 8 7 6 5 4 3 2

ISBN 13: 978-1-78227-360-8

Author photo © Pekka Holmström

Offset by Tetragon, London
Printed and bound by CPI Group (UK) Ltd, Croydon CRO 4YY

www.pushkinpress.com

Da bi se jasno videla i potpuno razumela slika kasabe i priroda njenog odnosa prema mostu, treba znati da u varoši postoji još jedna ćuprija, kao što postoji još jedna reka.

In order to see a picture of the town and understand it and its relation to the bridge clearly, it must be said that there was another bridge in the town and another river.

—Ivo Andrić,
Na Drini ćuprija (The Bridge on the Drina),
translated by Lovett F. Edwards

I

The first time I met the cat was something so utterly mind-boggling, like seeing the bodies of a hundred handsome men all at once, that I painted it on a thick sheet of watercolor paper, and when the painting was finally ready and had dried properly, I carried it with me everywhere I went, and not a single person walked past me in the street without answering the question, "Your Highness, may I introduce you to my cat?"

0:01 blackhetero-helsinki: anyone up for some fun and
        games???????
0:01 Chubby-Sub28: mature dom—wanna chat dirty?
0:01 sneakerboy-jyväskylä*: . . .
0:02 OuluTop_tomorrow: skinny guy for meet?
0:02 Kalle42_Helsinki: younger in Turku? bj next week?
0:02 Järvenpää: anyone nearby?
0:02 Helsinki_Tourist: butch guy to fuck my face . . . ? NOW!
0:02 Rauma_BTM: porcelain cheeks need stiff cock. any takers?
0:02 Tampere_guy for younger: tampere
0:02 N-Oulu: three-way fun? couple in Oulu
0:02 Tampere_guy for younger: tampere city center
0:02 Cam30: chat / cam2cam?
0:03 EasternLad_btm24: HOOK-UP?? MY PLACE!!
0:03 VilleHelsinki: fit top/vers guy 185/72/18/5 looking for fit vers/
        btm guy for meet NOW

When Ville's message popped up on the screen, I stopped reading. An hour later Ville was standing at my door saying hi, and I said hi, and he eyed me up and down from my toes to my hairline. Only then did he pluck up the courage to step inside.

"You're good-looking," I said.

Ville mumbled something. His movements were awkward. He took a step backward. At times he leaned against his right arm and at others he held it behind his back. But I knew how to play this game. No, I mean it, I said, you're really good-looking, I was a bit surprised when you turned up, I'd imagined something else altogether, imagined everything you'd said about yourself was a lie. *That's what I would have done.*

"I can go if you want."

His voice was timid and bashful, as though it belonged to a small child, and he turned his eyes away and gave a somewhat demonstrative huff, as though he was trying to convince me of something. *I don't normally do this kind of thing,* perhaps, or *I only signed in to the chatroom on a whim, I don't know what I was thinking.* As though he wanted me to know that he'd already thought of everything that could happen. *He might have an STD, he could be anybody, he might hurt me, you never know.*

"I don't want you to go," I said and tried to grab him by the hand, but he snatched it away and hid it behind his back.

I understood him better than anyone else. Why would a man like him do something like this? Why didn't he go back where he'd come from? He was a successful-looking man of just over thirty, he had combed his hair back, and his handsome, angular face appeared from the folds of his scarf and coat collar in such a way that he could have had anyone, he could walk into any room and choose whomever pleased him the most. He took off his shiny new leather shoes and expensive-looking coat and hung it on the rack. His clothes smelled clean, his pin-striped shirt was made of thick, smooth fabric, and his jeans hadn't even creased around the knees, though they fitted his legs like a pair of tights.

For a moment he stood in front of me without saying anything, until the forced silence began to bother him and he slipped his hand around my lower back, pressed me firmly against the wall, and kissed me roughly. He gripped my wrists in his palms and pressed his thigh against my groin, as though he was afraid I might say something like I fancied him or that I knew how angry all this can make you feel, how I understand him and the world he came from: professional parents, I know, you can't tell them you like men, oh I know, it's not the kind of thing you just tell people.

I hate this too, all of it, I wanted to tell him, ask him how we ended up here and why it has to be like this, but that's not something to say to a remorseful man, because loathing is so much stronger than anger. You can give in to anger, you can get over it or let it take over your life, but loathing works in a different way. It burrows down under your nails, and even if you bite your fingers off, it won't go away. But I didn't say anything to him, because between men there are no questions. There's no abuse, no reasoning.

His long nails scratched my back and shoulders, his neat row of teeth knocked against mine; I caught the smell of strong cologne on his neck, the feel of moist deodorant in his armpits. He pressed himself tightly against me and wrapped his legs around mine, his muscular thighs squeezed at my sides, and there was a sense of determination in his rounded shoulders. How beautiful he is, I thought for a moment, and how lucky I am that he's come. His wrists with fair, downy hair, the backs of his hands covered in bulging veins, his straight, smooth fingers and well-groomed nails, the fitted shirt, its top buttons undone and beneath which I fill my nose with his scent, his collarbone propping up his chiseled pectoral muscles, the elegance of his tapering chest and the seduction of his waist, his tight but well-fitting jeans that sit so snugly round his thighs that the contours of his leg muscles look like they were etched with a blade. I thought, How perfect a man can be.

He kissed my neck in the dark hallway, and though nobody could see us, though we could barely see each other, I started to see him differently as he slid a warm hand beneath my shirt. I wanted to believe that I could let go of my inhibitions because ultimately we're all animals, we can't do anything about it, it's what we're programmed to do. And judging by the strength of his grasp and his short, agitated breathing, he thought so too.

He tore off his shirt in the hallway and nipped at my shirt so that I could feel the warmth of his breath through the fabric. I pushed him away for a moment, pulled myself from his hands; he staggered against the wall and stood looking at me with his

large blue eyes. Then I pulled him with me over to the bed, my
sheets still smelling of detergent, and I looked at Ville and forced
myself to take from this encounter everything I could. Now that
it was finally going to happen.

He took off the rest of his clothes and started to smile. *D'you
want it,* he asked, winked at me, held my shoulders, and pushed
me down.

"Everything okay?" he asked once I'd finished.

"Everything's okay," I said and thought of all the messages
Ville must have received after posting in the chatroom. And of
all of those messages, he chose me, because my message was the
most striking, the most desirable, my strategic measurements the
most alluring. Everybody wanted him, but he wanted only me,
and I loved that.

He turned me upside down to return the favor.

"Does it feel good?" he asked, his sharp tongue almost dangling from the corner of his mouth.

"It feels really good," I said and instinctively pushed his
head down.

"You're good-looking," he said.

"What was that?"

"You're a good-looking guy," he repeated.

Afterward the room began to smell. He and I. We smelled. What
we had just done smelled, our thoughts smelled. The whiff of
latex was on our skin, the sheets, every surface, it clung to the
air throughout the flat. The sheets were damp with sweat. As he
stretched his arm behind his head, I noticed that his deodorant
had faltered, and his breath was different now. Heavier, smelling
of meat and onion.

"Thanks," he began, eventually.

"No problem."

"You okay?"

"Yep."

"Good," he said and gave a cough. "I'd like to see you again."

"Yeah, maybe . . . Coffee?" I asked quickly and stood up even more quickly, wrenched the window open by the handle, kicked into a pile the clothes he'd shed across the floor, picked up the duvet, which had fallen beneath the bed, and switched on the lights.

"At this time of night?" he said, sat up almost startled, and pulled the covers over his legs, pressed a hand against his abdomen, and squinted his eyes, somewhat bewildered.

His skin gleamed against the bright light like a freshly roasted joint of pork. He scratched his shoulder and asked me to turn the lights off.

"Yes, at this time of night. Want some?"

"I can't," he said, seeming to judge me again.

"You'll have to go now," I said.

"What?"

"I want you to leave."

He stood there gathering his clothes as I went into the kitchen to put the kettle on. I placed a coffee mug on the drain board, measured two teaspoons of instant coffee, two sweeteners, and a drop of milk.

"Could you go, please?" I asked.

He'd switched off the lights and seemed to flinch at the question, at the voice that broke the silence, or at how quickly I'd appeared at the bedroom door.

"I'm going, all right?" he said as he pulled a sock over his big toe.

I went back to the kitchen, poured water into the mug, mixed the coffee until it was smooth, and tasted it. Then I poured it down the drain.

1

I proceeded with barely perceptible steps, as though I wasn't quite sure what I was looking for. I'd been there once before but hadn't dared venture farther than the entrance. But there they were for anyone who wanted them. You could buy them, just like that. Anyone could acquire one and do with it as he pleased. Nobody was asked to explain why he was buying one, or what for; was it a spur-of-the-moment decision or had he been thinking about the project for a while already?

Anyone could lie once he reached the desk: *Yes, I've already got all the equipment. It'll be coming to a good, loving home, a terrarium three feet by three feet by six feet. I've got everything it needs: a climbing tree, a water bowl, places to hide and plenty of wood chips, everything you can think of, mice too. I've been thinking about this for as long as I can remember.*

I could feel their presence in the soles of my feet, which were tense and clenched. There's no mistaking that sensation— the shudder that runs from the base of your spine and down your legs, that winds its way along your neck into the back of your head, the muscles as they tense until they are numb and unresponsive, the hairs on your skin as they stand on end as if to attack.

The woman behind the counter quickly appeared beside me. I was standing by the gerbil enclosure and looked in bewilderment—no, in admiration—at the creatures' complex silhouettes and wondered how they got through life with their stumpy legs and long tails.

"Been thinking about a gerbil, have you?" she asked. "It's a nice, low-maintenance pet, doesn't need much looking after. You'll have it easy."

"No. A snake, actually," I replied. "A large snake." I watched her face and expected a different kind of reaction, surprise or astonishment, but she simply asked me to follow her.

We walked down into the basement, past freezers and shelves of dried food, past cages and specially designed toys, past glass cubes of terrarium animals, cockroaches, locusts, banana flies, and field crickets. The smell of death hung everywhere, hidden beneath the cold-warm aromas of wood and hay and metal.

They were kept in a darkened cellar space because the air was damper and the conditions imitated their natural habitat. The door wasn't opened and closed all that often, and they weren't on display. Many customers might have declined to go down there for fear of stumbling across one of them. Their mere shape was enough to drive many people into a panic.

The snake department was divided into two sections: poisonous snakes and constrictors. There were dozens of them, an entire storage unit full of them, stacked one on top of the other, the bulkiest and strongest on the lower shelves and the smaller ones on top. They came in all different colors: the lime-green tree pythons gleamed like bright neon lights; the thick yellow-striped Jamaican boas appeared before my eyes like the tastiest cake at a banquet; and the small orange corn snakes and brown-striped tiger boas had wrapped themselves into tight knots.

They were in glass terrariums, stripped of their might, wrapped round their climbing trees. Some of them had stretched out along the length of the terrarium, bathing their skin in the water bowl and digesting their food. They all shared a sense of profound melancholy. Their lazy heads turned slowly as though they were bored, almost humbled. It was sad. To think that they had never known anything else.

"These have been imported from a breeder abroad; you can't catch these in the wild," the woman began. "So you can handle them freely, but bear in mind that snakes generally enjoy being left to their own devices."

An image of the place they had come from appeared in my mind, because I'd seen videos on the Internet of the factories in which they were bred. They looked like the back rooms at fast-food joints: full of tall shelving units, stacked tightly with black, lidded boxes where the snakes lived until they grew large enough to be sold. At the bottom of each box was a small layer of dust-free wood chips and a single branch. They had never seen daylight or felt the touch of the earth, and now they were put on display in spaces mimicking natural conditions. Do they ever learn that all lives are not equal?

I ordered one there and then. A boa constrictor.

The terrarium arrived first, and I assembled it myself. Its new resident was delivered to my apartment separately in a temporary box. *Where do you want it?* Yes, that's what the driver asked. Where do you want it? As if it was of no significance whatsoever, as if the delivery box contained a flat-pack bookcase and not an almost fully grown boa constrictor. I asked him to leave it in the middle of the living room.

For a long time the snake remained silent and still. It hissed faintly and moved cautiously as I prized open the lid, letting in some light, and I caught a glimpse of its lazy, clammy body, the triangular black patterns along its brown skin, its noble movements. As it squeezed against itself, its dry skin rattled like a broken amplifier.

I'd imagined it would be somehow different, stronger, noisier, and bigger. But it seemed more afraid of me than I was of it.

I own you now, I said. Eventually I built up the courage to open the lid fully. And when I finally opened it, the snake began writhing so frantically that I couldn't tell where the movement started and where it ended. Its forked tongue jabbed back and forth on both sides of its triangular head and it began to tremble as though it had been left out in the frost. Soon it poked its head out of the box, and its small black eyes flickered as though plagued by a relentless twitch.

Once it had slowly lowered its head to the floor, I lifted the box and tilted it, the quicker to get the snake out. It slumped to the floor like a length of play dough and froze on the spot.

It took a moment for the snake to start moving. It glided smoothly forward in calm, even waves. The motion seemed unreal, timid and slow but purposeful and vivacious all at once. It explored the table and sofa legs, raised its head to look at the plants on the windowsill, the wintry landscape opening up behind the window, the snow-covered trees, the brightly colored houses, and the undulating gray blanket of cloud across the sky.

Welcome home, I said and smiled at it. *That's right, welcome to your new home.* When the snake withdrew beneath the table and coiled itself up, as though it was afraid of my voice, I felt almost ashamed of the place into which I had brought it. What if it didn't feel at home here? What if it felt shackled, threatened, sad, and lonely? Would what I could offer it be enough? This pokey apartment, these cold floors, and a few pieces of furniture. It was a living creature for which I was now responsible, a creature that didn't speak a language I could understand.

Then I began to approach it. I checked from the reflection in its small dark eyes many times that I was in its line of sight, before slowly sitting down on the sofa in front of it and waiting for it to come to me.

. . .

And eventually it unraveled itself and slithered up to my feet, sniffed my toes, and finally twined itself round my legs. Then it raised its head into my lap, pressed it into my groin, under my armpit, and behind my back. Everywhere.

I gripped the snake with both hands and wound it round my neck, and as its scaly sides touched my bare skin, as it touched my neck with the tip of its tongue, goose bumps appeared all over my body. Its slow progression across my bare skin felt like a long, warm lick.

And for a while we remained there, sitting on the sofa, its head beneath my chin, its body around my body like metal armor, my arms extended to the sides, the rhythmic, tense, considered movements of its forked tongue against my quivering skin.

We will be together forever, I thought, me and it. We would never stop loving each other. *Nobody must ever find out about this. I will guard this like I do my own life,* I thought. I will give it a home, everything it needs, and it will be content with me, because I know what it wants. I will learn to understand it so well that it won't have to say a single word, and I will feed it and watch as it digests its food, watch as it grows and grows and grows.

PEOPLE ON A MOUNTAIN

As someone well respected by the locals in our village, my father assured me that love for the man with the beautiful smile and the stubble that barely showed against the light, the man whom I was to marry at the age of seventeen and who strode along a dirt track winding away from the main road toward a cluster of three houses, that love for that man would come later if it wasn't there to start with. And as the eldest of seven children, I trusted my father.

Because my father was like fathers in the cinema: handsome, western features and a face that narrowed toward the chin, a commanding voice and a military posture. He was loved and admired, a Kosovan man of the highest caliber, a man people trusted and valued, *burrë me respekt,* and his face was always clean, he changed his undershirt daily, he never allowed his beard to grow beyond a thin stubble, and his feet never stank, like those of men who have lost their self-respect or care nothing for it.

He was well mannered and handsome. One of his many good quirks was the way he always said, *Everything will be fine.* He said this even when he knew things were going badly, when it was perfectly clear to everyone that we were in for a long winter and that the pickled vegetables would barely last until April. Another quirk was his habit of stroking my hair, of smoothing and straightening any stray strands of hair and massaging my scalp with his long, chunky fingers. He did this a lot, because doing household chores had started giving me the same headaches as Mother always had.

My father didn't so much speak with his mouth but with his face, which was glorious and expressive. You never tired of a face like that. You could sink into it, stare at it forever. You could always forgive a face like that. He only ever began talking once he'd decided what to say. For instance, he used to say that the poor have the best and the most imaginative dreams. There was no use wasting time daydreaming if you were too close to your own dreams, because there was a greater likelihood that those dreams would come true, and then you'd have to accept that making those dreams come true wasn't quite everything you'd imagined. And that—the disappointment, the anger, the bitterness and greed—that was a fate far worse than never making your dreams come true at all. *A man should always strive for something he can never achieve,* my father used to say.

He told me that when he was younger he'd wanted to be a musician, to perform on great stages, or to study hard and become a respected brain surgeon, because his large, steady hands were made for detailed, painstaking work. Then he held out his hands and winked at me. That's right, his hands were like two sculptures, strong and unfaltering.

After getting married at the age of eighteen and having his first child at the age of nineteen, he gave up dreaming and began hoping instead. He hoped for the small things in life, fatted calves, muscular horses and hens that shot out eggs, a rainier summer, and the sea, because he believed it was the only thing that everyone should see in his lifetime. The only thing that truly bothered him was that Kosovo was nothing but a little blob of land in the middle of the Balkans without even a sliver of coastline to call its own.

Over time he learned the same thing everyone had learned before him: people from villages like ours didn't move to the cities through hard work or by immersing themselves in learning. That only happened in the movies.

I would wake up at five in the morning to take care of the animals on our farm. After that I'd help my parents in the field. The field was enormous, as we grew almost everything by ourselves: lettuce, cabbage, watermelon, peppers, onions, leeks, tomatoes, cucumbers, potatoes, and beans. In fact, the field was so big and hard to look after that it was no surprise my mother had had her work cut out having seven children in twelve years. After my chores I left for school and I was always home again by half past two. Each day was precisely the same.

My mother was a typical Kosovan mother and housewife. She was hardworking, good to her husband, and strict with her children. And my siblings were typical, daydreaming Kosovan children. My sister Hana was a year younger than me, a sensitive and emotional girl who always looked as though she had a secret that nobody would ever find out, while Fatime, eighteen months younger than Hana, was the polar opposite.

I spent my evenings dreaming. I would sit on a large boulder on the cliffside and dream, lean against the oak tree in the copse behind our house and think, listen to the radio and fantasize. Listening to my favorite songs I imagined I could have become a singer for all I knew. Or an actress. I could learn to act, I thought, and they'd show pictures of me on the television, people would talk about me on the radio, and my life would be so interesting that people would write about it in the newspaper, talk of my red dress would be on everyone's lips, my legs would be long, slender, and smooth as a baby's. Nothing would be impossible or beyond my reach, just as long as I made the right choices, and that's why I dreamed so hard that I was moved to tears by my own imaginings.

On Sunday evenings we gathered round the television to watch music programs on the Radio Televizioni i Prishtinës channel. These programs usually consisted of men sitting cross-legged on mattresses on the floor and singing, dressed in national costume: *tëlinat,* long trousers ringed with black stripes, a *xhamadan,* an embroidered vest, a *shokë,* a red scarf round their waist, and a *plis,* a white felt hat on their head. They sang songs about love, war heroes, and honor, and accompanied themselves on the *çifteli.*

We watched lots of films too, mostly war films about the partisans during the Second World War. One of them was set during the Battle of Sutjeska in Bosnia, when the Nazis besieged Tito's partisans on the plains near the village of Sutjeska. We sat in a row in front of the television, crying our eyes out as we saw what longing and agony can do to a person, and how we empathized as the partisans' honor turned first to patriotic spirit and then to rage.

But more than anything I was waiting for Zdravko Čolić, quite possibly the most handsome man in the universe, to start singing, or for the station to show videos of his songs. I knew every song on his album *Ako priđeš bliže* by heart, though I didn't understand the Serbian lyrics in the least. But it was the emotion with which he sang the song *"Nevjerna žena"* that convinced me he was singing about a woman who had broken his heart. *"Produži dalje,"* on the other hand, was a more upbeat song, his voice so much more self-assured that it must have been about something more fleeting and superficial than love. Only love can make a voice quaver like that.

When Zdravko Čolić finally started to sing, we all fell silent and sang along in our minds. I was jealous of his background dancers who could all talk to him after the performance, of the photographers who could return home and tell people they'd seen Zdravko in the flesh, of the male TV hosts whom Zdravko embraced after the show.

Then one perfectly normal day, when I was about fifteen years old, I awoke to the realization that I lived in the middle of the countryside, that I was at best an average student, and that I wasn't even a very good singer, though I wanted to be the best in the world. I realized that I couldn't speak convincingly and that I couldn't write my own thoughts clearly enough. I couldn't draw or count, because I found it hard to concentrate on prolonged activities. I couldn't run very far, and I couldn't cut hair. I was only pretty and good at housework, or so I'd been told, and after writing down the things I was good at I shuddered, because neither of them was an achievement but rather a self-evident truth.

I looked at myself in the mirror and wondered whether I was stupid. It was a hard question to ask, but asking it wasn't half as hard as the later realization that I probably was, a stupid and unimportant person. I didn't understand anything about politics or society; I didn't know how Yugoslavia worked or what had happened during the Second World War, though I'd watched all those films about the partisans. I could only barely remember which nations made up Yugoslavia at all.

When people on the television talked about the disputes between the Albanians and the Serbs, I didn't bother listening; the news anchor might as well have been speaking Chinese. What's more, I felt as though I lacked the potential to become any the wiser, lacked a teacher to tell me about politics, lacked parents who wanted their daughter to become a singer.

I'd spent my entire life until then on altogether the wrong

things—chatting with friends, gossiping about the boys, learning to do housework and cook food, fretting about what I looked like at school and at parties. When I realized the only reason I went to school in the first place was because an illiterate woman had no chance of marrying a decent husband, the bile rose up to the back of my throat and my food no longer tasted of anything. And when I realized my life would be no more extraordinary even if I got top grades in all my subjects, I started to feel physically ill. I had never heard of a single female politician, a female teacher or lawyer, I realized, and I gripped the edge of the table and took deep breaths through my nose.

I shook my head and began wondering what I could hope for instead of dreams. And with that I hoped that my future husband would be good to me. And I hoped he would be handsome, that he'd organize the biggest, most beautiful wedding anyone had seen, and that his family would treat me just as well as he did, and once I had gone through this list of hopes in my mind, I ran into the kitchen, grabbed the mixing bowl, and vomited.

Our village nestled at the foot of a mountain. The road leading to the village didn't run between the mountains but wound its way back and forth across the mountainside. On one side of the mountain the road was long and winding, and on the other side, our side, it descended almost in a straight line. My father was in the habit of cursing the people who had built this road every time he drove along it.

On one occasion—as he kept a tight grip on the narrow steering wheel of his red Yugo Skala and wondered out loud why on earth the road was so badly built, so that people heading for the village first had to drive all the way round the mountain—I bit my lip and answered his question, though it was never intended as a question.

"Maybe it's because it was built by an Albanian," I said and turned to look right at him.

At that he got angry. I knew he would, I knew it before I'd even decided to answer him. He raised his hand between us, as if to strike me, and pulled his lips tightly together. He said I shouldn't use language like that, shouldn't speak ill of my own countrymen, because Allah is great and he makes a note of everything I do for the final day of judgment.

But I knew why he was really angry. He didn't care for the road or who had built it any more than I did. We had spent the day at the Old Bazaar in Prishtina, where my father used to buy great quantities of wheat and corn flour, sugar, oil, salt, and meat. I always tried to give the impression I didn't care for our trips to Prishtina. When we came home I would tell my siblings that the city was a dangerous place, that the rickety stalls looked like they might collapse at any moment, and that the entire bazaar area was covered in thick tarpaulins, which brought the temperature up to almost 120 degrees Fahrenheit, making the air thick and muggy.

I was afraid that, if I showed him how much I enjoyed our trips to Prishtina, he would no longer ask me to accompany him. And I had nothing else to look forward to except those visits when I could watch all those city folk, those handsome young men, those beautiful young women who went to work and wore such stylish clothes. I wanted to be just like them, I wanted their lives, their clothes and looks.

I held my father tightly by the hand as he walked through the city, always dressed in the only suit he had, and looked inquisitively around me, though I was scared to death of accidentally tripping over people's toes. The stalls were full of wares—black leather shoes, shirts, trousers, an array of spices, fresh vegetables, and meats—and some stalls held items designed for girls and women, such as lipsticks, eyeliners, and pretty dresses. The bazaar succeeded in smelling of everything all at once, but in the baking heat the only smells that stood out were fake leather, tobacco, and sweat. Small flies swarmed around the meat, and the vegetables' skins were damp and shriveled, so that the vendor had to wipe them dry with a paper towel. All around there was the drone of loud, emphatic speech, arguments, the clink of coins, the creaking of wood under heavy piles of goods.

When my father stopped to negotiate with the owner of a meat stall, I slipped a few stalls farther on. I imagined I'd have plenty of time to look at the items on the stall, the tights and the beautifully cut gold-embroidered dresses, because haggling with a stall owner could take anything up to half an hour. Giving way always meant losing—even when it meant that the stall owner ended up getting more than he'd asked for. I'd be back by my father's side before he even noticed I was gone.

I picked up a small handheld compact from the stall table and looked at myself in the mirror on its lid, adjusted my hair, and turned my face from side to side, until I noticed that the stall owner, a man of about twenty, had been eyeing me for an unsuitably long time. I raised my eyes from the mirror, the better to see him. All of a sudden he winked at me. *Po ku je moj bukuroshe,* he said in a loud voice and licked his lower lip. I didn't understand quite what he meant—nobody spoke to little girls like that, and it was highly improper to refer to them as *bukuroshe.* The man lowered his eyes to my chest, raised both hands to his cheeks, shook his head, and shouted, "O-paa!"

I froze on the spot. My back curled and my shoulders hunched up toward the corners of my chin so that the small mounds, which had been growing on my chest for the last year, might be hidden. I gripped the compact in my hand and tried to pull the long sleeves of my blouse down, but my body wasn't listening. I began to tremble, hot sweat started trickling from my scalp, and my knees quivered like those of an old woman. When the man licked his lower lip for a second time, I dropped the compact to the ground. I crouched down to pick it up, and at that the man gave a loud whistle—and all at once the attention of the men standing at the surrounding stalls turned to me.

"O-paa!" he shouted between wolf whistles. "So young?" he continued and burst into a volley of laughter.

It was then that I noticed my father, who had left the haggling behind and now wrenched me by the wrist. *Pthui,* he spat on the items the young man was selling and dragged me bullishly out of the bazaar. The journey seemed to take forever. He yanked my hand, and in his rage it seemed he had momentarily lost his sense of direction. I stumbled over people's feet and apologized. I didn't try to resist him, but above all the noise I tried to apologize to him too, to tell him how sorry I was, but he didn't hear me.

When we came out of the bazaar the sun was beating down above Prishtina like an immense spotlight. I tried to commit to memory everything that I saw around me, because I knew this would be the last time I went to Prishtina with my father. The tall, ten-story buildings, their façades painted with white slogans. The men and women with their shopping bags striding past little children selling tobacco, chewing gum, and lighters on the street. Long lines of one and the same car, the Yugo Skala 101, the car that my father and every Yugoslav adored. The newly paved roads, the smell of asphalt, the small newspaper and tobacco kiosks, the gardens outside great shopping complexes, the old men sitting in cafés playing chess and *zhol*.

My father bundled me into the car, then walked round to sit down in the driver's seat. Before starting the engine, he asked me, "Do you know what happens after death?"

He started the car just as I opened my mouth to give him the answer he wanted to hear.

"I'm sorry, Father," I said and lowered my head. "I know what happens after death."

"Never do anything like that again," he said.

We drove for a long time without speaking to each other. The city and all its people fell into the distance behind us, and ahead of us was nothing but a long straight road with orange-roofed houses on both sides and behind them tall mountains that looked almost as though they had been etched into the landscape. Only once the city was long behind us did he stop grinding his teeth.

He allowed me to open the window. A cool breeze fluttered inside. The chill felt liberating, my sweaty forehead soon dried, and the sun's warmth wrapped around my skin and face like soothing music.

"I'll never do anything like that again," I swore.

I knew that making excuses would have been pointless, because it wouldn't have changed his mind in the slightest. For a long time he'd talked to me about how unfair it was to my siblings that he always took me with him on these trips.

If I'd had the courage to defend myself the way I would today, I would have said that after death we meet God, but that meeting God means the absence or lack of God, because you cannot describe God, you can't fit him onto a sheet of paper, into the universe. God is something so immense that his presence actually means his absence, and his absence his presence. God will decide whether or not to reach out his hand to the dead; that is the correct answer. God will decide where the deceased shall spend the rest of eternity, for all this, these roads and these trees and these mountains, this time and this land, are simply an illusion, they are a test in which, according to my father, there is only one question: *Have you been dutiful to your God?*

My father smiled and placed his hand on my thigh. It was warm and clammy; I could feel the damp of his hand seeping into the fabric of my trousers. The wind whipped my hair around my head; cars driving past beeped their horns as they saw my father.

I don't know why, but I thought of the man at the bazaar. Everything about him, his expressive face, the confidence of his gestures, his brown shining eyes, his masculine shoulders, what his short stubble, his strong hands would feel like against my skin.

There was a tingling at the bottom of my stomach, something I couldn't have imagined in my wildest dreams. I closed my eyes, and for the rest of the journey I thought only of him, and I thought of him throughout the following years, for after that I never again visited Prishtina with my father. Every night and every morning I thought of the man at the bazaar, until one day I met another man.

THE FIRST MEETING

From my vantage point on the boulder you could see the whole small village, its unfinished houses and fields, their edges marked with razor-sharp precision. Behind them the low-standing mountains rose up like soft pillows covered with dark-green forests. There were clusters of houses, small orange-roofed houses. It was my favorite place in the whole world, and I've never found anything to match it.

One April morning, when the sun was still rising and I'd finished my morning chores earlier than usual, I climbed up the mountainside and sat down on the boulder on my way to school. A moment later a car pulled up on a dirt track a short distance away. I couldn't see the driver's face. All I could see were his hands, his muscular, hairless, sturdy hands.

The driver craned out of the window to take a closer look, as though he didn't quite believe what he saw. He blinked until he finally plucked up the courage to gesture to the girl sitting on the boulder; she quickly turned her head and looked away. As if by design, a gust of wind caught the girl's long, nut-brown hair, and the sight was like something from a film in slow motion. And behind that hair was a face all the more beautiful: symmetrical, strong, and flawless, and the man clearly liked what he saw, as he began to shuffle his feet restlessly beneath the steering wheel.

"What are you up to?" the man asked warily before adding a smile that revealed his white, straight set of teeth and deep-set dimples, which the girl quickly peeked at and which she liked very much, though at this point the girl wouldn't dare admit it even to herself.

The girl quickly clambered down from the boulder, as though someone had discovered her secret hiding place, irrevocably violated its sanctity. For a moment the girl wondered whether the boulder would ever be the same for her, now that someone had seen her there, though the view down into the village and the girl's fascination with it were no secret to the local villagers.

"Nothing," the girl answered quietly after walking back to the road. "I'm on my way to school. Have a nice day," she added bashfully.

It was only a few miles more to the school. After walking past the car, the girl continued with determined steps; class would be starting soon and she would be late if she didn't walk more briskly, and she didn't want the teacher to rap her on the knuckles.

She hadn't walked far when she heard the car she'd left behind turning. Her father had warned her about this, she thought. He'd always said you couldn't trust young Kosovan men, that they stopped young girls in the town, at work, anywhere, and distracted them, dishonored them. *Për me ja marrë fytyrën,* he said, placed a cigarette between his lips, and lit it with his left hand while stirring a cup of tea with his right.

The car soon caught up with the girl, who felt too nervous either to run away or to face the man.

"Can I give you a lift to school?" he asked and bit his lower lip as he looked at her back.

"No, thank you, I'm nearly there. Have a nice day," the girl repeated in an attempt to indicate to the man that she had no interest in continuing the conversation.

The man drove alongside her all the same.

"Suit yourself," he said cockily. "This might sound embarrassing, but I think you're the most beautiful young woman I've ever laid eyes on. I'd like to know your name."

Her whole body warmed and her guts seemed to melt. With that the girl's nervousness lifted, and a few seconds later she turned to look at the man, still smiling from inside his car. The girl tried to replay the encounter in her mind like a roll of film, careful not to break it, for she quickly came to the conclusion that the encounter was perfect in every way. She had just been called the most beautiful woman in the world. The girl thought how wrong her father had been. Miracles happened all the time, and not all men were devious.

"Emine," she replied.

No! She suddenly let out a noise somewhere between a gasp and the sounds she was trying to enunciate and quickly clasped her hand across her mouth as though she had just said something she should not have uttered under any circumstance. It was as though the girl wanted to slit her name's throat and give another name instead, so convinced she was of what telling someone your name really meant.

"Thank you," the man replied, winked at her, and turned his car in the opposite direction.

The following week an old man arrived in the village. He went from door to door until he found what he was looking for: the house where there lived a young woman by the name of Emine. The old man asked to speak with the head of the family, and when he appeared at the door, the stranger explained that a certain young woman and a certain young man had encountered each other by chance and took a liking to each other, and for that reason the young man's father now suggested the youngsters marry each other. The young woman's father contemplated this for a moment, but when the young man's father assured him that his son would promise the young woman a decent life, food and happiness, enough work and a loving family, beautiful children and a large house, the young woman's father consented to give his daughter's hand in marriage without further explanation. The two men shook hands and agreed to meet again in a few weeks' time to discuss details of the wedding.

It was a definitive moment in both their lives: the girl's father ceased to be the girl's father and the girl ceased to be her father's daughter. The girl wondered whether everything her father had said about love and happiness must have meant something else, for once they had met each other a man and woman weren't always able to get to know each other in peace; they couldn't go to a café or the pictures first and get married afterward, and love didn't start when they first looked each other in the eye. At most it was a fascination that had started, she thought, but it was a long journey from fascination to love. And the girl's father shook his head and deemed the girl's ideas of love and happiness childish and unrealistic, because what's most important in life is not love and happiness but peace.

And so the girl's father took the girl out of school and began adding up his assets, and together with her mother and sisters the girl began preparing her trousseau. The girl's mother began telling her daughter about the wedding ceremony, making sure at regular intervals that her daughter was listening because, despite her adroitness at household chores, the girl often seemed so absentminded that her mother wondered how on earth she'd get on. Didn't she appreciate quite how many different traditions and customs there were, or that they differed from one village to the next? Or how important it was to keep your husband satisfied?

Eventually she gave her daughter a little slap and told her she didn't know how lucky she was, because only a few decades ago traditional weddings used to be full of acts of indescribable cruelty.

"Like what?" asked the girl.

About a week before the wedding, the villagers snared a cat. They kept it locked up, waiting, the girl's mother explained in passing as though this was a detail that didn't require any explanation. But because she wanted her daughter to prepare for any eventuality, she told the girl that in some places it was customary for the groom to bring the cat to his newly wed bride on their wedding night and kill it with his bare hands to demonstrate to his wife his supremacy, to teach her to fear him.

The girl was shocked at the story. She imagined the sound of a cat's neck snapping, what the cat would look like as the groom tore it apart with his bare hands, and how much blood would pour out of it, what the room would smell like after the killing of the street cat. The girl shuddered, the fair hairs on her neck were suddenly like damp wool, and she started scratching her fingertips with her thumbnail.

Finally, the girl's mother advised her daughter not to smile or get a tan, because there was nothing more beautiful than a serious-looking, pale-skinned bride.

2

I tried to convince myself that sinking all my savings into a snake, a terrarium, a climbing tree, a heated mat, a water bowl, and frozen mice was a sensible decision, though our first days together didn't go particularly well. I don't know what the snake had been fed at its previous home, but thawed mice from the freezer didn't arouse the slightest reaction. I placed them right in front of its rubbery snout, but it blinked its eyes as though it was far more interested in wrapping itself around my arms or my body. It did this from morning to night; it was following me.

After shedding its initial timidity, it slid across the floor like a block of wet soap and found its way into every imaginable place. That morning it had wound itself round the toilet bowl, in the afternoon I found it on the hat rail above the coatrack, and in the evening it had folded itself across the back of my office chair like a pile of clothes. I had received detailed instructions on how to look after it: a happy snake requires love, calm, and above all boundaries. But no amount of love and calm, no amount of boundaries could make the snake what it was destined to become.

I'd understood that snakes should be left to their own devices and that they would come to trust their handlers over time. It would acquaint itself with the terrarium first and only then begin to explore larger sections of the apartment; otherwise it would become agitated at the size of its new territory and would be unable to protect it. However, as I placed it in the terrarium and switched on the heated mat it started wriggling and writhing so aggressively that the terrarium's glass walls all but shattered at the force of its agonized spasms.

When I let it climb into my lap, it wrapped itself around me tightly, almost as though it was escaping something, and when I tried to uncoil it and put it back on the floor it gripped me all the harder, meaning I was forced to show it who was boss by vigorously clenching its jaw. It often hissed, and I always gave in and backed off.

It bit me. It would nibble the back of my hand, my face, and though I raised my voice and chided it in no uncertain terms, though I clasped its springy jaw, my nails white from the pressure, it didn't learn but always bit me again so that I could feel its curved fangs and the two tips of its moist, forked tongue against my skin.

A few days later, life simply had to go on. The time reserved for getting accustomed to each other, acquainted with each other, was up, and I had to leave it in the apartment by itself. As I walked to the tram stop in the cold November morning, as the ground gray with frost crunched beneath my feet, I realized that I missed the snake, missed its timidity, its dependence on me. And its appearance, its beautiful, symmetrical, zigzag patterning. Of all the snakes in the world my snake was the largest, the strongest, and the most beautiful, I said and watched as my words billowed in clouds of frozen air in front of me, because my snake had the smallest head and the slenderest jaw and the tightest scales, the most mysterious personality, and the thickest skin, which my snake shed faster than any other snake of its kind.

I stepped onto the tram, sat down by the window, gave a

heavy sigh, and closed my eyes. I arrived at the stop in front of the university and walked in through the doors of the main building. I opened the door of the lecture hall and sat toward the front; a few condescending nods from the other students and the lecture began.

The lecturer started by talking about a change in the assessment of this course; instead of a final exam we would have to work in groups, produce a thirty-page study of one of the subjects covered in the course. My stomach felt as though I'd just swallowed a stone the size of a fist, and once we'd been split into groups of four and forced to sit with one another I didn't introduce myself to the other members of the group but said I felt ill, high temperature, and that unfortunately I'd have to go home. *In fact,* I said, *I feel so weak I'll have to go right away.*

I didn't enjoy my time at the university, though I'd convinced myself that study was my path to a better life. When I was accepted to the university to study philosophy, straight out of high school, I imagined that's how I would meet the right kind of people and so on and so forth. When I saw my name on the list of accepted candidates, I was so proud and overjoyed that I believed it was something in which I would find satisfaction for the rest of my life. I would study cultural theory, history, foreign languages, and linguistics. I would become wise and influential, able to formulate coherent arguments in German, English, and Swedish. I thought that in doing so I would be able to make different choices from those of my parents, who arrived in this country and had to start their lives again from scratch. I would find work and achieve a good life, affluence and a decent pension, the freedom to do everything differently. And friends whose encouragement would give me the determination to do just that.

But the more I studied and the more job applications I sent

off, the quicker I realized that that doesn't happen to people like me. *Immigrants have to grow a thick skin if they want to do something more than wait hand and foot on the Finns,* my father used to say. *Go ahead, do as they do. Ruin your life by being like them, but one day you'll see that if you try to become their equal, they'll despise you all the more, and then you'll end up hating yourself. Don't give them the satisfaction.*

And he said this too: *Don't do your work too well, only to notice that it won't lead to anything. Why is it so important to get good grades? To sit up night after night learning things by rote, things that are of no use whatsoever? Is there any sense in that? Sitting up at two in the morning, your eyes swollen from your reading lamp, giving yourself headaches and winding yourself into a fit of rage and tears at such a young age, just because you can't remember words in a foreign language, the names of plants and birds and trees, dates, turning points, historical figures, equations, conjugations, eras, genres, terms for parts of the heart, the lungs, the kidneys, the bowels? I'll only tell you this once: never try to be better than them.*

I didn't get to know anyone and didn't have a single friend. I did odd work in shops and for a maintenance company, cleaning hospitals and delivering the mail. The chitchat I occasionally picked up in the university corridors sounded meaningless: everyone was talking about student loans and the cost of food and rent and badly paid jobs, income levels that were too low, dilapidated student housing, the dreary program of events at student parties.

I couldn't stand it. Each student was a clone of the next. Their lives were one way, mine was another, and their conversation was so painfully boring that I had no desire to spend time with them.

Don't people in this country understand how desperate life is for the majority of the world? That people die every single day, that they are thrashed with leather whips and made to eat rat poison, that bandits force their way into their homes, desecrate, steal, or burn their possessions, and cart the victims off to dark cells or work camps where they spend such a long time that they forget where they have come from?

I treated them with disdain, contempt, I despised their life-styles, their choices and problems. I rolled my eyes at them, openly loathed their public discourse, and laughed at the books they wrote. For what did they know about real life and real suffering? Absolutely nothing.

They even asked me about it. When are immigrants going to get off their asses and do something? When are they going to stop shafting the welfare system, lazing about, and harassing women? *Sure, they're not all the same. Like you, I mean, you're an exception, you're just the kind of immigrant we welcome here. But most of them.*

And I said it's because of people like that that the world is becoming ill. *It keeps coughing, won't stop, because it's got carbon monoxide poisoning from the filth you churn out. Imagine having to abandon your family, having to witness your loved ones die in an explosion. Or imagine being so desperate that you turn to God though you don't believe in him. You would, and don't say otherwise.*

And don't interrupt me. Tell me, what would you do if you were forced to move to a country that despises your faith and you'd never be able to go home again? If you had to learn a foreign language taught in a foreign language, how quickly do you think you'd be able to land a customer-service job? No, don't answer that, because I never want to hear your voice again. Don't ever speak to me again. This is it.

I wanted to punch them, grab them by the hair, and smash their heads against the wall or the table, push them into a revolving door or under a car, run a cheese grater down their sickening faces.

The worst of it was that I started thinking the same kinds of things as they did. I wondered what job I might end up doing, how much work I could do, how long it would take for my career to pick up. I wondered what grade I'd get for my thesis, I lost sleep wondering whether it would make more sense to work for a few years and then go back to my studies. And I wondered whether I should take out my student loan immediately and buy an apartment there and then, or whether I should wait until I'd found someone with whom to share the expenses.

After this outburst I was sitting in a tram wondering what to do with my life. I could always leave, start afresh somewhere else. I could leave everything behind, refuse to look at anyone or listen to anyone, I could change my name and get new official documents. I could have a nose job and get cheek implants to make me look completely different. Then nobody would know the first thing about me because I wouldn't look like anyone with those looks and a name like that who had ever achieved anything or ever existed. There might be nothing to leave behind and nobody to tell that I was leaving, but a fresh start, a clean slate would help me realize that I don't really need anything, that there were only a few things that I could never live without.

I could travel the world, I thought. I could wash dishes in Spanish tavernas, pick South African passion fruit on sun-drenched farms, look after stray dogs in an American shelter, bring aid to people caught up in natural disasters. I'd ask them to listen and look them in the eye as I repeated what I could tell them. *We will survive.* I'd take them by the shoulders and smile, and they would smile back at me with such power that I would feel to my core how close I was to the essence of life.

I started to laugh at myself. So that's what you're going to damned well do, I scoffed. Are you thinking of leaving because you imagine you're different from other people or because you think you're above them?

A young woman got on the tram and sat down next to me. She was beautiful and well dressed, her perfume smelled of freshly picked berries, and a strip of bare skin was showing beneath her all-too-short jacket. She pressed her leg against mine and pretended to look elsewhere. I turned to look at her. I could have invited her to my place, and she would probably have come. Or I could have reacted in a different way altogether. *What the fuck are you doing,* I could have asked, she would have turned to look at me, and I would have looked down at her leg, which by then she would have moved away. *Sorry,* she'd say absentmindedly.

I left the tram without saying a word, closed my apartment door, hung up my coat, and walked straight into my bedroom. I looked around at the bright white walls and my cluttered desk, the ceiling-high wardrobes and the snake, which had moved from the living room into the bedroom and had climbed up to the windowsill. It looked like a bunch of darkened bananas.

My clothes started to constrict me, clinging to my limbs like tight nylon. I slipped them off, huddled beneath two duvets, gripped the snake by the tail, and pulled it down from the windowsill. And little by little it slithered next to me, without struggling or thrashing, and eventually positioned itself around me like a protective wall, a halo, and it was cool and rough and its skin gave to the touch like a ripe avocado.

"I've no idea," I said after a while as I stroked the snake's skin. "No idea what to do."

I wanted to tell it that I was lonely. So lonely that I sometimes spoke to myself in the apartment, that every now and then I walked to the park, sat down on a bench, and spent hours watching people who had come there with their loved ones, and I wanted to tell them how small and insignificant I felt when they started to eat and laugh together, how it never ceased to amaze me how people could find a shared rhythm like that, and I wanted to tell the snake that all those years of loneliness had been so brutal that sometimes it felt as though nobody knew I even existed.

In response the snake turned slightly and slid its head across my chest so that I could see myself reflected in its eye.

THE SECOND MEETING

The man's name was Bajram, and his name meant "celebra-tion." He was a broad-shouldered man, his body was big and muscular, there was a masculine swagger to his steps, pro-nounced chest muscles could be seen through his dark-red shirt, and his hefty buttocks barely fit in his trousers as he strolled along the path leading to our house and peered around as if he was trying to locate me. Sand crunched beneath his feet, and the tobacco smoke billowing from his mouth hung in the air like a thick cloud of dust.

I'd left the front door ajar and stood watching them approach the house. My breathing was heavy, and I tried to remain as quiet as possible because I was afraid that Bajram or his father, whom I now saw hobbling along behind him, might hear me. My stom-ach was churning like a pot of boiling water, and my hands were clammy with sweat.

I had learned to believe that women shouldn't think things like that. I must have been ill or going mad—to be so excited at the thought that I might soon touch his skin or smell him, that he might touch my skin, that I could press my lips against his lips and wrap my arms around his powerful body. I imagined that if it was natural to think about things like *that,* let alone to experience them, I would have heard people speak of them before.

On the one hand I wanted him, but on the other I was ashamed of the place they had come to meet us. The flaking paint on the walls of our modest white house showed that we didn't have much. The incomplete building work on the house revealed that we'd run out of money. The large field behind our house suggested that in the summer months we lived on vegetables we'd grown ourselves and during the winter we ate the same vegetables preserved in vinegar.

As they approached the terrace, I snuck into the kitchen. A moment later Bajram and his father stepped inside and walked into the living room to discuss my future life. I hadn't seen him since he'd asked my name there on the boulder, *te guri i madhë*, and now they had arrived to talk about the wedding, which would be held on the first weekend of May, to discuss how and when I would be fetched and taken to him, what would happen through the course of the day, for there he was. My husband.

After greeting them I listened to their conversation from the kitchen, though I couldn't make out the words. I couldn't hear Bajram's voice; he didn't have permission to speak over them. He could only speak once his father had finished, and he was supposed to shake hands first with my father and then with me. He had to step into the house with his right foot, accept the cigarettes that would soon be offered to him, the juice and the tea, though he mustn't be seen to eat too many of the nuts, salted sticks, and *llokum* laid out on the table.

I was holding a tray with assorted savory and sweet nibbles, three glasses for tea, and two Turkish teapots, one with brewed tea leaves and the other with boiling water. I had tied my hair back and dressed in a black sweater and a long black skirt.

I wrapped my fingers around the tray and lifted, but when I noticed that the bowls were clinking against one another I put the tray down again. My hands were still trembling.

It was only then that I realized I would live with that man for the rest of my life, and the thought struck me in the side like a wrecking ball ripping through the walls of a building. My cheeks were burning as though someone had rubbed them with hot *biber*. I felt stupid, betrayed, cheated. What if we never learned to love each other? What would happen then?

The thought of living with him and bearing children tugged at me like an angry farmer pulling up weeds. I began to worry that I would be unable to live up to his expectations, that I wouldn't be able to give him children, that I wouldn't even be able to live by his side. I wondered how I would greet him in the morning, how I could tell him about my women's problems. But what worried me even more was the thought that he was just as worried. If he was thinking the same things, we would be like two factory workers thrown into an operating room and expected to perform heart surgery.

I swallowed the thought, gripped the tray, and walked into the hallway but came to a stop outside the living-room door. I gave my head a shake, cleared my throat, pushed the door open with my foot, and walked into the living room regardless of the trembling, and what a happy surprise it was to see how divinely handsome my groom was. Up close he looked much better than from a distance. There's nothing to it, I thought, nothing difficult at all; it's not as if I'd be marrying an ugly, hairy man. His face was smooth and symmetrical. He looked like a model: full lips, a straight nose, brown eyes like pastilles, shiny white teeth, and neat eyebrows. What more could a woman wish of her husband's appearance?

The passion, the attraction that I felt for him at that moment was something almost supernatural. How did love ever flicker into life, if not from a meeting such as this? I wondered.

My father was sitting on one couch, and Bajram and his father were sitting opposite him on the other.

"You are a good man for her, Bajram, the right man," I

heard my father say and saw him clap Bajram on the shoulder. "This is God's will."

Bajram watched his future bride, as was customary. He assessed the order in which I placed the teacups on the table in front of them, watched whether I handed the first teacup to his father, then to him, then to my own father, scrutinized the way I poured the tea, watched to see whether it was strong enough, whether I stopped pouring at the right point, at the last line, or whether I had been brought up carelessly, whether my mother might be *e dështuar,* a worthless woman who had failed the task of teaching her daughter how men should properly be served.

Once the guests had made themselves comfortable and sat down, depending on the time of day they were to be offered either dinner or tea or coffee with something small to eat, either sweet or savory. Before dinner began in earnest, guests were served a glass of lemonade, mineral water, or natural water. If guests were to be served dinner, before the meal the youngest women in the family—generally the wives of the younger brothers in the house—carried in a pail of water, a jug, and a towel. One of them would have a towel draped over her left wrist while she poured water with her right hand in order for the guests to wash their hands. The water was then collected in a large pail held by another of the young women, which she emptied at regular intervals. Or: when guests drank their tea from Turkish teacups, the cups emptied quickly because of their size. The women had to be quick on their feet and fetch fresh water from the kitchen. Tea should be poured generously; the women should only stop pouring once the guests said *mjaft,* enough. Leaving teapots in the room in which the tea was to be drunk was a sign of indifference, disrespect, and laziness, while pouring tea sparingly showed greed and miserliness.

Once the tea I was pouring was a perfect shade of brown and red and precisely reached the last line in the cup, and when I'd done everything just the way I should, Bajram squinted his eyes, gave me a trusting smile, and looked at me even more piercingly than before, as though he remained oblivious to how uncomfortable his scrutiny made me feel.

Stepping backward, I began taking the teapots back into the kitchen. As I turned in the doorway, I felt his gaze burning my back. Once I had returned to the kitchen and placed the teapots on the counter I had to catch my breath. I looked out of the window at my siblings running and playing at the edge of the field, my mother peering expectantly toward the house. She was annoyed that my father had driven her out of the house while Bajram and his father were visiting.

I drank a glass of water, and when a moment later I returned to the living room carrying a tray, Bajram was still smiling his charming, magical smile. I wanted to press my fingers against the wrinkled corners of his eyes, caress his dimples, stay there with him, alone, touch his arms, because I couldn't believe what I saw in front of me was real. Can a man really look so handsome when he smiles?

"How are you, *zotëri*?" I asked his father as he dropped three lumps of sugar into his teacup. I held the tray in front of my hips.

"Very well," he replied.

"And how is your wife, *nana*?"

"She is in good health," he answered and stirred his tea.

"And Bajram and the girls?"

"They are well too, healthy," he said.

"And the cattle? The field?"

"Very well."

"God's blessing."

He asked me the same questions, as etiquette required, and I gave him the same answers. Then we went through the same list of questions with Bajram, he replied the same way as his father and asked me exactly the same questions, and I gave the same answers I had already given his father. All was well. It's a good thing there were only two of them, I thought. Greeting everyone individually took a frightfully long time, and standing in front of everyone felt like being on stage performing a role without knowing the right lines.

After hearing my answers, Bajram turned to look at my father. I saw his profile, his angular chin, the straight line of his nose and his round head, and what an attractive silhouette they formed, but also I noticed how there was now something different about the way he was smiling at my father. His smile was modest, timid even. The smile meant for me was personal, he lowered his jaw slightly, as though he didn't care for the conversation going on around him. He sat on the couch, his hands on his thighs, and his forehead shone; he was surely as nervous as I was.

Again I left the room but stood behind the door listening to their conversation.

"You shall treat my daughter well in your house," my father began.

"Of course," said Bajram's father.

"Bajram," said my father and turned to look at Bajram. "I do not accept gambling or other women," he continued, his tone serious.

"I'm not that kind of man," Bajram tried to assure him.

"You have seen my daughter. You don't come across girls like that every day. What's more, Emine is good with her hands, she is hardworking and careful, she has been the answer to my prayers, and I believe she will be the answer to yours too," my father continued every bit as seriously, and as he said this I began smiling to myself.

"A good man works hard, and after work he returns home to his wife and children. And his wife shall keep the house in order," my father continued.

"Then we understand one another," Bajram's father said confidently. "Bajram has yet to complete his studies at the university in Prishtina. As you see, he is handsome, but more than that he is wise and upstanding, and one day he will end up in a well-paid job."

"I assure you, *zotëri,* I will take good care of your daughter," Bajram added.

"Good," my father said contentedly. "Because I am not afraid of prison, and neither am I afraid of death," he said, and for a moment it was so quiet that I knew my father was giving them a very meaningful stare.

I must be a hardworking, obedient wife to him, I thought. My mother had told me countless stories about the various reasons for which women were sent back to their own homes. One had accidentally farted while pouring the tea, one had neglected to iron her husband's shirts, a third had washed her husband's feet in almost boiling water because he hadn't shown her due respect. Such rejection would be shameful, the whole family's reputation would be destroyed, and nobody wanted a woman who had already been driven out of one home.

Then my father asked whether they would be staying for dinner.

"Unfortunately we are unable to stay for dinner," said Bajram's father, and they began to take their leave.

Once we had said our good-byes, held out our right hands in the all-important order, first to the oldest man, then to the younger men, after that to the oldest woman, then to the younger women, my father said he'd never met a family as fine as this one. He praised their speaking skills, their ability to take care of things quickly, the way that they didn't brag about their possessions though they had good reason to do so, and how their handshakes were firm and unflinching.

"Did you know that your husband's family just agreed to pay for everything? They even asked how much the wedding preparations have cost us. Do you understand what this means?" he asked and propped both hands on his hips as he stood on the terrace and watched them leave.

"What does it mean, *Babë*?"

"It means you are the luckiest girl in the world, Emine," he answered, smiled, and took me by the shoulder. "Did you know that Bajram studies Balkan languages and literature in Prishtina?"

I knew he didn't mean this as a question, for after he had said it he exhaled wistfully. For a moment he stood silent, listening to what he had just said.

"At the university," he added and cupped his hands over his forehead to shield his eyes from the light of the setting sun.

He sounded happy and smiled again. *A poor little girl like you. It's just as well you're pretty and good at your work; there's no other reason a fine family like that would have you,* was what he was probably thinking.

"Did you hear that, Emine? The university," he repeated and shook his head in disbelief. "You can wake up next to him every morning and share every day with him."

At that I smiled too.

My father then went off to fetch the engagement presents they had brought and shouted to everyone to gather in the living room. There were clothes for everyone: smart shirts for my father and sweaters for my mother, shoes and socks for my siblings. Eventually my father laid a dress and two sweaters in my arms, fastened a silver pendant round my neck, and placed an engagement ring in the palm of my hand.

I slipped it onto the ring finger of my right hand, and it fit perfectly, the most beautiful ring I had ever seen. All day long I fingered the pendant, and just as many times as I touched the pendant I touched the ring too, took it off and slipped it back on again.

3

Most of the time I think of my father's absence with a sense of indifference. He never really got to know me, I imagine, and I never got to know him. There was too little time; we glided past each other like distant acquaintances. If he knew me now, I imagine he would introduce me to his friends, show me off like a trophy. I would sit next to him, he would place his arm round my shoulders, and as for me, I would smile at the sight of his smile, I would smile so broadly that my face muscles would start to ache.

Sometimes I'm so angry that I wonder how it's possible for someone to carry this much anger inside. It's like a beast bound up in a straitjacket, tearing at the jacket's fabric and loosening its straps, hurling all the books from the bookshelf and breaking the furniture and the dishes by throwing them against the wall before forcing itself into an ice-cold shower. Then suddenly, out of nowhere there's more, and eventually there's so much anger that it feels like I'm choking on it. It's so dense, teeth that want to break as I clamp my jaws together long and hard, hands that clench into fists with such power that my fingers go numb, food stuck in my throat that comes flying out again.

Sometimes his absence doesn't feel bad at all, like a bowling ball resting on my stomach or my muscles wasting away from sitting still too much.

At its worst his absence can be sensed at night, the nights I spend awake from start to finish because I'm so bitter that my whole body feels about to burst into flame.

Sometimes I miss him, his voice, and sometimes I can barely remember what he looked like. Then I have to pull the photographs out of the drawer in the hallway, and each time I take them out I refuse to look at them. I only glance at them because I don't want to see him after all, and when I still find myself thinking about him, dreaming of his presence, I do something else altogether, put the photographs back into the drawer and clean or read or go for a run.

And still he manages to push his way in between the lines, in particular words, in the letters in both his name and mine, and he jogs alongside me, jumping across my steps, he is there when neither of my feet are touching the ground, and when I wash up the same glass so long that it cracks, he is there in the cut on my hand spitting blood down the drain.

In its simplest form, his absence comes as tears. Sometimes there's only a little bit, my eyelids moisten when I remember something insignificant about him, like the fact that he always wanted to watch all the TV advertisements and wouldn't change the channel for their duration. But sometimes there are lots of tears. At times like that I can't leave my apartment, and though I try as hard as I can to make it stop, it won't stop, because then I'll remember something important about him, like the night when he came into my room and told me he was dying.

He knelt down, gripped my shoulders, and told me to wake up. And I looked at my father but couldn't see his face because he pressed it against my chest and wrapped his arms ever tighter around me, and I asked him what was wrong and he began to cry, and then I asked him when, when are you going to die and why, and his body began to tremble in time with his limp sobs.

"I have lung cancer," he said and blew his nose. "I found out today. I only have a few months, a year if I'm lucky."

I looked at him through tired eyes, and at first I couldn't understand quite what these words meant. I can't remember how long I looked at him, but I remember that I didn't say anything to him. At some point he stood up, dried his eyes on his shirt, and made to leave the room. *But this is between you and me, it's our secret, you mustn't tell anybody,* he said after a moment. *I had to tell somebody, because otherwise I don't think I can cope. I don't want to die alone. But you're not to tell anybody, is that clear?*

"You are the strongest of us all, I know it, I can see it in you. And I need you now," he said and switched on the lights. "Did you hear me?" he continued. "I need you now more than ever before."

"I heard," I said and pressed my wrists against my eyes.

Then he turned off the lights and left the room.

And I began waiting for his heart to stop beating. I watched him, constantly offered him cigarettes and made him sandwiches with plenty of margarine and salt, and I never told anyone about his approaching death, neither my siblings nor my mother. And though my father coughed in front of us as sharply as though he were about to draw his last breath, I wanted him to enjoy his final months. And I waited and waited, I waited months and eventually I turned twelve, then I waited another year and turned thirteen, then I waited another year, and a third, but it never happened. The day never came.

Instead there are days that don't feel like days at all but simply relics of what was once his presence in our lives, because people like my father get to live forever.

THE HOUSE ON THE LEFT

On the day before the first day of my wedding celebrations, Thursday the first of May, given the circumstances I awoke surprisingly calm on the threadbare, yellow-brown sofa in the living room, which at night became a bed for me and my sister Fatime. My parents slept in their own room, my three brothers had their own room, and the four of us girls slept in the living room.

More than anything our house was impractical. Kosovan homes were not designed to meet the needs of their inhabitants; quite the opposite. There were no beds, only mattresses folded on the floor to form couches or sofa beds one after the other. There was no kitchen, only a room with logs, a wooden stove, and cupboards where we locked away even the few items we used every single day: brushes, napkins, pots, and oven trays. Leaning against one of the walls was a *sofra,* a low round dining table that we rolled into the living room with each meal and sat on the floor around it.

According to my mother, a Kosovan home should always look tidy and shouldn't look lived in. There were two rules of thumb: the house should be tidy enough to photograph at any time should anyone walk in, and second the house should echo.

In a way a home was a reflection of its hostess: a tidy home made a woman whole and made a girl a woman. In a clean home there were no secrets.

American homes were my favorites. The magazines on the shelves at Mehmet's village store, in particular *Kosovarja,* were like train tickets to far-off places. I turned their pages, pored over the images of all those homes that adapted to the needs of their inhabitants. I dreamed of a shower that ran hot water, of appliances to take care of the dishes and the laundry, of wooden flooring and venetian blinds, of another life. I dreamed I lived in a country where homes were large and beautiful. I dreamed of a kitchen full of pots and ladles, a place where life was on display and where there was nothing to hide, of couches that were just couches. I dreamed of floors that didn't need to be covered in rugs and where people didn't sit on them to eat, of dishes laid out on a high dining table around which people sat to enjoy their meal.

We cleaned the house every day, because a cluttered house was *marrë,* and no self-respecting person wanted to bring shame on his or her family by living in an untidy house. Even houses had face that they mustn't lose. It was a matter of honor. An Albanian is prepared to die to preserve his honor and keep himself from losing face, because losing face was a fate many times worse than death. This was something the other Yugoslavian nations didn't always appreciate. A girl found indulging in inappropriate behavior or a boy caught gambling and drinking alcohol would permanently scar the family's reputation, which people would often salvage by evicting the culprit from the home. Albanians refused to feel any form of shame. They would rather flee from it, run to the ends of the earth, while at the same time dedicating their lives to showing that they had nothing to be ashamed of in the first place.

· · ·

I woke early, prepared my share of the breakfast, and for the last time walked the half mile to Mehmet's store, which stood by a large, rusted bus shelter on the main road running through the village. Anxiously I thought of the coming days; I went over the order of events in my mind and prayed I'd be able to do everything at just the right moment.

Set up in an old warehouse building, the store sold tobacco, spices, flour, frozen meat, and little else. In the summer months there were vegetables for sale. Along one of the walls was a set of small shelves reserved for sweets, savory treats, and preserves. It was sweets we craved the most but could afford the least, but this time, for once, I had some money because my father had given me five dinars to celebrate the wedding. *Buy yourself something sweet,* he'd said.

On the top shelf were large boxes of confectionaries adorned with pictures of beautiful women, while on the lower shelves there were cartons of juice and bottles of lemonade. Each time he visited Prishtina, Mehmet bought one copy of every newspaper and magazine. Customers were allowed to read the magazines as long as they bought something else.

I stuffed a bag of sweets beneath my arm, picked up a jar of fruit jam, a box of chocolates, a bottle of lemonade, and the latest edition of *Kosovarja*. My cousin Mehmet, the thirty-year-old owner of the house next door who, as the only son in the family, had inherited the store, the house, and five acres of land from his father only a few years ago, congratulated me from behind the counter.

I slid the money across the tabletop. As I nervously gripped the new *Kosovarja,* he chuckled at my absentmindedness, as I'd only put the jar of jam into the plastic bag dangling from my fingers.

Through the store window I looked at my own house standing shy and almost apologetic at the edge of the green field and held the magazine open beneath the panorama outside. I realized that I was ashamed of the house. Why on earth would Bajram fall for the daughter of a poor small family? I wondered. What could I possibly give him?

The first floor of the house, with an identical layout to that of the ground floor, was still unfinished. And the third. My father had never gotten round to buying windows, doors, or floorboards for the upper stories, though he'd been talking about renovating the house and getting the job finished for what seemed like an eternity. On the upper floors there was nothing except the walls.

One floor for each son, he'd said and given my brothers a victorious, self-satisfied smile. They would bring wives into the house, and each would settle on his own floor, have children, and look after him and my mother, and thus they would be able to grow old and die with dignity.

I leafed through the magazine, its black-and-white pictures of brand-new ovens whose temperature could be adjusted as needed; I read columns about knives so sharp you could use them to cut wood and articles with illustrations of men watering the small gardens outside their beautiful houses while their wife and daughter hugged each other in the background.

I folded the magazine, handed it back to Mehmet, and put the rest of my purchases in the plastic bag. I walked home slowly. The sun squeezed its way between the great mountains, turning the green leaves orange and the gray earth yellow, and the chocolates I picked out of the box melted in my mouth like nut butter. I had enough sweets to last me all evening, I thought, and licked my lips.

4

I met the cat in a bar. And he wasn't just any cat, the kind of cat that likes toy mice or climbing trees or feather dusters, not at all, but entirely different from any cat I'd ever met.

I noticed the cat across the dance floor, somewhere between two bar counters and behind a couple of turned backs. He loped contentedly from one place to the other, chatting to acquaintances in order to maintain a smooth, balanced social life. I had never seen anything so enchanting, so alluring. He was a perfect cat with black-and-white stripes. His soft fur gleamed in the dim lights of the bar as though it had just been greased, and he was standing, firm and upright, on his two muscular back legs.

Then the cat noticed me; he started smiling at me and I started smiling at him, then he raised his front paw to the top button of his shirt, unbuttoned it, and began walking toward me.

It wasn't long before he was standing in front of me in all his handsome glory. It was as if the cat had got my tongue and at first I was unable to speak at all. The famous hits of yester-year were playing in the background, and the cat clearly felt an affinity with the lyrics, as he was singing along to songs by Tina Turner and Cher with such gusto that I thought he might burst with the force of his own memories.

Give me a lifetime of promises and a world of dreams
Speak the language of love like you know what it means

And then:

Do you believe in life after love?
I really don't think you're strong enough.

The cat leaned his head back and grinned so widely that his chin formed three different chins. The expression on his face was as dramatic and fateful as that of an opera singer arriving at a climax: his eyes had creased shut, his mouth was wide open as though he were about to sneeze, and his knees bobbed in time with the chorus from "Believe." One paw was clenched to his heart and the other reached out as if to take a lost lover by the hand.

After praising his extraordinary rendition, I looked him in the eyes and smiled.

"I know," he began. "Nothing short of astonishing, isn't it?"

The cat's white stripes shone in the dark, and the flashing of the strobe lighting sometimes made him disappear altogether, as though he weren't there at all. The cat was such a wonderful, beautiful, gifted interpreter that I took him in my arms without waiting for any indication to do so, and straightaway I noticed that his silky smooth fur smelled good and that his body was muscular from top to tail. The mere sensation of touching it was so magical that, goodness me, I needn't have touched anything ever again.

In a flash the cat bounded back onto the dance floor, leaving my arms momentarily embracing nothing but thin air.

I prowled round the bar a few times and started to get agitated. I realized I wanted the cat so much that I'd already decided I would have him. My upper lip tensed, my head was pounding, and my focus sharpened. And just then his magnificent, arched back appeared from round a corner, his long black tail wagged up and down, and he stepped forward as though he were stalking fresh prey.

The cat stopped a short way away. He peered discreetly—seductively—over his shoulder and looked me right in the eyes. With his front paw, he gestured for me to follow him, winked at me like the other men in the bar, and disappeared once again round the corner.

At his command I began following him, and before long I was standing right behind him, and I felt like saying what a beautiful cat he was, a truly wonderful kitty cat. After walking across the corridor, the cat found a free table. It was one thirty in the morning, music was blaring, and the dance floors were crammed with party animals. The cat leaped onto a sofa and settled himself by the table with a look of pride: his eyes were closed and his stately head slanted up toward the ceiling in a truly aristocratic pose. When I sat down on the sofa beside him, he made room for me but still didn't look at me directly.

"Well, well," he quipped, nonchalantly scratching his chin. Suddenly he was wearing glasses, of course. "And who have we here?"

I mumbled something indistinct, stumbled over my words and stammered. Eventually I managed to spit it out, told him we'd just met, *over there, on the dance floor, you hugged me and I hugged you, do you remember?*

"You look positively awful," he exclaimed in grandiose fashion. "I don't know you and I certainly didn't hug you, *pthui,*" he said as though spitting in the other direction. "A brute like you."

I was so shocked by the cat's judgmental manner that all I could do was sit quietly next to him.

"Come on, *ha ha*—that was a joke, you idiot! We don't *know* one another, so don't talk as if we did," the cat reprimanded me.

"But we can get to know one another, *ha ha;* I'm open to suggestions. Do you want to get to know me or not?"

As soon as I said yes, the cat wanted to know things. Everyday things: my name, my date of birth. And I told him my name, and he said he'd never heard such an odd name, such a *frightful name,* he continued, *utterly dreadful, ha ha,* laughed the cat. *Bekim. It's such a dreadful name I'm sure I never want to hear it again!*

Only now did the cat turn his head toward me, peer through his narrowed cat's eyes, and find a face for the name he found so disagreeable, ears and eyes, a mouth and body. He crossed his legs, all the while brazenly gawping at me, and started guffawing, his mouth set in a grimace.

"Nomen est omen," he said. "Did you know that? The name is an omen, *ha ha*."

Of course I'd heard that, I told him, it's just a collection of letters and, by the way, my name means "blessing." But before I could continue, the cat burst into a volley of such raucous laughter that I could no longer think anything at all, and he rolled and writhed on the spot without trying to control himself in the slightest.

"Well, in that case it's the worst possible name you could have!" shouted the cat through the roar of his laughter.

"Well. It might well be quite a bad name, but isn't that a little impolite?" I said, trying to affect a mature, adult tone of voice.

"Well, now!" the cat shouted and sat up straight. "Sourpuss. It wasn't the least bit impolite," he said, trying to imitate my tone of voice, and continued laughing as though he didn't care how uncomfortable he'd made me feel.

"Oh, do forgive me, *monsieur,*" he began, raised both front paws into the air, and with a pout began straightening his whiskers on both sides. "Or should I say, *mademoiselle, ha ha,*" he continued. "I didn't realize I wasn't allowed to joke about your name. This is all deadly serious, *meow*!"

I gulped. "Do you want a drink?"

"Of course I want a drink," he replied. "And only now you ask me—how rude!"

I stood up and fetched us both a gin and cranberry juice, and when I placed the tall drink in front of him, the cat muttered something to the effect of how bloody long it had taken me to bring the fucking drinks.

"There was a bit of a line," I said in my defense. "Sorry."

"Ooh, what beautiful eyes you've got, what beautiful dark-brown hair," said the cat once he had relented. He leaped onto my shoulder and began stroking my hair.

The tender, soft touch of his paws made my skin tighten into goose bumps, but after only a short moment the cat jumped back to the sofa again.

"So, what do you do for a living?" the cat asked, now serious, and pressed his fingers against his lower lip.

And so I began to tell him this and that, talked about my studies and my lowly job as a postman, my apartment and all the various classes I'd taken in all the various departments, my hobbies, my likes and dislikes, my free time.

The cat didn't seem to think my story sufficiently interesting, as his attention drifted and he stared at other men in the bar, their bodies and their bottoms. His eyes were half shut and drool trickled from the corner of his mouth.

"Ugh," he said as though he were about to vomit.

"What?"

"Gays. I don't much like gays."

I was astounded. People don't normally come to a place like this if they don't like gays. When I asked the cat why he didn't like gays, he explained he had nothing against homosexuality per se, just gays. Before I could ask him another question and point out that people usually liked gays but not homosexuality, the cat clarified his answer.

"Obviously, I like all kinds of toms, but I hate bitches!" he said abruptly and crossed his paws on the table. "You have to decide whether you're a man or a woman," he continued and leaped suddenly onto the table, raised his backside in the air, and stretched his front paws.

"Just look at that," he said quickly, fixed his eyes on the men on the dance floor, and wagged his tail. "How repulsive. Men's hands don't move through the air like that, and men don't talk the way women talk. And men don't wear such tight tops or wiggle their bottoms like that—like a prostitute, a whore!" the cat snapped so loudly that the dancers turned to look at us.

The cat wound his way between the pints of cider and jumped back onto the sofa. *Christ alive, and sex between men is even more disgusting! Unnatural through and through. Horrid, absolutely horrid!* he declared. Wouldn't it be easier just to leave people in peace, I asked, and let them be themselves?

"Hippie," said the cat pointedly. "It so happens the world works rather differently. People have expectations and opinions, there's no getting away from it."

"Yes, I think you're right," I said.

"That would hardly be a surprise," he said, wallowing in self-satisfaction; he smugly stretched out his paws and gave a brazen smile.

The cat assured me that his opinion of gays wasn't based on mere hearsay but on bitter personal experience, for he had once met two gays. He had been backcombing his luxuriant fur in the bathroom of a local restaurant when two gay men had cornered him. According to the cat, the men marched up to him, stood on either side of him, and began pointing at his handsome flanks and shiny tail as they might a piece of meat, and the cat had felt so objectified that he'd been forced to stop his preening and cover up his sweet curvature.

A moment later the cat said I should tell him something that would make me special, someone worth getting to know, because otherwise he would go straight home. Apparently everything I'd told him was meaningless nonsense, as boring and predictable as the government's budget proposals, *pthui,* again he almost spat. *Good grief, you certainly know how to bore a person so completely and utterly!*

"Now, tell me something you've never told anyone else!"

At this, as if by accident, I began telling the cat about my past, the country I had come from, about the situations in which people moving from one country to another find themselves, and about the small Finnish town where I had grown up. The cat sensed that I don't normally talk about my past, because now he was listening more intently; he narrowed his eyes and cupped his paw at the edge of his chin the better to hear through the music.

I told the cat about people for whom my name was always something I had to explain, people who, when I answered their questions and told them where my name came from, were always disappointed. *That's why I'm so insecure about it; surely you appreciate that a name can cause more bad than good.*

I told the cat that it always feels as though people are scrutinizing my behavior at school, at work, everywhere, watching how much food I take for lunch and checking whether I remember to thank the people working in the cafeteria, to see whether I write my essays in flawless Finnish and how often I change my clothes.

Whenever we talked about Islam, dictatorships, or foreign languages at school, I always lowered my head, as I could feel them all turning to look at me. And when they asked me to say something in my mother tongue, some of them even said out loud what a shame it was that speaking such a language was useless here. And whenever I was late, I often heard it was high time I learned this wasn't a third-world country. *Living and going to school in Finland is like winning the lottery. Remember that.*

SHE WANTS ALL THE LINEN

By Thursday afternoon everything was almost ready. I sat in the middle of our living room and looked at the piles of linen that would eventually bear the porcelain cockerels from the glass cabinets in Bajram's home, tablecloths on which he would eat his meals, sheets on which he would lay his skin. It was customary for the bride and the women of her family to prepare all the linen the new couple would need throughout their years of marriage. Handmade duvet covers, pillowcases, sheets, tablecloths, bedspreads, hand towels, and bath towels, all of which formed the *qeiz*. They represented a new start for Bajram and his family, a life as yet untouched.

My siblings looked at me with fascination as I sat among the linen. They were doubtless thinking about their own futures too. *Is this what it will be like when my time comes?*

At that moment I felt a strange sense of closeness to them, now that their task was to serve me, to make sure I had everything I needed. They woke early to prepare food for the guests, to clean the house and pack, relieving me from my chores. For the duration of her wedding preparations, the bride was not allowed to work at all; she was a queen who had to be kept happy.

The bridal linen was ready. Duvet covers, pillowcases, sheets, dozens of towels, hundreds of hours of work. Fatime and Hana admired them, saying they were practical and would last for years to come.

"And eventually you can cut them up and use them as cloths," said Fatime.

"Though this linen will last many years," Hana added.

The three of us stroked the sheets. All I could do was imagine the moment at which they descended onto a proper bed, covering up the squared pattern of the upper mattress and hiding its ragged corners, leaving the room smelling clean and fresh. The kind of bed that was only a bed, that didn't double as a sofa, the kind I'd seen in the pages of *Kosovarja*. Bajram would lie down on it, and the sheets would stretch and shape around his body, and his skin would smell of my home, our shared home.

"Can you leave me alone?" I asked and they respected my wishes.

I looked at the glass cabinet, which ran the length of the living-room wall, the three threadbare sofa beds along the walls, the wooden table with the scratched legs, its surface scuffed, and I was so exhausted that it felt as though I'd run home all the way from Prishtina.

"They're coming!" Hana ran to the door and shouted.

"What?"

"The clothes, *motër,* the clothes!" she shrieked and clapped her hands. "They're here!"

Bajram's family had bought me so many clothes and belongings that they had to be delivered in two cars. I didn't recognize the men in the driving seats, but when we introduced ourselves it turned out they were Bajram's uncles.

My father showed them inside. My sisters and the relatives gathered at our house began carrying the clothes into the boys' bedroom. I secretly wished they would all leave straightaway because I wanted to get my hands on the clothes immediately, but we were expected to serve the guests something to eat and drink.

It was only a few hours later that they started getting ready to leave. Once we had said our good-byes and they had driven out of sight, my siblings, my mother, and I dashed toward the clothes like a herd of animals.

I'd wanted to examine the clothes in peace, but my sisters started rummaging through the plastic bags, reading out the names of the brands, the materials and sizes. *Look how much he's bought! Oh, what a pretty skirt. If only I could have one like this. They really have splurged.*

"Stop it," I said, but they didn't listen. They carried on, thrusting their hands into the plastic bags and shoe boxes, holding the clothes up against their own bodies.

"Stop it!" I shouted at the top of my lungs.

They froze on the spot and looked at me, bewildered.

"Get out!"

I don't think I'd ever shouted the way I shouted then, because they quietly laid the clothes aside and left the room apologetically.

I closed the door behind them and looked at the array of dresses and shoes for everyday use and special occasions. There were dozens of them, as there were dozens of sweaters, scarves, pairs of trousers, tights, and underwear.

And when I thought of the following Monday, when all my friends and relatives were invited to Bajram's house to look, green with envy, at all the clothes, the perfumes and makeup, all the gold that my husband had bought for me, there was no one else and nowhere else I would rather be.

5

The cat was visibly shocked by what he'd heard. He blinked his eyes as if to make sure he'd heard right.

"How unpleasant," he said. "That some people can be so black-and-white about things."

"Not really," I said and looked at the cat, who seemed to be seething on the inside.

After a moment the cat asked whether I had any other stories like this to tell him. He was very interested in this; he'd been waiting for a long time to hear stories about such things.

I promised to tell the cat more next time and decided to ask him something instead. I asked where he had come from, what his family was like, whether his mother had similar black-and-white stripes, but the cat refused to tell me anything. Instead he said we shouldn't talk about that just yet, because there were so many incorrect preconceptions about cats that should be addressed first. For a start the idea that cats aren't really independent, they're just lonely.

Once I got going, I couldn't stop introducing myself, because now the cat was listening intently, nodding encouragingly, punctuating my monologue with follow-up questions and elongating their final vowels in strange, fanciful curls.

I explained to the cat that I avoided people, avoided talking to them, eating in large restaurants, sitting in lectures, standing in crowded trams or long lines or at bus stops with a steady stream of cars speeding past.

The cat burst into laughter.

"Surely nobody behaves like that!" he exclaimed and picked his teeth with a long claw.

I disagree, I replied. People can be afraid of anything. Walking on a blustery street, for instance, worried that a traffic sign might fall on your head, that its sharp edge might slash your jugular. You'd bleed to death and die. Or you might worry that the wheels of a passing car could burst right next to you and that flying pieces of rubber would strike you in the face and that you'd never recover from the blow. All through winter and spring there was the risk that lumps of ice might fall from the roof and land on your head and split your skull open. You could trip on the curb, slip on an icy pavement or a step and break your arm, your leg, or your mind. And every single day, all year round, there were dangerous people out and about, strange, unpredictable people who could do or say anything at any moment. They don't ask. Pavements don't ask, and neither does the ice.

The cat thought such fears were irrational. He didn't seem to appreciate all the things that could happen once you realized you ought to be afraid. The cat interrupted my rebuttal and asked whether I should be concentrating on my studies instead, because my studies were something he thought particularly special. *Finnish isn't even your mother tongue,* he said, somewhat sycophantic, and waited for me to praise his extraordinary powers of perception and his keen eye.

"Yes, you're absolutely right," I said.

"I most certainly am right," he retorted and commented that most immigrants are stupid and brash and that when they walk past the smell is enough to knock you out.

"Try to teach them something, but they'll never learn. Give

them a job and they'll steal your money. Give them an apartment and they'll trash it, though they don't even have to pay for it themselves," said the cat sternly. "Good God," he continued contemplatively, assuming a truly bizarre position: one paw on his hip so that his fur now looked like a tulle skirt, while the other paw fumbled blindly at the air in front of him, making him a great, clumsy, furry sight in front of me. "If it was up to me, I'd ship the troublemakers back where they came from."

I squirmed uncomfortably on the sofa, flicked back the hair that had fallen across my brow, and gave a forced smile.

Eventually I told the cat that things were different in our house. Nothing else was considered as important as studying and educating oneself. *We spent all our time reading and studying. My parents were doctors. They cured the sick and brought them back to life. Did you hear? Doctors who spent their evenings reading books.*

"Hmm," the cat mumbled pensively, his expression as mysterious as that of a secret agent. "What genes you have!"

The cat retreated into his own thoughts like a Renaissance philosopher. His cheeks were round and drooping like Jeremy Bentham's, and the Jeffersonian tufts of hair behind his ears made his head look like a cauldron of unfathomable depths. The only problem was that nobody listened to what he had to say, for what could a cat possibly know about politics, economics, or other sociological issues.

"It's a shame you can't pass on your genes," he said. "At least, not very easily." He paused for a moment. "Unless someone desperately wants to create problems for her child with a father like you!"

At that he burst into a volley of cackling laughter. He beat his paw against the table, shook his head, and waggled his hind legs like a madman. *Kaboom! Here comes the cat! Hahaha!*

Once the cat had spluttered out the last of his guffaws, he asked me to continue. So I carried on with my story until I'd tied up all the loose ends, until there was nothing else to say about me. An entire life fitted into such a small collection of words that when I reached the end of the story it felt as though I hadn't said anything at all.

The cat seemed to recover from my story as he nudged me with a long, sharp claw, its edges caked in plaque, and urged me to tell him more about myself and my family, more still.

"This is all fascinating," he said.

I told him that all my siblings were academics, they'd studied communications, photography, economics, information technology, law, psychology, and computer programming—*we're not like other immigrants that turn up here and laze around, don't even think that.*

"Hmm!" The cat seemed suitably impressed, fiddled with his thick-rimmed sunglasses, and pulled his face so that his two incisors appeared at the sides of his mouth like two anchors lowered from the deck of a ship. "It seems you're quite a catch," he said.

Apparently it hadn't occurred to the cat that I was telling him the first things that came into my head, that I was tailoring my story to what I thought he wanted to hear. The cat wanted a story whose protagonist's life began from a set of impossible circumstances, a story that would be so heart-wrenching that it might make him shake his head at the state of the world. But he wanted the story to end in such a way that he was able to applaud the protagonist's ability to take matters into his own hands—despite the fact that the protagonist had learned that skill specifically so that he could shake off the burden of other people's pity—and in order to reaffirm his own beliefs. *Anyone can change the direction of his life, any time at all, if only he has enough motivation:* that was the moral of the story. The cat found it easier to believe this than to think about what it actually meant: that the word *anyone* actually referred to a very small group of people, that time has no direction, and that motivation is rarely the salient difference between people.

The cat then asked where my parents were now. Instead of answering I was silent for a moment, picked up my gin and cranberry, and drank.

"My parents are dead," I said eventually, placed my drink back on the table, and stroked my chin. "When they were alive they still mattered, they had a meaning, a life, and a job. But now they're gone and nobody will ever need them again."

The cat's eyes popped wide open. And he looked at me, and for a long time he didn't say a word.

"Well," he said eventually and squinted his eyes. "I'm sorry," he slipped into the conversation. "It must have been tough," he continued and paused.

"But!" he shouted, his voice ominous. The cat's eyes bulged even more than before and his cheeks filled with air. He paused again, jumped from the sofa onto the floor, *hop,* then quickly leaped up again, *hop*.

"I'm bored," he said all of a sudden.

Pff, the cat exclaimed, an extension of his show of protest, then scoffed a *meh* to underscore how little he was interested or could be bothered to listen any longer. He pulled a pink straw between his narrow lips, stroked his long cat's whiskers, and with sunken cheeks he sucked on his tall drink, though he seemed bored by the taste.

"Do you want to come to my place?"

The cat pushed the straw away with his tongue. His little cat's eyes brightened, his groomed paws tensed, and his coat fluffed up, so thick and bushy that he looked unbearably overweight.

"So, you finally asked me!" he shouted excitedly, pulled off his glasses, put them in their case, and ran his tongue along his lower lip, making his whole body seem to crackle like baking paper.

"Keep good hold of me," he said. "Because without my glasses I can hardly see in front, only to the sides, and only bright pastel colors."

THE MOIST EARTH

It was Friday, the first official day of my wedding, a day I was supposed to use to grieve and say my farewells. I was leaving my family and our village behind. Instead of grieving, however, I felt restless all morning, couldn't bring myself to concentrate on anything. I glanced furtively around and was certain that I'd forgotten something terribly important.

I stood at the front door and looked at the pretty flower beds in our yard. Rain was battering the leaves of the plants, whipping them. Droplets of water ran between the rocks, splashing from one stone to the next like crickets. The earth succumbed to the water, turning in front of our eyes into an inviting garden bed purring for yet more water. I sat on the edge of the terrace and pressed my bare feet into the soil. I had always loved the rain, its smell. It made everything seem fresh, extinguished the piles of burning rubbish at the edge of the field, and washed the dust back into the ground.

I pressed both hands into the soil and rubbed my feet. I imagined them covered in soft sand, moist from the sea. I closed my eyes, and the earth yielded to my imagination: now I was sitting somewhere else, I was on a beach where it never rained, where the sea foamed and splashed around my feet. The cold rain whipped my skin like a sigh, as though it had delayed its arrival so long that people had already given up all hope.

And then, a cool droplet on my hot skin.

I'd heard that a certain time after death there is nothing left of the body but the bones. In contrast to what I had imagined, the body was responsible for its own process of decomposition: the bacteria in the gut grow into long worms and begin eating the very creature that had once given them life. For the human body, the process is uncomplicated: all it can do is carry on living until one of its parts stops working.

I had often thought about my own death, but never as much as on that morning sitting on the terrace outside our house. How it would happen, how comfortless it would be. How brutal and quick, unrecognizable, a small flash somewhere, a hiss. My body would bear no sign of life, no evidence whatsoever.

Soon I heard the sound of determined footsteps clomping inside the house.

"What are you doing out here?" asked my father.

He was standing in the doorway, his expression unhappy, grave, and distrustful. He was wearing his dark-brown pajama trousers and a white sleeveless shirt.

"I was fetching tomatoes from the garden for breakfast and tripped," I said and smiled at his stony face as politely as I could.

"You can't make breakfast today, girl," he said as if to put an end to the matter.

I was about to say that it didn't matter, that I wanted to do something to keep my mind off what was about to take place the day after tomorrow. I wasn't expecting him to place his hands on my shoulders and to speak to me the way an adult speaks to one who needed support, to his equal.

"I know you're frightened about getting married," he began and turned for a moment to stare out at the road leading away behind me. "It's only natural because everything feels new. Fear is the most natural of all human emotions. It's the same the world over," he continued and paused, though not long enough to allow me to speak. "Just you remember, Bajram is frightened too. I am sure you're going to be very happy with him. Do you hear? I'm sure of it."

He held his hand into the rain and closed raindrops into his fist, letting the water trickle gray to the ground. "The earth has treated us well, don't you think? Our generous partisan leader has been righteous to his people."

His eyes gleamed. He took me by the hand and pulled me closer, pressed his lips against my forehead, and sheltered me between his chest and arms. His bristly chest hairs scratched my cheek and his faint heartbeat, calm yet full of pomp, drummed in my ears like the strophes of Aleksandër Stavre Drenova's *Himni i Flamurit*.

When I was little, my father told me a story about the Balkan peoples, explaining that they were all distinguishable by their own specific characteristics. Bulgarians were good when it came to business negotiations but were bad judges of character; Serbs were crafty, devious to their heart and soul; Macedonians had a self-assurance verging on self-destructiveness and were easily conned; Bosnians lied through their teeth and had a finger in every pie; but an Albanian, you could trust an Albanian like a rock. Albanians helped those in need, while the other Balkan nations swooped after money and possessions like vultures.

My father continued by telling me the story of how a Bosnian, a Bulgarian, and a Serb put their wise heads together to trick a Macedonian living in the United States by selling him faulty car parts. Still, the devious Serb, the lying Bosnian, and the greedy Bulgarian couldn't decide what to do with their ill-gotten gains and ended up destroying one another.

Money leads to envy, he said. Envy leads to lies, and lies lead to deviousness, which in turn leads to violence and death. When the unarmed encounter the armed, the outcome is clear, but when the armed encounter other armed people, nobody wins. A motley crew of Bosnians, Bulgarians, and Serbs is doomed to failure; it's an impossible conundrum. And my father explained this in the only way he knew, leaving not a single stone unturned. His final word was a full stop, the end of the story, and for every question he had a perfectly absurd answer. But it was always the right answer.

The Macedonian of the story lost his money and was forced to return to Macedonia via Albania. In his simpleminded naïveté he had counted his money incorrectly, and in fact he had only enough to get him to Albania. But as soon as he stepped off the ferry across the Adriatic Sea at the notorious port of Durrës, he met people who helped him home, helped him back on his feet, and with their genuineness, their meekness and generosity of spirit even strengthened the Macedonian's self-esteem. The story ended with the familiar aphorism: an Albanian's word is his bond.

"It's what's always happened to us Albanians," he said. "People always abuse us and our good-heartedness. In some ways we're like the Macedonians, because we're too good-natured, too strong and trusting," he said. "That's why it's so easy to kick us."

My father let go of me, took a few steps, and stood on the spot. He sniffed the clean air, sniffed it as he might a freshly washed shirt, filled his lungs with it as though he'd been cooped up in a prison cell. I looked at him, the holes along the seams of his sleeveless shirt, the stretched collar and the thick white hairs jutting out from beneath it, hairs that I could still feel and smell on my cheek and beneath which his heart was beating in time with the second hand on the clock.

THE WOMEN WHO
WISHED HER LUCK

The following afternoon there came a knock at the front door.
My mother beckoned the guests inside, women from the village, extended family, and some of my girlfriends. They paraded
through into the living room, where my mother kept them company while I waited in the kitchen. I was sitting in front of the
woodstove. I'd opened one of the hatches and was watching the
logs burning inside. First they turned black and began to crackle.
After that they snapped in two, then into even smaller pieces,
until all that was left of them were flying black strips.

"Emine, come here!" my mother shouted.

I pretended I hadn't heard her.

"What are you up to?" Hana asked.

She was leaning nervously in the doorway because I hadn't
appeared in the living room after being called twice. I could hear
my mother telling the women of the village that preparations for
the wedding had clearly taken their toll on me. *Only this morning
she was so absentminded that she tripped in the yard, imagine, and came
in covered in mud like a wet dog. I don't know how such a clumsy girl ever
caught the eye of a man like Bajram.*

I thought of Bajram and our marriage, because there were
men, and then there were some men we called *Llapjan* after the

place where they lived. That's where Bajram was from, a region renowned for its traditional ways, its violent men and unhappy women. I'd rather die than live with a man like that. I'd kill either myself or someone else, I thought, that's what would happen. Killing someone would be easy; you could kill your husband without him knowing. I'd pick up a large knife and drive it through his chest in the middle of the night. I'd choke him to death, cut off his penis with a pair of shears, or slit his throat and run off into the woods. Either that or I'd slit my own throat if all else failed.

"Please just go away," I said once I noticed out of the corner of my eye that Hana had no intention of giving up.

Hana stepped into the room, pulled up a wooden stool standing next to the door, sat to my right, and started staring at me. She looked exactly like my mother; reading her expression was impossible.

"What do you want?"

Hana took my hands and held them tight. I tried to pull my hands free but my struggles only made her tighten her grip. Then she hugged me, as quick as a flash, as though she didn't want anyone to see her doing it. She wrapped her longs arms around me. Her whole body was trembling. After that she let go of my wrist, quickly looked behind, and pulled me toward her.

"You have to get up now," she said, stood up, and tugged at her blouse to straighten it.

I continued to gaze at the burning logs. The surface of the wood looked almost moist.

Hana breathed gloomily and told me to pull myself together. *Please, why are you making this so difficult? Get in there, now.*

After a moment I stood up and forced myself into the living room. I took my first steps surrounded with encouraging smiles, and my sisters cheered me on as they might a sportsman. I held out my hand, thanked the guests, and forced myself to respond with a smile to their well-wishing.

. . .

I waited in the kitchen, my face covered, and I was wearing the long dark-blue evening dress with silver sequins at the top that Bajram had bought me. On the Saturday of the wedding festivities, it was traditional to hold a *kanagjegji,* the women's party during which the bride wept in front of her relatives, friends, and the women from the village. The bride was to cover her face with a red veil, curtsy in front of each guest in turn, hug her, and weep. The closer the friend or relative, the more noise the bride was to make. This was how the bride said good-bye to her friends and the other women in the family. After this, the bride spent the evening with the guests, the women painted one another's nails, looked at the clothes the bridegroom's family had bought, and, naturally, talked about the bridegroom, his family, and his wealth.

A large group of women had congregated in the living room while the children set up chairs for the men in the yard, where they sat smoking, talking about politics, farming, and the economy, and eating the snacks laid out for them: salted sticks, salted nuts, chocolate candy, coffee, tea, and *llokum.*

My mother had explained to me that if for some reason I couldn't cry, then I had to pretend to cry. She was walking around the room dusting the windowsills, lifting ashtrays to wipe beneath them. *You'll just have to pretend. Lie so much that you can feel it throughout your body and soul, right down to your fingertips.*

"Though I'm sure you will cry. It's that kind of occasion," she continued.

She placed the final ashtray back on the windowsill, folded the cloth in her hand, and threw it toward the cooker before starting her performance. She gripped the side of the stove and suddenly began writhing and moaning. *Like this. You can mumble, wail, or whimper, so long as it's broken, as if you're really crying.*

Remember to breathe every now and then. If you tense your arms, your hands will start trembling, and there won't be a soul left unconvinced.

Now there were dozens of women, young and old, sitting on the sofas, on the floor, wherever there was room, staring at me as though a creature from beyond the grave had stepped into the room. The murmur of the men's conversation came bubbling in from outside. There was very little space to move on the floor. Everybody was staring at me, pricking her ears to hear the moment I started weeping.

I stepped forward, my back hunched. Hana stood behind me, holding my skirt and guiding me toward the guests because the veil was thick and I couldn't see through it properly. A bead of sweat trickled down my forehead. My heartbeat boomed in my ears, on both sides of my throat, throughout my upper body. Then we began doing the rounds.

When I gripped the hands of the lonely widow living next door, who had always been so genuinely happy at other people's joy, and hugged her, I thought it wouldn't be long before I would no longer have to pretend. I'd be crying soon. It would happen at the very latest once I'd seen enough wet eyes, once I'd received enough encouraging embraces, or once I'd touched enough hands, once my friends started singing the wedding lament accompanied by the *defi,* the tambourine, and with the words:

> *Never again will you see your family.*
> *Why do you leave us?*
> *Why do you leave all this behind*
> *And go to your husband?*
> *From tomorrow you belong to another family.*

But all I wanted was for these sad dirges to end; I wanted to pull my hands away and wipe them on the hem of my skirt, because my hands soon stank of the grime on the guests' hands, of ingrained sweat and old grease. The smell pushed its way through my veil, and time went so swiftly that the weeping was almost over before I knew it.

Once we had finished the round of guests, I had to wait for Hana to give me permission to sit on a stool placed in the middle of the living room and reveal my face, my red swollen eyes that I had rubbed with a raw onion before we started.

When I revealed my face, a long sigh filled the room, as if performed by a choir.

6

The morning after we met, the cat was next to me when I woke up. The night before, when we'd arrived back at my place and gone to bed, I was sure that once I closed my eyes and drifted off to sleep, I'd never see him again. I imagined he would carefully pick up his clothes in the morning and skulk outside, close the door so quietly that it would barely make a sound. He wouldn't want to wake me because he thought I might ask him for something he was unable to give.

I glanced at his delicate head, which was like a sculpture as it rested on my checkered pillow. His thick whiskers extended into the room like sharpened pencils and his breath cascaded into the air with a gentle wheeze. The cat had placed his paws beneath his head. He had curled up beneath two blankets to keep warm because he hated the cold and even the slightest chill made him shiver. What's more, he'd already commented on how terribly cold it was in my apartment; apparently it struck him the minute we stepped inside. He'd made a show of looking for a suitably warm spot. He thought it was extremely uncouth and downright despicable that something so obvious had been overlooked.

Then he woke up. He stretched his limbs and muscles, taking all the time in the world, yawned long and hard, and eventually stood up as if to show off his beautiful silhouette.

"Get up," he said curtly. "Up, right now," he continued when I didn't obey him. "I want to wake up and eat and bathe and take a walk and do things!"

The cat's smell had clung to my sheets, and I kept finding his fur for weeks. He had seen everything: my apartment, my secrets, the fact that my cupboards were full of all different kinds of detergent and that my walls, floors, windows, and tiles were all sparkling, not a speck of dust in sight. And now he was lying next to me telling me to get out of bed, humming a tune he'd heard on the radio and licking his coat as though to rid himself of a tick. When I didn't get up at once, the cat never thought of waiting but leaped onto the windowsill, gripped the curtains, and pulled them demonstratively to one side. *Serves you right! Ha ha!*

"Don't be lazy," he said eventually. "Laziness is truly unpleasant."

I wanted to be good to the cat, to meet his needs and requirements, so I pulled on a pair of black pajama bottoms and brown-leather ankle boots, slipped a gray woolen sweater over my pink long-sleeve T-shirt, took my jacket from the coatrack, and left the apartment, because the cat had already turned his nose up at the porridge I'd tried to offer him.

"I'm not eating fucking porridge," he'd said, demanded to be given a clean towel, and disappeared into the bathroom.

I stepped out into the cold, biting February morning and pulled a packet of cigarettes from my pocket. After the previous night there were only three left. With a sense of routine, I gripped one of them between my dry fingers and fumbled with my other hand for the matches. I lit the cigarette and took a first, dizzying toke, and in a matter of seconds my whole being felt lighter.

Naturally, I couldn't possibly smoke in front of the cat. He was too sensible to smoke and far too intelligent to understand such an obnoxious habit. In his opinion cigarettes smelled disgusting and were almost amusingly unhealthy.

I headed to the corner shop, a cigarette in my hand. I'd had a headache all morning—after all, the cat and I had been knocking back tall drinks at the nightclub and we'd had to shout at each other over the music.

But at the very first pedestrian crossing, there between the ice-covered ground and the houses surrounded with snow, I stopped in my tracks as though someone had pointed a gun at me. My heart sank and seemed to plummet down my trouser leg and burning sweat oozed from every pore of my skin.

I reached my front door, wiped the sweat from my brow on the back of my hand, panted in and out in an attempt to steady my breathing. I pushed the key into the lock and turned it slowly so that the cat wouldn't notice my return or take fright. I opened the door as quietly as I could and peered inside my apartment as though I were breaking and entering. To my relief I soon realized the cat was still in the bathroom, still singing the same song, "Grenade" by Bruno Mars. The cat couldn't properly pronounce the English lyrics, though he thought of himself as a full-blooded citizen of the world.

I dashed into the living room and looked around in a panic. I checked the radiator, all the corners of the room, all the cupboards and cubbyholes where the snake might have curled up—they slither into hiding when they are afraid—but I couldn't find it in any of the usual spots. Then I noticed it peering from beneath the sofa. I dropped to my knees in front of the sofa and looked underneath: the snake was stretched out behind the sofa. Its skin was rough and had begun to turn gray. It would shed its skin at any moment. Its eyes were dim but otherwise it was in the same position as always.

I grabbed its tail with both hands and began dragging it away, but it had been in the same spot for so long it was stuck to the linoleum floor. I shook it and tried again, but it only started thrashing and slid out of my grasp like a slippery eel. It was so large and powerful that it could decide for itself where to lie. You couldn't move it as easily as all that. It slept wherever and whenever it pleased.

When I heard the cat turn off the shower, I dropped the snake's tail and sat down again, placed both feet against it, and pushed it as hard and far as I could behind the sofa, and though its irritable hissing made me worry for my feet, the most important thing was the cat didn't see anything.

I went to the front door again, slipped into the corridor, back outside, and hurried to the shop, because I wanted to surprise the cat by buying him all kinds of delicacies while he was getting ready. I would have liked to tidy up a bit, put fresh sheets on the bed, put things back in order, and spray air freshener round the apartment.

I was already home again by the time the cat finally stepped out of the bathroom, where it became apparent that he enjoyed spending especially lengthy periods of time. He licked his paws and smoothed his eyebrows and whiskers with his own spit.

I was sitting on my fake-leather sofa, nervously biting my nails, because I couldn't think how to explain the empty terrarium to the cat in case he asked about it. Or what I'd say if the snake suddenly decided to slither into view, for that matter. Fortunately, the cat didn't notice it. Instead he ordered me to my feet, saying, *Aren't you fat and lazy, lounging around like a slab of meat!*

I stopped biting my nails and decided not to respond. I

fetched a cloth from the kitchenette, picked up the bits of nail, and wiped the edge of the sofa, a place the cat might like to settle down.

The cat watched me for a moment, combing his fur, then hopped onto the coffee table and stood between the cans of cat food I had left there.

"What are these?" he asked, his voice skeptical.

"I went to the shop," I answered, as though it hadn't been the least bit of trouble, as though I'd sorted everything out in the time it took him to wrap a towel round his waist. "I thought you might like to eat something different. The porridge was a bad idea. Sorry about that."

The cat examined the cans for a moment, sniffed them and felt them and read the advertisements on their labels. When he realized that there were all different flavors, he eagerly began reading the ingredient lists. He began pacing round them intensely. After watching all the pacing and sniffing for a moment, I came to the conclusion that going to the shop had been one of the brightest ideas I'd had in a long time.

"Such rubbish . . . ," the cat said eventually, leaving enough room for his next comment. "I certainly won't be putting that anywhere near my mouth!"

"What do you want to eat, then?"

I looked at the cat and he looked at me, first curiously then more intensely.

"They're full of all kinds of additives. I've got a reputation to uphold and I won't eat rubbish like this!" he retorted aggressively. "Got any meat? Fresh meat?"

"I'm a vegetarian."

"Of course you're a vegetarian. Christ, how embarrassing," said the cat and rolled his eyes.

At that he irritably knocked over a can of chicken-liver pâté, pointed at it with his paw, and turned to look at me.

"Open it!"

I opened the can and scraped the contents onto a plate using a spoon. I placed the food on the coffee table and wished the cat bon appétit, though the smell of chicken liver made me want to retch. He didn't answer, but he seemed to eat his food contentedly enough after all.

I took a container of yogurt from the fridge, joined the cat, and wondered whether I should give up being a vegetarian and start eating meat. After gobbling down his food, the cat astutely noticed that I hadn't moved for a short while.

"What the hell? Give me that!" he snapped, grabbed the container, and began pouring yogurt into his mouth. "Liar. Christ almighty," he muttered between mouthfuls. "Don't put on a face like that. You're ugly. Butt ugly, if I may say so. That's a bad expression for you. Change it this instant," he continued and buried his head in the narrow container and licked it clean.

The cat wanted to spend the morning at the apartment. *Pretty good service here,* he'd said after stuffing himself so full of food that he slumped on the sofa rubbing his swollen belly. I'd taken it upon myself to put the cat's clothes in the washing machine, I'd ironed his shirt, polished his shoes, and aired his woolen coat. That's how much I liked him already.

After his nap the cat asked me to recommend a book that would make him happy, because that was the subject I knew best of all. I fetched him a copy of Günter Grass's *Cat and Mouse* because I thought the cat might enjoy that. After all, he seemed to love all kinds of games, pursuits, and tomfoolery.

With the book in his mouth the cat leaped up to the windowsill—and how lightly he leaped, like a hang glider. He lay down on his back, opened the book, and leaned against the window, gave a sigh of boredom, and peered around for a moment at the bookshelf along the opposite wall, the light-green rug whose tassels I'd already had to straighten out after he had clawed at them.

"Bring me my glasses," he said. "This minute."

I rummaged in the side pocket of the cat's satchel, took out his glasses case, and handed it to the cat, who was staring at me like a murderer.

I tried to peer under the sofa as regularly as I could, and to my relief the snake was always in exactly the same position.

"What an awful book. Quite dreadful," he scoffed after finishing the first chapter. He folded his glasses and put them in his breast pocket. "I'm bored with such absurdity," he added and opened his mouth in a wide yawn. "Bored to death."

Before leaving the cat placed his card on the hall table and told me to call him the following week. *Let's do something nice, go to a nice place for dinner maybe.*

When the cat finally closed the door behind him, I was relieved.

I took the card and began turning it in my fingers like a bunch of five-hundred-euro notes. I wanted to call him right there and then and not wait until next week, because that was days away. I would spend too long thinking about our encounter, mulling over the things I'd told him, and that would mean I'd never have the courage to pick up the phone and ask him out. What would he say when he found out about my snake? Or when he finally found out the truth?

My head felt like I'd immersed it in a pot of boiling water.

I fanned myself with the card and dashed outside, went to the store, and walked straight up to the dairy shelf. I placed a tub of yogurt in my basket, went to the checkout, and came straight home. I fetched a spoon from the kitchen drawer, sat in the middle of the floor, and started eating.

The snake joined me and tasted some, though it didn't know how to eat yogurt; it just smeared the stuff all over the place and made a mess.

Once I'd eaten I gripped the snake with all my strength. It wound itself round my wrists like a length of rope and struggled, and when I started walking toward the terrarium it began nibbling my fingers, constantly trying to escape.

When I dropped it into the terrarium and saw how painful it was for the snake, heard what a dreadful noise and commotion it made, watched as it thrashed against the glass, looking crushed and trapped in its own body, like a child having a tantrum in a candy store, it broke my heart.

THE CUTICLE

I hadn't been able to sleep that night. It was only in the morning light that I noticed how the floors in our house were trampled, dirty, and covered in litter. Packets of West cigarettes had fallen to the floor, and the tables were strewn with empty chip and cookie wrappers and ash flicked here and there. As usual I got up early and slipped quietly out to the veranda, my feet slapping against the cement floor.

I sat down, raised my knees firmly against my chest, and began nervously chewing my nails. I stared at the silent landscape around us, the chairs populating the yard. It was still cold. The late spring morning was spitting out its final chilly winds, trees in fresh bloom swayed along the blurred mountainside, and my skin tightened into goose bumps. I bit through my cuticle, and blood instantly began to flow from beneath my nail.

I looked away from my bloodied finger and stared once again at the yard, pressing the wound with another finger. My mother had already hung out old tattered clothes, worn-out pairs of jeans and torn shirts, on a cord strung between the apple trees. White chairs were dotted around the yard like a frightened shoal of fish, and the lawn was awash with cigarette ends that looked almost like small pieces snapped from the white plastic chairs. The mountains rose wide and tall, to the right and to the left, which made it look as though the world began and ended on the veranda where I was sitting. And yet nobody knew about us. None of us was anybody special, none of us spoke any languages, and everybody had less than everyone else. The world felt like an impossibly small place.

My mother opened the front door and leaned against the doorjamb. *The most important day of your life,* she began. She had raised her eyebrows exceptionally high and the lower half of her face bore a broad smile. There was still plenty to do, she continued—too much perhaps: food, drinks, dress, hair, makeup, cleaning, food, drinks, dress, hair, makeup, cleaning, she repeated, paced up and down the veranda, and eventually gripped my hand and tried to haul me to my feet.

"Food, drinks, dress, hair, makeup, cleaning. Don't just sit there, girl. Go and get yourself ready."

"In a minute, *Nanë.*"

"Right this second. Now! *Nxito!*"

Mother stomped back indoors.

When I tried to stand on the step up into the house, I felt dizzy. I took a few hobbling steps across the veranda, pressed my forehead against one of the supporting beams, and closed my eyes. In addition to the sounds of nature around me, I could hear my mother rattling the dishes and picking up rubbish. I gave a resigned sigh and stepped inside.

By ten o'clock everything was ready: I'd been to the hairdresser, and we had collected all the litter, vacuumed every last corner of the house, ironed and folded the laundry, washed all the dishes, thrown all the plastic bottles, cans, and pieces of wrapping paper into a black garbage bag and begun burning it at the edge of the field.

.   .   .

At around midday I was standing in the middle of the living room in my white wedding dress, with patterns embroidered in golden thread decorating the shoulders. It had a round neckline and fitted chiffon sleeves, a wonderful pleated hem, and the train was made of translucent, shiny lace. The dress was unbelievably beautiful, and though it swallowed me up so that it almost felt as though I was made for the dress and not the other way round, I felt like the prettiest woman in the world.

By one o'clock I was wearing more gold than any woman I'd ever known. There were rings on every one of my fingers, my golden earrings were large and impressive, and there were so many necklaces round my neck that I almost had to hunch my shoulders. The sun shone diagonally from between the clouds, though the forecast had promised us a cloudless sky. My entire family had gathered to wait for the guests and the highlight of the afternoon when, as custom dictated, I would be fetched and taken to my Bajram in an entourage of several dozen cars whose drivers would blow the horn throughout the journey in honor of my wedding day.

I'd imagined everything differently, assumed it would be so oppressive that I'd be unable to stand for shock, unable to speak for the choking sensation in my throat. I'd imagined I wouldn't even be able to breathe, that my wedding would leave me with memories I would rather not revisit, that I'd sweat so much my dress would be soaked, that you'd be able to wring it out like a wet towel, but there wasn't a single person who saw me that day who didn't marvel at my glowing, serious expression, my sheet-white skin, and how beautiful I looked.

"Give me the veil," I told my sister.

There was only one piece missing from my reflection in the full-length mirror. Then it would be perfect. I placed the veil over my head, positioning it carefully until it was securely fastened to my hair, which flowed prettily down to my shoulders.

I looked at myself in the mirror. From beneath the two layers of the veil it was hard to make out the contours of my face or lips, now drawn boldly with bright red lipstick. It was hard to recognize the people who had come to watch me being fetched.

"Are you ready?" Hana asked, a little anxiously. Her bright voice broke off halfway through the question.

For a moment I looked my sister in the eye, and in reply I smiled at her long enough for her to pull herself together and ask the question again.

"Of course," I said. "I'm happy now."

I lifted the veil over my head, kissed her on the cheek, and lowered it again.

7

My father had nothing to his name when he arrived in this country. He had a wife and five children, a wallet containing the sum total of his worldly possessions, his head full of fear and hatred and plans that, if he followed them to the letter, would turn him once again into the same man who had left Kosovo.

In this way my father had planned the course of our life before it had even properly begun. His three daughters would grow into good, obedient, honorable wives and his two sons would become strong, hardworking men who would return to Kosovo as soon as it was safe again, they would marry good Kosovan women and build grand houses next to each other. The plan flickered in his mind like stars, like small bonfires burning in the sky, because to his mind there was nothing about his plans that was remotely unrealistic.

I learned to speak and read in a language he didn't understand, to live among people whose culture he despised, to talk about subjects he couldn't fathom. I learned to avoid him and everything to do with his life. Over time I forgot the most basic words in my mother tongue and started speaking Finnish to my siblings, and though he punished us harshly for it, we carried on because none of us wanted him to understand.

He urged me to go to technical college and study car repair, electronic engineering, or information technology, the building or printing industry, and the minute I said I wanted to do something else he interrupted me and said I would study whatever and wherever he told me. *I've always been fair to you,* he said and asked me to fetch his cigarettes from his coat pocket. *Don't try to defy me. Defying me will have severe consequences. You know that. I'll hit you so hard your face will never look the same again.*

I dug the cigarettes from his pocket, my blood boiling. I'd been avoiding him since I was a small child, because he saw our desire to live life the way we wanted to as selfishness that should be punished.

I declined his suggestions and handed him the cigarettes, furiously shaking my head. My father's lips tightened like a rubber band stretched to the extreme. I could feel his blood beginning to boil too.

Fine, I said eventually, I'll go to the technical college if you say so. *You've always been fair to me, and there's no sense doing anything except what you have decided.* As I said it I felt almost as though I were bursting into flames.

I pulled the wool over his eyes for as long as I could: in addition to my high-school books I ordered books on the basics of electronic engineering and read up on the subject just enough to be able to isolate the problem with a broken lamp or television, a computer or mobile phone, and to fix them. Everything else was straightforward—after all, my father didn't particularly care how or where we spent our time. As long as it looked like we were doing what he'd said, he was happy.

A few months later I moved away from home. I slipped a piece of paper into a pile of bills and managed to get him to sign it. *The school is too far away and I won't graduate in time. I'll become an electrician if I can live in the school dorm. You need to sign this consent form, then I can get a job and give you part of my monthly salary.*

My older siblings had already moved to different towns and had nothing to do with him any longer. But he continued lying to me, telling me he was still in touch with them. *I saw your sister today. She hates you. That's what she told me, to my face. What do you think of that?*

I carried the final box of stuff to my friend's car, and in a deviation from my original plan I went back up the stairs to the top floor of our apartment building to destroy his dream and see it come crashing down. I wanted revenge, wanted to hurt him so much that he would turn in his grave for all eternity out of sheer bitterness. I wanted to say something so appalling that my words would scratch and bloody his skin.

I've tricked you, I began. *All this time I've been tricking you, getting you to believe my lies.* Now he was listening, his ears pricked. He looked at me, his eyes prowling and predatory, his body backing up as though he were getting ready to attack. *There never was a technical college. I asked for money for those two books, but I spent it all on cigarettes and clothes, wasted it on tattoos and piercings and alcohol. How does that feel? Tell me. I want to know how that feels.*

He said nothing but leaped toward me in two enormous steps before I had time to take a step backward. He pulled his arm back to gather as much force as possible.

I fell to the floor and gripped my jaw. It felt somehow detached, dislocated, warm, and it smelled of his strong aftershave. I stood up and tried to dive out of his way, to run out to the balcony, swing one of my legs over the railings and slide down the gutter, anyhow, anywhere, but my father grabbed me. He laughed at my indecision: Why had I stopped to ponder the best way to get down from the third floor? *Not that smart after all, are you?*

He closed the balcony door after dragging me back inside. He had always been like this, I thought. *He'll never change.* He flicked the venetian blinds shut. Then he walked up to me, pressed his forearm against my throat, and stood in front of me huffing and puffing.

For the majority of my childhood, I'd wished my father would die. I prayed. Whenever I saw him thrust his empty plate in front of my mother's face without saying a word—she was supposed to realize this meant he wanted more food—or whenever he threw his stinking socks in her lap, when I listened to the unpleasant comments he spouted, saw how judgmental and opinionated he was about everything around him, I knew he would never bring happiness to anyone.

Don't you ever bring Finnish people into my home.

Don't you ever tell anyone that we don't have money.

Don't you ever call me a liar.

I wanted him to suffer for as long and as painfully as possible. I wanted him to choke underwater, suffocate in an airless wooden box, thrashing like a fish on dry land. I wanted him to take his last breath in a coffin that reeked of his own sour, tobacco-stinking breath. His bones would shrivel inward, he would split like a watermelon dropped on a concrete floor, collapse like a house of cards. They'd find him frozen to death beneath a snow-drift, naked, without any identification, and nobody would ever know who he was or what had happened to him because nobody would ask after him.

"You're mad!" he shouted, shook his head, and finally threw me to the ground. I took a few croaking breaths as though a sheet of tissue paper had been held up against my mouth. "Mad! Do you hear me?" he raved and punched the wall.

I'd fallen in front of him, propped on my knees, which had thudded to the floor like a pair of iron bars. The trickle of blood oozing from the corner of my eye had reached my jaw. He was about to leave when he decided to take a step toward me and look at me one last time.

He laid his hand on my head and stroked my hair, and for a moment I thought he might be about to apologize to me. Instead he wrenched my head back with such force that I heard something crack in my neck, and all I could see were his yellowed teeth and red face as he spat at me.

"Get out of here, *o qen*, you dog, *o gomar*, you donkey."

That was the last time I saw him; after that we were both free of each other. I returned to my friend's car, smiled, and said that everything was finally all right. As for my father, I never saw him again because he soon returned to Kosovo and never came back.

As a child the first emotion I fully recognized was the feeling of shame. When my parents asked for driving directions in mangled Finnish I sank into the backseat and tried to make myself so small that nobody would see me and felt utterly ashamed. When they asked whether there was any pork in basic groceries, the storekeepers glowered at them like criminals and didn't understand a word. I hid beneath the counter and waited until they had walked a short distance ahead. Only then did I follow them, careful that no one accidentally thought I was with them.

When they were forced to come to parent evenings at school, I prayed that they would be quiet, that they wouldn't speak to anyone. When they had an appointment at the social-security office, I prayed again and hoped they wouldn't ask me to come along and interpret for them.

For a long time, I believed that they simply didn't understand how other people saw them, why people gawped at them or why talking loudly in a foreign language elicited such reactions, stares, and shakes of the head. Only much later did I realize that they only pretended not to understand, because it made living that bit easier.

We were allowed to come and go as we pleased and we didn't have curfews. There were only two rules in our house: we weren't allowed to make a racket and we were certainly not allowed to challenge our parents.

Sometimes, not often, my father talked to us about God—as if every now and then he awoke to the thought that it had been a while since he last wondered what God would say about the choices he'd made. He would stand behind us to make sure we were praying, though he wouldn't pray himself. He told us that everything, the whole universe, humans, animals, and all their movements, deeds, and words, were foretold in the word of God. He drew the globe in the air with his fingers and said, "*He* is everywhere, *he* who will save us, *he* who will show us mercy and forgive us our sins. Right now he is sitting up there with a pen in his hand writing out the future of everything in the universe. Your future, and yours, and yours."

He took a breath as though he was moved by his own words.

"You should be afraid of God because he has an eraser too, and he'll use it if need be. Though he might have written out a glorious future for you, he can just as easily take it away. Your belongings, your health, your family and friends. Then there will be nothing you can do but cause pain to those around you, because there will be nobody up there to forgive your sins."

FIRST REVELATION

It was half past four when I heard the sounds of my wedding, the incessant tooting of car horns. Everyone must hear and know that somewhere a bride was about to be fetched. A moment later a white Zastava swerved into the yard. Before long there were five cars, and soon the yard was filled with the clamor of cars.

A man stepped out of the white car, straightened his tie, slowly turned his head toward the front of the house, took off his sunglasses and looked around, then slammed the car door shut with a resounding thump.

When people realized that the man was Bajram, time seemed to stop. For a few seconds not even the clocks ticked and nobody moved; not even the wind blew. It was as though everyone had been asked to stand still and pose for a photograph. We were an empty blackboard and Bajram a wet rag splatted right in the middle. He turned and began slowly walking up to the house like drops of water trickling down the board.

Why is he here? What on earth is he doing here? I asked my mother. The groom wasn't supposed to fetch the bride; that was a job for the men of his family. But now here he was. He waved a greeting to my father, sitting in his chair in the yard, and walked up to him.

"I don't know," answered my mother as my tearful sister Fatime whispered something in her ear. "I truly don't know," she repeated and a strange expression came across her face, as though she had just heard that someone had died.

She had never heard of a man who arrived with his wedding entourage. The groom was supposed to wait at home and the entourage would bring his bride to him. Why wasn't he afraid of what people might say about him? she asked herself in disbelief and gripped the hem of her wedding dress. Why is he going around causing a panic like this?

Bajram shook hands with the girl's father and quickly exchanged the customary greetings. After being given permission, Bajram sat down next to the girl's father. The two men looked serious. A moment later Bajram took a cigarette out of his pocket and lit it with his left hand, while sheltering the lighter from the wind with his right. His head leaned to one side as though he had pulled a muscle in his neck.

"Sunny day," he said eventually, sucked on his cigarette, and blew the smoke out of his lungs. "I absolutely wanted to come along, *zotëri*. I couldn't stay at home. Not on a day like this."

"I understand," said the girl's father, though he didn't know whether to be flattered or offended by Bajram's audacity.

Her father was taken aback that the man struck up conversation with such ease, as though he were taking care of everyday business. He looked at the man's leg, which was stretched out into his personal space. Was the man insane, thought her father, or did he simply want to give a certain impression of himself: here is a man who carries himself lightly and does not take matters too seriously. Or could it be the case that the man had joined the entourage on a moment's whim? After all, on a day like this anybody could lose his sense of judgment or even his mind.

Her father lit a cigarette in a show of friendship and cleared his throat. The cars parked outside were like mosquitoes seeking out a trickle of blood, she thought as she stared at them through the window. The men stepping out of them smoked cigarettes and slowly made their way toward the food laid out on the table.

"Have the festivities here gone well?" Bajram stretched his leg out even farther and put one of his hands in his pocket. "Ours have been excellent."

"Yes, indeed," her father said, cleared his throat again, and shifted position in his chair, as though he were talking to Bajram with his body.

"Back home my grandparents and my mother are eager to see Emine. My parents know your fine family well. They have no reason to doubt my judgment, because your name is unblemished and highly regarded. I am a very happy man. Allow me to assure you that Emine will be every bit as happy. She is in good hands. I am a good man, of that you can be sure," Bajram said in a single breath before filling his lungs once again with smoke.

People gathered round the tables, foremost among them the men of Bajram's family, for whom the girl's siblings poured juice, coffee, and tea. But their speech was quiet and expectant, not nearly as brash as she had expected.

About an hour later Bajram suddenly stood up. This made everybody stop in mid conversation. His confidence was like a wave the size of an entire building, thought her father. He too stood up, wiped his dirty trouser leg, and held out a hand to Bajram.

"Thank you. Your words are music to my ears. Your parents have raised you properly. Emine is inside. We can fetch her together. I wish you both well and hope you will enjoy your life together, enjoy each other, your children, your riches."

"Zotëri," Bajram began. "May I fetch her alone?"

The girl's father looked at him in bewilderment. Then he looked around and saw that nobody was speaking. People were sitting quietly in their chairs; everyone had stubbed out his cigarette and now sat staring at the two men. Eventually her father smiled.

I was sitting in my parents' bedroom and waiting. I could hear his steps making their way indoors, clacking against the concrete floor, the creak of the doors. At the last moment I straightened my skirt and hid my face behind my veil.

Bajram appeared in the room alone and immediately fixed his eyes on me as though he hadn't noticed my sisters in the least as they stood looking at me and Bajram in turn, as though they were looking for answers, waiting to know what it was natural to feel in a situation like this. We had all assumed that my father and little brother would take me out to the car driven by Bajram's relatives, but now Bajram was leaning carefree against the doorframe, his black sunglasses dangling from his fingers, and looking at my dress.

He was wearing a neat, snugly fitting dark suit. His brown hair was thick, wavy, and attractive; it was shaped with quality hair products and finished off with a shiny lacquer. He had a white shirt and a black tie, which together with the black suit jacket and his black leather belt made for a stylish and carefully preened overall effect.

Bajram began to smile. His cheeks lifted up into a broad, handsome curve. His teeth were every bit as white as they had been a few weeks ago by the boulder, and they sat neatly in his mouth like glittering diamonds. Judging by those teeth it was hard to believe that Bajram chain-smoked just as much as my father.

At last he held out his hand. A strip of sunlight glinted from behind him like a halo.

"Shall we?" he asked and stood up in the doorway, moved forward a fraction.

His sculpted arm pointed at me like a rifle. His skin looked taut and firm. That was an arm that would protect me, I thought, one that would build a strong, lasting home, wrap it around our shared life, our children, and our world of happiness. Gently I reached out my arm like another rifle, gripped his soft skin, his fingers, smooth as satin, and left everything without so much as glancing behind me.

We finally arrived at his white car. The drivers threw their cigarettes to the ground, stamped them out, and climbed into their cars. The fug of gasoline hung in the air, a cloud of gas built up above the yard, and the swirls of cigarette smoke slithered toward it like leeches.

Bajram's car was decorated with bows and flowers. I was supposed to be in the backseat with his relatives, take hold of the headrest in front of me to keep myself from falling over, and bow my head until my parents' house had disappeared from view. If the bride sat down and made herself comfortable in front of her family and the local villagers, this was a sign that leaving her family behind didn't cause her great anguish after all. And that, in turn, meant that the bride was haughty and lazy.

And then, with everyone watching, Bajram asked me to sit in the passenger seat. I was standing in front of him, rigid, and didn't dare look behind me. I thought I was going to die. *Really?* I wanted to ask him. *You really want me to sit down? What will the others think when they see there's nobody else in the car but us?*

Bajram began to laugh, repeated his invitation to sit down, and gestured toward the passenger seat. *Don't think about them,* he said as though he were able to read my thoughts. After this I obeyed him; what else could I do but obey my husband? I began to settle myself in the car. Bajram held the door open, carefully folded the pleats of my skirt inside the car, and asked whether I was comfortable. I didn't answer him because I was not comfortable. I tried to wiggle myself forward slightly, gripped the dashboard with my right hand, and stuck the nails of my left hand into the back of the seat. *Right,* said Bajram, gave another laugh, slammed the door shut, and walked round to the other side of the car.

He winked at me and started the engine. The other drivers swerved back out onto the road and last of all we drove out after them, a convoy of ten cars and the gray sky ahead of us, to the sides the rows of closed windows along the road, and behind us the battered, rickety asphalt and the unfinished house, which eventually disappeared from view. Once we were farther along the road the horn tooting started up again. It was relatively warm for the time of year, May at its most beautiful.

My breath felt like warm steam beneath my veil. I could feel drops of sweat pulling the powder from my cheeks and getting it stuck in the gauze of the veil. I slid my hand beneath the fabric to give myself more air, but the car was baking hot, quiet and empty, like a shuttle sent hurtling into space.

It was only once the landscape slowly became less and less familiar that I realized Bajram and I hadn't said a word to each other in almost fifteen minutes. I looked away from the landscape, where the mountains rising in the distance turned to gently sloping forest, and looked at him. Through my veil I could make out the contours of his muscular thighs, where they started and where they ended. The suit fitted him just the way a suit should fit a man. His posture was upright as a pistachio tree; he even sat upright in the car.

I wanted to place a hand on the hand resting on his thigh, because he had tensed his thumb and stretched his other fingers out straight as if to make room for my hand, but I didn't dare touch him. I unclasped my own hands and laid them on my thighs. Bajram took the hint and took off his sunglasses. He began to smile.

"Could you put these in the glove compartment?" he asked and held out his right hand, the sunglasses dangling in front of me.

I took the glasses without saying anything. I smiled back at him and hoped he wouldn't notice how such a small gesture seemed able to numb my entire body. He was closer to me than at any time before, and this was the first time we were alone together. I took his glasses and put them in the glove compartment.

But Bajram's hand did not return to the steering wheel but came to rest on my left thigh as though it had found a home, and my leg felt so warm it could have melted. *I have two options,* I thought. I could leave his hand where it was or I could take hold of it. I could decide to start loving him from that moment onward or I could wait for the same thing to happen later. Of these two options I chose the latter and laid my hand on top of his hand.

And for a few moments I was the happiest woman on earth.

Look at me, I wanted to shout out. I wanted to climb up the minarets and skyscrapers and tell everyone about us, about how our fingers intertwined and clenched one another so that we didn't know whose fingers belonged to whom. His hand was soft, his grip was gentle and warm, and his face was beautiful and chiseled.

But he hit me, even though he walked so upright, though he had promised me a happy life.

A moment earlier Bajram had slid his hand from under mine and placed it on top of my hand. Then he took my hand, briefly closed his eyes, and laid it on his groin.

Startled, I pulled my hand away. I was shocked at his lecherous behavior and frightened for my life, as the car almost swerved into the oncoming traffic. He gripped my hand again and did the same thing. Again I pulled my hand away. When Bajram's eyes opened a second time, I no longer recognized his face. His eyes were so wide open that I felt almost nauseous; his upper lip curled toward his nose and his eyebrows toward his hairline, then he looked at me at first angrily, then with disgust, and finally livid with rage. *There's no need for that,* I wanted to say. *To wait so long and take a shortcut at the last minute.*

The back of Bajram's head began to tremble as he clenched his teeth, and sharp spikes appeared at the edge of his jaw. For a third time he took a firm grip on my hand, yanked it between his legs, and began rubbing his groin. By now he was squeezing my hand tighter than before and pressed it down to show me that this is where it belonged now. Then he moved his hand and began fumbling between my legs beneath the layers of lace. I could hardly believe such a handsome man was capable of something so unpleasant.

"Don't," I said quietly.

Beneath my skirt Bajram's hand found my petticoat. He clipped two fingers around the elastic like a pair of pliers, pulled it back, and eventually located my panties. He began rubbing me. Then, using his middle finger, he pulled my panties back and began rubbing with his forefinger.

"Don't!" I shouted and grabbed his hand, clenched it as forcefully as I could, and looked at him furiously.

You're hurting me.

He pulled his finger out and slapped me so hard that my head almost turned right round. Instead of his face, all I could see now were the painted, bare mountains. I could feel my pulse beating on my cheek, which now smelled of his fingers. After that he menacingly slid his fingers into his mouth and laughed.

8

The next day the cat sent me a text message. He told me he was homeless and needed somewhere to sleep. I was writing him a response asking him to come and live at my place when my phone beeped again.

I'm moving in. That's all it said.

By all means. Be my guest! I answered.

I followed this immediately with another message explaining that I had another pet, a boa constrictor. *You don't mind, do you?*

Not at all! the cat replied, and he moved his things in a week later.

Our shared life began promisingly enough, though until then I hadn't lived with anything except the snake. We shared all our expenses, and gradually the cat got used to the presence of the snake, even dared to touch it, and I thought that perhaps our love could be just like in the cinema: strong, powerful love that needed no questions and wasted no time.

We walked through parks hand in hand, we read the morning paper together, we told each other the things you only tell your loved ones. The cat asked about my previous relationships, and I told him I had been with both men and women but that nothing had ever come of it, and now I was more than content to be with a cat.

I told my cat about my hopes and fears, and the cat told me about his dreams and family. *It's a perfectly normal story. I'm a perfectly normal cat from a normal home and everything about me is normal, normal friends, normal job, yada yada. Not worth worrying about.* I never asked the cat why he was homeless, because I sensed that he didn't want to talk about his financial situation or social position. He would tell me everything when he was ready.

We took baths together and I would read him extracts from my favorite novels. We went hiking and visited spa hotels; we tried our hand at bowling and mountaineering and squash. And every evening we returned to our shared home, both of us convinced that this time it was different, this was fate, these two beings had finally appeared in each other's lives to make them more worth living.

The cat loved films. He could have watched them all day. He dragged me to the cinema several times a week and became irritated at me or other people in the theater if someone spoke too loudly. Once he climbed onto the back of his chair and shouted at a dark-skinned man sitting a few rows behind us.

"In Finland people sit quietly in the cinema! Now shut your mouth back there!" Then the cat dug his paw into his popcorn and began throwing it at the man, though we were only halfway through the advertisements.

The cat had a firm understanding of films and the history of cinema, actors and screenwriters, directors and galas. He spent time on the Internet reading about films and making lists: films he should absolutely see, films he wasn't yet sure about, and finally films that didn't interest him in the slightest.

He then learned the contents of his lists by heart in case anyone ever asked him about them. And this wasn't just a hobby for the cat. After living together for a few weeks he told me he dreamed of changing profession. He no longer wanted to be a cat; he wanted to be a film director.

"You're just like me," I said with a smile and placed a cup of coffee in front of him on the table where he sat examining his lists. "That's what I do too. You've got to have your finger on the pulse, to be alert at all times. Someone could ask you a question at any moment; they might ask about that film there, and you'll know the right answer straightaway."

The cat gave a sour smirk. "This is in a *slightly* different league from you and your silly books," he commented, "books that no sensible person can understand at all."

"Don't talk to me like that," I snapped. "That's disrespectful and I don't like it."

The cat threw his glasses on the table, gripped his coffee cup, and turned to look at me. He crossed his hind legs, sat upright, and placed a paw on the back of his chair as though someone had just erected a 1920s Parisian set around him.

"Look at it another way," he said arrogantly. "What's disrespectful is that I still haven't met your siblings," he continued through gritted teeth.

"They're busy. I've told you a hundred times."

"Always the same story," he said, his voice now surly. "To be honest, the only disrespectful act in this entire conversation is going to be this one." At that the cat held his front leg out straight—the one holding the coffee cup.

Then he dropped the cup. There was a clatter as the cup smashed, which startled the snake. It was sensitive to sounds and thuds, and the cat knew this.

"Clean it up!" he shouted wildly, a ferocious rage glinting in his eyes.

The snake began hissing and thrashing against the floor and the wall, and soon its small head peeped out from beneath the sofa, eventually followed by its whole body. There was coffee everywhere, all over the floor, on the rug, splashed up the walls and the chair legs. The cat sighed with ostentatious discontent and went back to examining his lists. By now the snake had slithered so close to the cat and the table that I picked it up with both hands and placed it round my shoulders, regardless of the cat.

"I knew it!" cried the cat.

"Come on. It could cut itself and die."

"I wish it would die," he snapped. "A disgusting creature like that deserves to die. I can't for the life of me understand why you want it in the house."

I took the snake into the bedroom, placed it on the windowsill, and returned to the kitchen, where the cat had sorted his lists into three separate piles. The lists were covered in bullet points and arrows, sums of money, annotations, the cat's expectations, attitudes, and opinions. I took a small bag from the kitchen cupboard and began picking up the shards of the coffee cup.

"You know, I've been thinking," I said as I took the shards to the garbage can.

"Well, well, do tell me what you've been *thinking* again," said the cat.

"I've been thinking of changing profession," I said, picked up a roll of paper towels and a cloth from the sink, and began mopping up the mess the cat had left. "Of quitting the university, and when vacancies come up in the spring I could apply to the same school as you," I said to the floor. "We would always be together. I've been thinking I'd like to become a film director. I think I'd be rather good at it."

For a while the cat was silent. I'd managed to dry the floor and fetch the vacuum cleaner before he started communicating again. He burst into laughter and laughed so much it sounded as though he could barely breathe properly.

"You? You, a person who knows nothing whatsoever about films?" he managed to say through the volleys of cackling.

I switched on the vacuum. As I vacuumed the floor I muttered to the cat that I could learn, I could know as much about films as he did.

Spring arrived, bright and sunny. Our first spring together when the sun was cool and light lasted long into the evenings. Snow dripped from the rooftops and disappeared down the drains, and the air was heavy with the scent of the moist earth. The trees gradually filled with light-green leaves that shone as if they were spun from pure silk.

To my surprise the cat didn't want to come and see it all, the thawed lawns whose grass was still a heavy shade of green, the dusty asphalted streets completely dry though all around was still damp. Spring made the cat feel almost ill, all that light and sun, and he slept until long into the afternoon. And on the rare days that he agreed to venture out of the apartment he guarded his winter coat as if it were his most prized possession and refused to take off his thick gloves, scarves, and ankle boots. He huddled beneath his clothes and buried his head under a tight hood though the temperature rose to over seventy degrees.

I had lived under the belief that the cat simply hated the cold and that's why he didn't enjoy going outside during the winter, but it seemed he simply didn't want anybody to see him. He didn't like the way people had started talking about us. At first he led me to believe that he didn't care about other people, but after a while he began to hear rumors, to read on people's lips words that he took very personally, and no matter how much he tried to dismiss what he heard he began to see himself in other people's words.

It's such a burden, being different, he said, crushed and despondent. *People just stare at me and you and wonder, they gawp at us—and wonder! First you try to become just like them, and when it doesn't work out you try to come up with the silliest jokes to cover our difference in laughter, and when the jokes stop being funny, that's when the lies start.*

And when that stops working, it's time to pack your bags and run for the hills.

The cat had put on weight too. When he leaped up to the windowsill to watch people, he had to use his front paws to hoist himself up, leaving his hind legs flapping in the air like two ungainly appendages. Only then could he haul himself all the way up, gasp for breath, *huh, pff,* and swear to himself. He hadn't become fat and happy but fat and bitter, and he began to find himself ugly. *Don't look at me. I'm a mess.*

And though I tried to convince him that he was still very handsome, he couldn't stop calling himself names, let alone stop blaming me. He blamed me for making him fat, for his greasy coat and swollen stomach, his badly trimmed claws, which he could no longer reach to cut by himself. He thought I fed him too much. *I'm a cat; I can't help my basic instincts. I'll eat whenever there's food available and drink when there is something to drink.*

For the rest of the spring the cat waited anxiously to hear whether he'd been accepted to the school where he had applied. He paced nervously round the apartment, as though that would make time go faster. I was waiting for the same news, though I'd had to keep my application a secret from the cat because he had no faith whatsoever that I would get in. *You can't just wake up one day and decide you want to be a doctor. These things take time to mature and develop.*

Of course you can, I wanted to say to him. That's exactly what you can do. You can open a book and read so much that you no longer have the strength to hold your head upright. The cat believed that time would make him intelligent and mature, that time itself, living from one day to the next, would give him experience that would in turn make him wise. That's not how it works, I wanted to say, not at all. Instead I held my tongue and encouraged him through every stage of the application process. *You can do it. You're a clever cat. Who are they going to take if not you?*

Our life began to turn to routine, and suddenly we knew

each other so well that we had run out of questions to ask. The cat knew not to talk to me for half an hour after I walked in the door; he let me read in peace and kept the sound on the television turned down whenever I went to bed before him, while I knew to lay out the clothes he needed for the next morning, as the cat was terrible in the mornings, whereas I was excellent.

Then one perfectly normal June day, the cat came to the decision that he wasn't cut out for such a life. *It's the same every day,* he said. *I have to leave you. I want to leave you. I don't want to do this anymore. A cat, in a world like this, a relationship like this.*

At that moment the old Kosovan proverb popped into my mind whereby too many good things can spoil a person. We can achieve good things and they can occur in a variety of ways. If someone has more possessions than he needs, if he is used to being treated too well or becomes too adept at something, he starts to believe that he deserves only the best. He refuses to associate with people other than those who are the same as he is. He becomes accustomed to good food and drink and wonders how it was once possible to drink sugary lemonade or smoke the cheapest tobacco. And all the while he thinks other people's pity is nothing but envy.

Did you really think that you and I would be together forever, just the two of us? How could you believe something like that? Surely you realize that you are like that and I am like this, and that together we're not like anything? People should be fined for such abject stupidity.

The cat wanted to move out straightaway, but when I said I thought he should reconsider, he stopped to think over his options. *You can live here even if we're not together. It's not a problem for me,* I said. At that he raised his head from the sofa, leaned it to one side, and smiled, and his eyelids were curved like in Japanese cartoons.

"Very well then," he said. "But I won't pay a penny in rent."

"That's fine," I said.

SECOND REVELATION

The car curved into the yard and the shadows cast by the freshly painted tall white concrete walls. At each entrance stood a small cypress bush surrounded with flowers in different colors, as though they had been fired toward the bushes at random.

Bajram's family house stood right in the middle of the yard all by itself; there were no other houses in sight. This enormous house was just the way I had imagined it, and the yard was filled with women and children waiting for us in their best outfits. Many of the women were wearing a *dimije,* which looked like wedding dresses and were bought especially for weddings.

The car pulled up right in the middle of the neatly trimmed lawn. At the other end of the yard stood the massive, three-story building with the orange roof. This place was only about twenty miles from my house, and still I felt as though I had traveled to the other side of the world. The house had been painted white. On the upper floor was a balcony the length of the building, and the family's land seemed to stretch as far as the eye could see.

I heard people standing outside the car giving melancholy sighs and talking to one another, though I couldn't make out the words. Bajram slipped out of the car and walked round to the other side to open the door for me.

I gripped Bajram's hand and slowly stepped out of the car, pulling the train of my dress after me, and as I stood up I felt as though I were the only person in the world. The guests gathered in front of us gave way to form an aisle through the yard, a route along which I would soon be brought to the house.

The women were singing and rattling tambourines while the men beat their *tupan* drums roped across their shoulders, and I held out both my elbows to the sides, the palms of my hands one on top of the other above my stomach and tried to concentrate on looking at the ground. Bajram gripped me by one shoulder and his sister approached us and took me by the other. Slowly they began guiding me toward the veranda.

Once we arrived at the front door it was time to anoint the upper part of the doorframe. Bajram's sister was holding a small bowl containing some sugar water.

"When you reach the door, dip your hand in the water and rub it along the top of the doorframe," my mother had instructed me.

In times gone by, it was a commonly held Kosovan belief that this would make the newly wed couple's shared life sweet. I dipped my fingers in the sugar water and tapped them against the doorframe as the guests looked on. After this Bajram opened the door. Waiting for me inside was my new bedroom, the bedroom I would share with Bajram.

As I stepped into the hallway I noticed that the layout of the house was identical to our house, just like all Kosovan houses. The hall rug was placed precisely in the center of the corridor, the porcelain cockerels behind glass vitrines in the living room had never moved from their spot, there wasn't so much as a scratch on the steel kitchen counter, and there wasn't a single crumb on the floor to disturb the perfect symmetry of the kitchen tiles.

Bajram reached out a steady hand and escorted me to the bedroom door. To my surprise, he was the one to show me into our shared bedroom instead of his mother. He had doubtless demanded to have it like this. After the anointment, the groom usually waited at the front door with his back to it until his bride joined him there. I stole a quick peek at Bajram before taking another step. He looked arrogant, as though he was enjoying the situation and the attention to the full.

The first things I noticed as he opened the door were the red curtains that made the room look dark and dingy, almost threatening against the light. The view from the window gave, exceptionally, into the garden. On the floor was a red rug, which had clearly been selected to go with the red bedspread. The wardrobe was made of dark wood, as was the bed and the tables placed flush against it. The ladies' dresser was from the same series. It was a typical showroom: the furnishings had all been bought at once, no doubt directly from a furniture-shop display window.

Everything betrayed the fact that lots of money had been spent on this wedding: both outside and inside the house was the smell of fresh paint, the aroma of wood and varnish would linger on the furniture for a long while yet, and the kitchen cabinets looked and smelled new and untouched.

Eventually Bajram asked whether I liked the room and the items he had bought for me, the countless shades of red and the view from the window complete with the fully grown pear trees in the garden behind the house, the field behind them, the dusty pathway between them, and the cluster of mountains behind it all. He wanted to know *this instant,* he said. *Tell me what you think of everything. I've bought you vast amounts of possessions. This is all for you,* he said and groped at the curtains. I looked at Bajram, nodded, and sat down on the bed.

"Quickly," he urged me after a moment.

"It's good."

I asked him where he had put the clothes we had brought here, as I had slipped a small box of caramels into one of the bags. Bajram shouted to his mother, who ordered the girls swarming around the house to fetch the bags that had been taken up to the top floor.

Once I had clasped a small bag of caramels in my hand, we stepped outside again.

The wedding guests had formed rows a few yards apart and stood waiting for the moment when the bride's veil was lifted and her face revealed to the crowd.

Almost without noticing it I took Bajram by the hand. He had bought me enough jewelry to last a lifetime and chosen me a red bedroom and golden earrings.

Then Bajram's father held a sweet little boy in front of me, his grandson. I noticed that the boy smiled at me cautiously, embarrassed that everybody was watching him. I wanted to smile back at him but I was expected to look serious. I crouched down to the boy's level, clasped his hand between my palms, and passed him the bag of caramels. It was the least I could do, because what he was about to do next would bring good luck and make me give birth to lots of sons.

"Thank you," said the boy.

Bajram's father held the boy up so that he could carefully lift the first layer of my veil above my head. Those with keen sight could already make out the contours of my face. Many of the guests held their breath and squinted to see better. I closed my eyes. My red-lacquered nails gingerly made their way up toward my chest. The boy took hold of the second layer of fabric and lifted it even more slowly than the first one.

Now everything was visible: my neck, chin, and lips, my nose, eyes, brow, and hair.

For a moment everyone was silent. Then the women began to clap and the men to whistle. A moment later I slipped both thumbs beneath my necklaces and lifted them up for all to see. Then I lifted my wrists into the air. The gold glinted like glaring sunshine. *And all this gold my husband has bought for me.*

At this the assembled guests began to rejoice, to sing and

play all the louder. Bajram and I must have stood on the spot for at least half an hour. People looked at us, took photographs of us, and Bajram's relatives began bringing me presents. They slid more jewelry on my fingers, round my wrists and neck, and stuck money in my veil. All the while I was gritting my teeth, trying to shut out the noise, trying not to look anyone in the eye.

After that the *temenet* began. The men resumed banging the drums over their shoulders and the women again rattled their tambourines while singing me songs with words to which I was to pay close attention, for they contained tasks the bride was expected to carry out.

> *If you like your mother-in-law,*
> *Go and embrace her.*
> *If you like your father-in-law,*
> *Go and kiss his hand.*
> *And if you like your gold,*
> *Show it once again.*

I will be the perfect woman for him, I thought as I went about my tasks impeccably. *Everything he wants, his wife shall give him.* The whistles of unknown men and the clapping of the women and children showed that people liked what they saw—the bride was beautiful, her skin was unblemished, she had thick hair, full lips, and so much gold that it could have blinded them. I felt prettier than ever before, as though I had taken a microphone and walked across a vast stage, as though the people in front of me were groups of my admirers waiting for my song to begin, as though their claps were the flashes of cameras taking my photograph.

And then I heard it.

Somewhere. The meow of a cat.

9

A few weeks later I found myself sleeping on the floor in the hallway. The cat said the snake stank and I stank because I handled the snake, so he wanted to sleep in my bed without me. *Either that or I'm leaving,* he threatened, and at that moment I realized there was plenty of room for me to sleep in the hallway.

I asked my employer if I could do some overtime and extra shifts at night and during the weekends because the cat wanted more space to itself, he asked for a new computer to edit his short films, a larger litter box to relieve himself, and expensive organic food.

And he ate so much that he soon grew into a giant. When he leaped onto my king-size bed, which we had once shared without any problems, the duvet and pillows bounced up to the ceiling and the bedsprings almost touched the floor, which trembled as he plodded around the apartment, his paws now as big as a bear's.

When I came home from work, the cat was sitting in the middle of the bed eating pistachio nuts (I was naturally expected to pick up the shells he had spat and strewn across the floor) and scratching his coat so frantically that every corner of the apartment was filled with dander and hair. He left crumbs at the bottom of bags of chips and cookies, and these spilled out over the bed each time he shifted position or went to the litter box, and he let out reeking farts and belched grotesquely.

The cat didn't care that my books were all arranged by language group in alphabetical order or that I kept my deodorant and bottles of aftershave in a pedantic, precise row. I wanted to ask him whether putting things back where he found them could really be so difficult.

If I'd known taking in a cat could be so expensive, I might have given it a second thought.

In June the cat received a thin letter from the university and I received a thick one. I'd hoped it might have been the other way round or that I could have given up my place and allowed the cat to take it instead.

You don't deserve it, he began. *You're just fooling around. You take, you steal, you lie. You probably cheated for all I know. Why else would you hide this from me?*

At first I thought the cat simply wanted to let off steam, to get over the bitter taste of being proved wrong, but he continued: *They're only taking you because you're an immigrant. There are quotas for people like you, though they'll never admit it. A bit of color, something exotic, you know, something different. How tragic. You're so pathetic I never want to see you again. I can't be with someone who doesn't even realize he's being used.*

"Don't end things like this," I begged him.

"Oh, I will," he said once and for all. "Because you know what?"

"What?"

"I hate immigrants," he growled. "Have you any idea how much you've received in this country? How many opportunities you've been given?"

We started arguing at the top of our voices. I sat down at the table and rested my head against the palm of my hand. The cat was sprawled on the sofa, staring at me sourly.

I replied firmly that I had been given just as many opportunities as everybody else. The cat burst into laughter. *Dear, oh dear,* he snapped in faux compassion.

"I never thought I hated all immigrants, but apparently I was wrong. And I never thought I hated you, but it turns out I hate you most of all," he snarled.

He suddenly jumped down from the sofa and up onto the table. He threw everything from the tabletop and grabbed my throat, and pressed his paws so tightly that they almost stopped the blood circulating in my body. He grimaced, and now for the first time I saw his full set of teeth. Four of them were as sharp as ice picks.

"You've been lying to me, haven't you?" the cat asked and tightened his grip further.

I placed my hands on top of his paws and tried to prize his claws open, but they were so hard and powerful that it felt as though they were made of metal.

"For your information, I've looked up the names of your brothers and sisters on the Internet. And guess what? There are no such people by those names! None whatsoever! I even called the magistrate's office, for Christ's sake, and pretended to be a fucking onomastics researcher!"

The cat laid one of his paws across my chin and gripped. He smirked at me. *Well? What do you say to that?* he asked, though he knew it was impossible for me to speak because my face had swollen up, the color of blood. I could feel the bulging veins in my forehead and sensed the blood draining from my body, the pressure in my head increasing.

When I didn't answer his questions, the cat placed his hind legs on the edge of the table and pushed. *Fucking poof.* My chair tilted backward and I went with it. The ceiling and the curtains came slowly into sight behind the cat's ferocious grimace, and eventually the whole room seemed to somersault around me. I fell to the floor like a series of fragile vases, my shoulder crashed into the edge of the sofa, and the chair's wooden backrest snapped in two.

The cat slid his hind legs beneath a kitchen knife resting on the table, rose up on his hind legs, lifting one of them so that the knife flew into the air and almost hit the ceiling. As the knife was on its way down again the cat grabbed it with one of his front paws and began adroitly spinning it in the air. All the while he looked at me unblinkingly; he didn't even have to look at the knife, which he whirled in his paws like a magician's wand. His eyes were like sharp-edged triangles, and his tensed muscles made his whole upper body appear swollen.

Then he readied himself. He stood up, the knife in his paw, as if in slow motion, and spun around like a figure skater practicing a pirouette. The knife followed him like a thin, dazzling strip of light, and his bulging stomach followed the rest of his body like a half-empty balloon—that's how fast he was spinning, like a samurai.

Finally, he pounced on me. His paws landed beneath my arms and the whole floor shook, the windows too. In a flash he grabbed my chin, the claws jutting from his paws scratching my skin. He pressed one of his paws against my throat, and I could feel the thin blade of the knife, how delicately it would slit my throat, like a fresh sheet of printing paper. *I'll do it,* the cat threatened me, his face recoiling into a ferocious snarl. *Tell me the truth or I'll fucking do it, you'll bleed to death,* he seethed between his tightened lips and pressed the knife deeper still, so much so that I sensed my jugular would soon give way under the pressure.

Just then the snake slithered out from behind the sofa and the cat turned his keen eyes to look at it. *Hm.* His ears pricked up. He hissed at the snake and eased his grip on my throat. The snake hissed back at him and edged closer, now only a few steps away from us. It wrapped itself into a bundle like a pile of small discuses. I tried to stretch a hand toward it and pull it closer, to wrap it round the cat's throat and ask it to strangle the cat with all its strength, but I couldn't reach it.

When he saw what I was doing, the cat quickly raised the paw that had been resting on my chin and slapped it down again with such force that the air cracked as though someone had thrashed a slender whip. After that the cat dug his massive paw into the middle of my face, and at that point I fainted.

When I came to a moment later, the cat and the snake were sizing each other up. The toppled chair, my body, the wall, and the sofa formed a battleground in which they were about to fight it out. The snake was curled up and hissing and the cat had risen up on his hind legs and seemed to widen in all directions, standing as tall as he could; his hairy stomach sagged so much that it was almost touching the floor. And he hissed too; they sounded almost identical.

The cat's claws were fully extended from his paws and he began to swing the knife around, to hit and scratch the air. He switched his body weight from one leg to the other like a boxer and held out his other paw as if to taunt the snake and make it move closer. *Huyaa,* he shouted to assist a sudden curving kick with his back leg, and his paw came down on the snake's bouncy head with a slap.

The snake's head flew backward in a beautiful arc like a jig cast on a fishing line, but it quickly recovered from the blow and curled up again. It attacked the cat a few times, trying to grab him with its jaws, but the cat was too fast and agile. He leaped onto the sofa, and from the sofa up to the windowsill. He climbed up the curtains, grabbed the lamp hanging from the ceiling, and swung himself on top of the fridge, where he hurled the knife at the snake but missed.

Then the cat made a mistake by jumping from the top of the fridge across the room to the table. Midway through the cat's graceful flight through the air the snake stretched itself up as far as it could, its whole body standing straight for a moment, and with the symmetrical patterns on its skin it looked almost like a ruler. Its jaws sank into the cat's furry side.

Before I even realized what was happening the snake had wrapped itself round the cat three times. The cat was completely buried within the snake. His head popped out in one spot like a man sinking in quicksand. The cat looked exactly the same as I had only a moment ago. Red veins started appearing in his narrow irises, and he was making the squeakiest sound in the world. *Mhhm,* he whimpered.

The cat tried to open his mouth and straighten his ears, to rub his cheeks and tweak his whiskers, but his movements only made the snake constrict even tighter.

I saw a tear trickle from the corner of his eye, then another. *Save me,* his tears seemed to beg me. I heard what he was thinking and I began to wonder whether the cat deserved to live or die.

I grabbed blindly at the cluster formed by the snake and the cat and pulled it between my legs. The snake instantly began to hiss. I took it by the chin and squeezed, but still its grip would not let up. I tried scratching its skin with my nails but even that didn't cause the slightest reaction.

The cat's eyes began to close. I could almost see that its heart would soon stop beating altogether, almost feel its organ functions slowing down, sense the blood stop flowing to its head and limbs.

I stood up, walked over to the tap, ran the water until it was ice-cold, and picked up a tall glass from the kitchen counter. I waited a short while without looking behind me, hoping the cat would hold out for a moment. Once the water was cold enough I filled the glass and hurled the water over the snake. It turned its head and seethed, and the cat gasped for breath as though he had been under water for many minutes. The snake was still tightly locked round the cat but had loosened its grip a little.

I threw several glasses of water over it; only then did it straighten its body out, release the cat, and slither back beneath the sofa, leaving the injured cat and a trail of water behind it.

The cat's fur gleamed from the exertion. He looked newly born, his limbs squashed against his body as though they had been broken and twisted out of place. He took a few shallow breaths, as though he wasn't sure of the world around him or of the fact that he was still alive. I knelt down beside him and stroked his little head.

"Are you all right?"

The cat lifted his head, bewildered, and looked up. *Ugh,* was all he could muster.

Minutes passed before he was able to react to anything. He'd forgotten my question; he probably hadn't even heard it properly or noticed that I'd been stroking and massaging his battered body. After a short while he began to stretch his limbs back into their normal positions, to breathe more heavily.

"I'm sorry," I said.

The cat waited for a moment, then his eyes flew open, and they had never seemed as wide and as round as right now.

"What the fuck is this?" the cat almost whispered.

"I'm sorry," I repeated.

The cat slowly began to haul himself up, still without really comprehending what I was saying to him. After struggling to his feet he staggered around like a drunkard, supporting himself against the walls and chairs, and gripped his sides because his ribs were broken. As he walked out of the room he coughed and spat blood on the floor. I followed him.

"Don't speak to me," he said cuttingly and began panting. "Don't say a fucking word."

Nobody will ever love you, he said once his breathing had steadied. And all I saw was his furry back; I could no longer see his face at all.

At this the cat wrapped a sweater round himself, held it

against his bleeding elbow. *Nobody,* he repeated and pressed his chin against his shoulder, giving me a glimpse of his eyes, now white again, his dashingly handsome profile, and pushed his doddery paws into his shoes. *You're going to die lonely, alone and depressed,* he said and opened the door. *And you deserve every bit of it. Wog.*

THE WEDDING NIGHT

The moment that only a week ago had seemed unreal and mindless was now upon us: Bajram and I were lying together for the first time.

Only a moment earlier he and I had been eating together, after which Bajram's sisters and aunts, who had prepared our meal, stood outside the bedroom and sang to us. *If your bride is pretty, come out and give us some sweets,* they sang, and as he sat on the bed Bajram opened the box of chocolates, stood up, and went to the door.

Once the women had finished their song and gone from behind the door, it was time. Bajram said he had to visit the bathroom.

The door opened. Bajram appeared in the darkened room carrying a small porcelain bowl containing raw white beans. Bajram then threw them into the air with a surprisingly subtle flick of the wrist so that, despite the force of the movement, the beans only rose a short way into the air. They flew in different directions and scattered around the room, on the bed, over the floor, and behind the furniture. They bumped against one another, hit the dresser and the walls like marbles.

I was to gather them up and put them back in the porcelain bowl Bajram was holding out. The groom was supposed to watch his wife, to follow this performance, to examine and size up the shapes and curves of his new beloved's figure. This was his way of getting to know his wife's body.

I got up from the bed and allowed the silken nightdress I'd put on to slip from my back to the floor. I held out my hand and Bajram gave me the porcelain bowl. Only now did I notice the letters B and E beautifully engraved into its side. I knelt on the floor and began gathering the beans and placing them one at a time into the bowl.

I placed the bowl in my left hand and peered under the bed and behind the dressers in such a way that my buttocks moved farther away from each other, my thighs formed folds as they pressed against the floor, and the hardened soles of my feet were facing upward toward Bajram's pensive stare.

I'd imagined I wouldn't be able to kneel down properly for shyness and shame, that I wouldn't be able to collect the beans with ease, but I could after all because this event had arrived as naturally as one harvest follows another.

Once the bowl was full and I had stood up again, my eyes were caught by the figure of Bajram, who now stood undressed at the other side of the bed and whose proudly engorged penis looked frighteningly large. His arms were muscular and the contours of his body were well defined, his shoulders broad; everything about him was symmetrical. He had a handsome washboard stomach and a back that curved into buttocks so round that they appeared almost separated from his body. The lower part of his back and his coccyx was covered in a thin layer of hair that seemed ready to thicken and conquer a larger area for itself at any moment.

I yearned to touch him, to rest my head on his chest, to caress his chest hair, to listen to the beat of his heart.

There was still one bean beneath the bed. I balanced on my right knee and reached toward it. When it fell into the bowl, the final bean of all, all I could hear was the sound of Bajram's heavy, lustful breathing. I turned to look at him. Bajram had begun to pleasure himself; with his left hand he was stroking his chest, while his right hand was frantically moving between his legs. He jumped onto the bed, grabbed my hand, and pulled me with him.

And I remember exactly what happened next. Every detail. The way Bajram forced his way inside me, rupturing my hymen. I remember the unpleasant, stuffy smell of his groin, the pain coursing through the bottom of my stomach, pain that felt as though someone had slit me open with a knife. I remember screaming with pain, Bajram's hand in front of my mouth, his shushing, the stink of his breath: tobacco, garlic, tobacco, leek, tobacco, and aged beef.

I remember how he pressed his body down on top of me, the small berries of spittle that trickled from the corner of his mouth, the sweaty hair clinging to his forehead. But perhaps most vividly of all I remember his face, frozen in an expression of the utmost pleasure: the inability of his eyes to focus, his lips slightly open, the panting moving in and out of his mouth, the quiver of his muscles from the exhausting back-and-forth motion of his hips.

Once Bajram had finished he looked casual and carefree as he wiped his groin on the corner of the duvet. He sprang up from the bed, muttered a word or two to himself as though nothing had happened, as if he had stood up from the bed like that a hundred times, and disappeared.

I remained sitting on the bed, pondering the extraordinary disappointment that had just befallen me, a few minutes of unpleasant smells, strange positions, and unexpected, uncomfortable surprises. I was at once calm and in an utter panic. I had nothing left to wait for. This is what it would be like always, I thought. Every time.

Then I looked beneath the blankets. When I saw there was only a little blood on the sheet I took the razor blade from beneath my armpit. Following my mother's instructions, I'd kept the blade in my bra and slipped it under my arm before undressing. Using the blade I made a little cut in my armpit, scraped up some blood and smeared it over myself and the sheets, careful not to leave smudged fingerprints. I licked my fingers clean, stashed the blade beneath the mattress, and pressed my arm against my side.

When Bajram came back inside he sat down on the bed without saying a word, pulled away the blankets, and looked between my legs. He gave a satisfied smile and slipped the duvet between his legs. There was something so self-assured, so easy-going about his behavior that I knew he would always do this, always come to bed in precisely the same way.

Then he opened the drawer in the bedside table and took out a packet of red Wests, pulled out a cigarette, carefully placed it between his lips, lit it, and filled the room with smoke.

The following morning our white sheet with its large red stain was hung out on the washing line for all to see.

The relatives who had been staying at the house looked at it, now convinced beyond doubt that the bride was indeed untouched. The sheet fluttered with the wind carried in across the undulating meadows. I looked at it through the kitchen window, relieved that the bleeding had stopped so quickly last night. By morning there was only a thin smudge of blood across my bicep and armpit.

Just then a black cat ran across the yard. It leaped up onto the wall and walked along until it reached the corner. The cat sat down and looked regal and dignified, the mountains rising up behind it like a cape, the walls surrounding it as though they were a part of the cat's armor in which the trees were embroidered decorations. The cat's long black tail dangled in an arch like an adder; it sat on the spot, not moving, and stared at the house, which seemed to stare back at it.

I wondered why the morning seemed so quiet and strange. When I had served the men of the family with coffee and handed them a slice of bread from the tray, they had put money on the tray and driven off to their own houses. Bajram's mother hadn't shown the slightest interest when I'd mentioned the events planned for the afternoon and evening and said how much I was looking forward to receiving my family.

When Bajram and his father drove off somewhere, I asked his mother to tell me the truth. *Is it true that we're not having any guests today?* A moment later Bajram's mother showed me into the living room, told me to sit down, and switched on the television.

The death yesterday of Josip Broz Tito marks the end of an era.

"Bajram didn't want to tell you," she began and dabbed the corner of her eye with a handkerchief. "He was worried it would ruin your day if you heard. That's why he wanted to fetch you yesterday in person."

When it transpired that I was the last person to hear the news, I realized that my wedding had come to an end. That day would not be a day during which the bride can receive guests at her new house, a day on which anyone can visit and see all the clothes and gifts that the groom had bought his bride and that were now laid out for all to see in the newly wedded couple's bedroom. The ball gowns would not cover the bed and the walls, the floors would not be covered with different pairs of shoes, gold would not be set out on the dressing table, pieces of jewelry would not be hung around the drawer handles, and rings would not be placed in a neat, pretty row so that the dressing-table mirror would make it look as though there were two of everything.

And I went back into the kitchen, pressed a hand against my chest, clenched my fist, and when I noticed that the cat was no longer sitting on top of the wall, I ran my fingertips along the windowpane and wept.

II

When you touch me, I die
I wonder if this could be love

—LADY GAGA, "VENUS"

10

Our trip to Kosovo each summer took us almost two thousand miles by bus, because my father refused to use the plane or the train. They traveled so fast that they would come to pieces, he said, their metallic bodies would fatigue and eventually fall apart and passengers would be thrown from inside like giant hailstones.

In Helsinki we took the ferry to Estonia, and from Tallinn we took a bus to Berlin. There we changed to the bus to Vienna, and in Vienna we changed to a bus bound for Prishtina.

Of those journeys I remember the hours spent sitting in buses, the searing heat, and the skylines of the cities. How primitive Tallinn looked compared to Helsinki, for instance, how forbidding and colorless Warsaw rose from the banks of the Vistula, how the sheer abundance of consonants in Polish caused me anxiety, every word sounding harsh and violent. And when I told this to my father, he explained that the Polish language is like that because the Polish people are like that, harsh and violent. They support Russia and Serbia. *Thank the Lord there's only another two hundred miles of this godforsaken country.*

Once we had driven through Poland and passed the seemingly endless lines of trucks, we arrived in Germany, where the roads had four lanes and were all brand-new, they smelled of fresh asphalt, and you could drive along them so fast that sitting in a bus suddenly felt even more frightening than all those Polish consonants.

I can recall how modestly the outskirts of Berlin began. The city didn't draw attention to itself but warmed up slowly like a jogger's muscles. And I remember the hurry in Berlin, how little time we had to change buses, it was the same every time, there was never any time to go to the toilet let alone stretch our legs, and how much my coccyx started to ache the minute the bus jolted off again.

But it didn't matter for soon we would arrive in Vienna, which was my favorite city of all. Its tall buildings were beautifully shaped: roofs with tapered turrets, curved buildings one after the other. They were built of shining glass, and the people standing at the foot of these buildings looked content and cheerful and beautiful and, above all, happy. The hours spent waiting at the bus terminus in Vienna were what I looked forward to the most, even though I was never given permission to explore the surrounding area by myself.

I admired everything around me—the modern benches we sat on, the patterns on Viennese shopping bags, the habit people had of lightly blowing smoke from their lungs, as though it had never been there in the first place, cars with hoods that gleamed and glinted and with tires that looked as though they were turning backward though, of course, they were moving forward.

I pressed my forehead against the bus taking us to Prishtina and dreamed that I would one day return to this city and really see it, go inside all those buildings that we never visited and that we left behind after ten minutes' driving. After a while the mountains came into view, mountains that looked very different from those in the Balkans, greener and steeper and yet gentler with cozy little houses built into the hillsides. They were connected to roads and villages and posed no danger to anyone. They simply existed.

All I remember of the final leg of our journey was the heat and the feeling of nausea. The buses were older and made more noise, there wasn't always a toilet on board, they rattled along the bumpy roads stretching across the Balkans, and the seats were upholstered with old, stale-smelling velour.

When we arrived in Slovenia my father told us that many people had died here. And when we reached Croatia he said the same thing: many people had died here. And when we arrived in Bosnia my father told us that here is where the most people of all had died. And as we drove through Serbia my father said that many people had died here—and a good thing it is too. People had died all around us, in Macedonia too, he said, in Albania, Bulgaria, and Greece.

So many people had died on this peninsula that it seemed as though my father wished to honor each and every one of them by using the word *death* as many times as possible.

When we finally arrived at our destination my parents smiled. It was different from the smile that my siblings and I smiled, for our smile was one of relief, a smile that after three days we no longer had to sit on a bus. But theirs was the smile of someone who hasn't smiled for a long time.

We stayed at my mother's parents' house in the countryside near Prishtina, and throughout our stay we did virtually nothing. We woke up in the mornings, ate breakfast, then dinner, and eventually went to sleep. I remember that time seemed to pass very slowly, that our father spent very little time with us, and that every day ended with my mother arguing with her parents.

"You promised to come back," they said.

And my mother said simply that it wasn't possible. She said

it almost in passing because my mother didn't argue with them at the same speed as they argued with her. She answered their questions calmly and slowly, and they presented increasingly provocative questions. And eventually they said to my mother that she had turned her back on her own country. The argument always ended when my siblings and I were summoned into the room and asked point-blank where we would rather live, here or in Finland, asked which was a better country, and we looked at one another and answered one after the other that we would rather live in Finland, though we didn't say why.

"See?" said my grandfather. "That's precisely what I mean."

Once I woke up in the middle of the night, and I was on my way to the bathroom when I bumped into my grandfather in the corridor. He went into the toilet first and I waited my turn behind the door. When I was finished, I saw that he hadn't gone back to his room but had sat down in the living room and left the door open. I had barely glimpsed his figure from the corner of my eye when he called me by my name and startled me.

"Bekim. Come here," he whispered.

And I did as I was told, sat on his knee, and asked him what he wanted. He gave a deep sigh and began to speak. He said he was worried about us, worried about what kind of people we would become. I couldn't say anything to him because the room was pitch-dark, and he asked whether I'd noticed that I had started to forget words in my mother tongue, asked why I didn't like the same games as my cousins, because he wanted to know, and he asked why I was so quiet, why I spent all day with the farm animals, why I didn't answer when I was asked if I liked the food or whether I had slept well, why I would rather spend the evenings reading a book than watching television with the family.

"And I'm worried," he said. "Worried that one day you

won't be an Albanian at all but something else altogether. And then you'll go to hell."

He pulled me closer, tight against his chest, and wrapped his arms around me. I could smell the old sweat beneath his armpits, the scent of garlic on his breath; his rough fingers clasped round my wrists. Then he said my mother had suggested that, if I wanted to, I could stay with them.

"You could help with the animals and go to school in Albania," he said and clenched my wrist tighter still.

I tried to wriggle free of his grasp, but he clenched all the harder.

"Think about it," he whispered eventually and let me slide down his thigh.

I lay awake all night, and when I heard that my mother had woken up I went to her and asked why she had suggested such a thing. I didn't want to live here, she knew that perfectly well.

My mother creased her brow, she scoffed and looked away for a moment, then turned and stared past my grandfather and across the room with a look in her eyes that I was unable to read.

THE ALCHEMY OF A NATION

I duly obeyed Bajram and his parents and never made a fuss, though the majority of the household chores and work in the fields fell on my shoulders. For a long while I was unsure of my status in Bajram's house, a feeling that only worsened when I didn't become pregnant at once. His father made only a few comments, but his mother more than compensated. *Shouldn't we do something with her,* she whispered to Bajram, making sure I heard. *Take her to the doctors, maybe? I'm worried. I want nothing else in this life than to see you have a son.*

Bajram had three older sisters who had all been married off to neighboring villages and who visited the house several times a month. There was nobody else in the house, only us and his parents.

At last we had our first child, who was a boy. Bajram and his parents couldn't have been happier, and they spent all their free time with the boy and were continually buying him new clothes from the bazaar.

As I looked after the child, I gradually realized that I was different from the other mothers. The other women in the village talked about their children all the time: how old they were when they started to walk, when they stopped breast-feeding, what kind of children's clothes you could pick up at the bazaar. Listening to the other women, I'd realized that having a child changes us. There is nothing we care for as much as our child and our child's well-being. Any extra resources would be used on the child, while we ourselves could survive on bread if necessary.

Once I got over the enormous sense of hollowness that the birth of my first child brought about, the other four came in quick succession. We had two girls one after the other, and Bajram became increasingly impatient until we had another boy and then a third daughter. Bajram was thrilled—two sons, both of whom looked exactly like him.

I loved my children with all my heart, of course I did. But though loving them made me see the world in a wholly different way, I still didn't love them as much as I loved myself. It's impossible for us to love another person in the same way as we love ourselves. There is nothing more tragic than a mother who talks endlessly about her children in an attempt to demonstrate that it's possible after all.

If I'd had the choice, I would have chosen not to have children. It was painful and messy, and the workload only increased with each subsequent child. In fact, one thing that Bajram and I shared was a disappointment in the monotony of parenthood and family life.

I was the wife of his dreams. I washed, clothed, fed, and looked after his children, scrubbed and polished his guests' shoes when they visited the house. I made sure there was always water in the bucket in the toilet for flushing—this I checked every time one of his guests left the bathroom. Every evening I laid out his clothes for the next day, I ironed his socks and shirts and washed his underwear in almost boiling water, otherwise they smelled of his groin.

I became pregnant without making a fuss and my bulging stomach only stopped me working in the final months of the pregnancy. I never gossiped with the other women and brought our children up to be quiet, the kind of children who didn't make a song and dance about themselves. They only spoke when they were given permission.

When cancer finally took Bajram's mother, who had looked after the family finances and delegated the household chores for three decades, I assumed her role and workload without the slightest protestation. Throughout the village my reputation as a wife, a woman, and a mother was second to none—nobody else was able to get so much housework done, nobody else prepared *pite* pastry as thin as mine, and nobody else's laundry smelled as fresh as mine. What's more, nobody's children obeyed their mother as dutifully as mine.

In all those years Bajram never once said thank you, though he had plenty of opportunities to do so. He didn't thank me that his favorite towel was always laundered and ready for him, didn't thank me for the fact that he never once had to go to work without breakfast, neither that his shoes always looked polished and new nor for the fact that our children never woke him up at night, neither because I never mentioned his snoring nor for the fact that I never left him in a situation in which he might have needed me, because in his life I was always present. Nothing hurt me as much as his lack of thanks. It hurt more than all the work, the endless drudgery of beating the mats, washing the floors and walls, dusting the shelves, and preparing food.

Did he have any idea how much time all this took? I often wondered. When it took me less than a minute to fall asleep next to him, did he understand that every part of my body ached? And when, despite my exhaustion, we made love, did he really think that nobody could possibly love her husband more than a woman waiting at home?

Bajram worked long hours at the ministry of education, and when he came home he expected dinner to be served immediately, followed by two hours to relax. During that time nobody was allowed to speak to him. The children were shut in their rooms.

Yet nothing pleased him, and he flew into a rage with increasing regularity. He often behaved violently for no apparent reason, slapped our daughters if they got in his way. He wanted the world to function according to his wishes. He lived out his days in his own mind and became frustrated when reality didn't match the life he had imagined.

Bajram's father died suddenly of a brain hemorrhage. He was a man who did lots of physical labor and who never complained of tiredness. One morning, as he was walking from the house out into the fields, he simply collapsed and fell onto his stomach. It was several hours until someone noticed him lying facedown in the overgrown reeds. *Death plucked him like a caramel,* said Bajram. *Now I see that everything can end at any moment. What on earth is the point of all this?*

We held a dignified funeral for his father, and once it was over Bajram suggested we move to Prishtina. He would be closer to his work and the children could go to better schools. *We wouldn't need to look after all this. It would be easier for you too.*

Bajram felt almost naked. He was left looking after the farm by himself, and before the age of thirty had been saddled with the kind of responsibility that men his age rarely had to shoulder. He went to Prishtina to look for an apartment and quickly found something suitable: a flat on the sixth floor of an apartment building.

City life came as a shock to all of us. From a young age I had wanted to live in the city, to visit jewelry and clothing boutiques, but the buildings were noisy and people thronged around us. It was impossible to concentrate on anything. There were shops on almost every corner, newspaper stands and tobacco kiosks, restaurants belching out the smell of boiling fat.

Everything was expensive, food in particular. In the countryside ten dinars could last you for weeks, but here it was gone in only a few days. The city was brimming with temptations, gambling, and drugs. Thieves who emptied the bags and pockets of people walking along the street. You had to be on your guard all the time, and you couldn't let the children out after dark because the roads were filled with black cars with tinted windows. Every day women and young children disappeared into those cars before being sold off for such brutal purposes that one could hardly believe the human mind could imagine such a thing.

We knew that there had been unrest in the city between the Albanians and the Serbs, but we had no idea quite how serious the situation was until we moved to the city. Every day somebody died, somebody's possessions were destroyed, houses, cars. Every day the front page of *Rilindja* was filled with gruesome headlines: someone was murdered on the way to work and someone else in the middle of the night, cars were driven into nearby lakes, and families entered long-lasting feuds with each other. Serbian children didn't play with Albanian children, the Serbs didn't eat in Albanian-owned restaurants, and the Albanians refused to sell tobacco to the Serbs. *Tito's death was the end,* said Bajram. *The Serbs will never give up. They want to see us on our knees, shining their shoes.* One of the reasons Bajram wanted to move to the city was so that he could follow the unfolding chaos up close.

The situation grew tenser with every passing day. Party Chairman Milošević diverted more and more government funds to building projects in Belgrade, millions and millions of dinars.

Everyone began to miss Tito because if Tito had still been in power the Serbs' demands would never have passed through parliament. The people of Yugoslavia had feared this moment for years, the moment when the man who had risen from a modest peasant family to lead us all finally died. Who would lead Yugoslavia once Tito was no longer around?

Only a few years after Tito's death, Prishtina became a dangerous place to live. Milošević gave speeches in which he promised to look after all Serbs in the province who lived—without any good reason—in fear of their position in society. *Nobody shall beat you again,* said Milošević. We followed the rise in nationalist fervor his speeches caused in a state of shock. Nobody had beaten the Serbs. Nobody had so much as touched them.

All of a sudden tanks and soldiers were filling the streets. When Albanians started being systematically removed from their jobs, from positions in hospitals and the police, and when it became impossible to study in Albanian, the situation turned desperate. There was no room in the city to breathe. The caretaker in our apartment building didn't bother to clean the floors with Albanian residents. The bosses at Bajram's office were sacked and Serbs were appointed in their place, and eventually Bajram too lost his job. Local authorities gave Serb-owned businesses tax cuts while general taxation for Albanians was increased. Albanians had to study in basements and private apartments, in secret, and teachers caught teaching Albanians were routinely attacked, gas grenades were thrown into civilian apartments, and innocent people were beaten up in the streets.

The air became thick and damp, heavy with the smell of burning, because it was breathed in turn by the desperate and the insane. I worried that I would wake up to find our apartment building on fire or that my children and I would be kidnapped and taken away, that we'd never see one another again. How was it even possible to experience hatred to such a degree that you altogether lost your sense of right and wrong?

When war broke out in Bosnia and we heard about the brutalities to which the Bosnians were subjected—they were driven out of their homes, their houses were bombed, pregnant women were tortured and raped and taken to concentration camps— I wondered what was happening to this planet. At what point had humans turned into beasts that mauled one another, that held their neighbors' heads beneath the water? People had died inside, the veins leading to their hearts were a mesh of mold, and their souls were black and sticky with filth. Do people who commit such acts deserve to live?

When I heard the streets rumble beneath the tanks, I wondered what it would feel like if my life were to end in the same way as that of so many Bosnians. I would look on as buildings were destroyed, the Biblioteka Popullore dhe Universitare e Kosovës and the Xhamia e Llapit would collapse like sand castles, and the city would no longer be a city but sand soiled and tormented with gunpowder, people would die in fires and explosions, and among the dead might be my own friends and relatives. And me too.

I couldn't help thinking these things, though they made me tremble with fear. I sweated with terror, had to change my clothes several times a day, and didn't dare go outside. I might wake up in the middle of the night and frantically check that my children were all still alive, place a finger beneath their noses and reassure myself that they were still breathing.

As I looked at the Serb soldiers' machine guns I realized that that soldier could end the life of any passerby in a matter of seconds, that tank could bring an entire building crumbling to the ground if the soldier sitting inside the tank decided to do so.

Death was the very clothes we wore, and the whole city was wrapped in sheets doused in ash. It belched dust and mortar, showering a ghostly fog all around, and it was so close that our entire lives assumed a new form. Life was no longer a unique journey; it was a short slit, a pinprick on a fingertip, a bottle to the head in a dark alleyway, and there was nothing unique about it.

One June day in 1993, when we arrived home from my parents' house, we realized that our apartment had been ransacked. The door had been rammed in. My jewelry had been taken, the furniture broken, and the appliances smashed to pieces. A large stone had been thrown through the television screen and the cable cut with a pair of shears. The windows were in smithereens. The oven wouldn't work because the flue had been knocked out of place. There was no warm water in the bathroom because the boiler had been knocked from the wall and had broken in two. The photographs had all been taken—they'd taken our photographs too, for no other reason than to cause added distress, all our wedding photos, photos of our children.

There was nothing left, not even a bed to sleep in. Bajram stood for a moment looking at the devastation, the shards of glass and the torn clothes, at what little was left of our world. *We have to leave,* he said. *If we don't leave, we'll die.*

Eventually we learned that our insurance would not cover any of the damage caused in the break-in. According to the Serbian eyewitnesses our front door had been wide open and a group of Albanian youths had taken advantage of the situation, and this was a good enough explanation for the Serbian police. Bajram paced agitatedly round the apartment, breathing heavily. He looked withdrawn, as though he couldn't get a firm grip on the decision he'd just made, and rubbed his overgrown hair.

He drove me and the children to my parents' house, fetched our suitcases the very next day, threw them into the hallway, and said he would go back to the apartment in Prishtina to see if there was anything we could salvage. He had a few thousand dinars in cash, which would help us to a fresh start.

We had heard countless stories of Albanians who had moved to Germany, Switzerland, and Austria, the Netherlands, but Bajram wanted to go somewhere far away, somewhere where there wasn't a single Serb. On a map he had bought he circled three countries: Australia and the United States because they were far away, but Finland he circled because he liked the name

of the country and because he'd heard people talk of how afflu-
ent the Nordic countries were.

Once he realized how many forms and applications he would
have to complete in order to move to Australia or the USA and
how expensive it would be he settled on the final option and got
his hands on a pile of books about the Nordic countries.

"It says here they have good schools and well-paid jobs.
We'll only be there a short time," Bajram declared and slammed
the book shut.

"Very well," I said. "We'll go there now and come back here
eventually."

"It will be best for all of us," he said and paused for a
moment.

Then he said thank you.

ABOVE THE BALKAN SKY

Bajram had never before been in an airplane. He put five pieces of chewing gum in his mouth, took me by the hand, and gripped hard as the jet engines right by his ears began to suck air through their blades to lift up the weight of the plane and its passengers. His hand was sweaty and felt unpleasant.

It was my first time in an airplane too, but I had to be a wife to him and a mother to my children, who were every bit as afraid as we were and whose ears hurt. The plane was a long, narrow tube, and nobody could get out of it. When the plane achieved the necessary speed and began rising into the air, higher and higher, Bajram pressed his hands over his ears. He was afraid that the floor might disappear from beneath him and he would plummet to his death, that the very fall itself would seem to last an eternity because it must take hours to fall from such a height.

Bajram leaned across me to look out of the window. His eyes widened all the more and his grip on my hand became almost unbearable. Eventually he closed his eyes and began to pray. *If humans were meant to fly like this, we would all have wings,* he said.

A month earlier we had traveled by bus to Sofia in Bulgaria, where we had been forced to wait several weeks. The city felt sweltering and massive, the volume of people seemed endless, they disappeared into brightly colored buildings like ants. We stayed at a cheap hotel and with the children in tow we didn't venture farther than the hotel's front courtyard and the shop round the corner because we spent every day waiting for Bajram to sort out our affairs.

When Bajram tried to book flights to Helsinki, at first the staff at the tourist office refused to sell them to him. When Bajram told them we were going to Finland to visit relatives, they didn't believe him and asked him to give the names and addresses of the relatives. Neither did they believe him when he said he had secured a job in Finland, nor when he told them he was a diplomat, and they took a particularly dim view of matters when he tried to bribe them. They knew we were Albanians. The city was full of us, and everyone wanted to fly somewhere out of Sofia.

Once we were almost out of money, I asked Bajram to be honest. *Tell them the truth. Please. Tell them you have an exhausted wife and five exhausted children, and tell them you're worried we won't survive this. Tell them you are a human being just like them, a father and a husband, and that you care about your family just as they do for their own.*

The following day Bajram ran back to the hotel. When he stepped into our hotel room he was panting heavily and stealing paranoid glances over his shoulder. Then he closed the door and pulled seven plane tickets from his jacket pocket, placed them in my hands, and kissed me on the forehead.

"You're a genius," he said and stroked my hair with a smile, and once he'd gone again I sat down and smiled more broadly than I had ever smiled before, and I didn't know whether I was smiling because we would soon be on our way or because Bajram had called me a genius.

All the people around us looked wealthy and important and they all spoke a different language. I didn't dare get out of my seat, not even to go to the bathroom. Bajram, on the other hand, didn't hear or see a thing until halfway through the flight when the plane began to shudder violently and sway like a rickety boat. It felt as if we were on a train that had come off its tracks. From the overhead speakers we heard speech that we couldn't understand, and yellow lights switched on in the contraptions above our heads. Bajram was certain we were going to die, though nobody else seemed at all nervous. Bajram opened his eyes, gave me a look of sheer terror, and placed his other hand on my thigh.

In the seat in front our eldest daughter stood up. She looked first at her father then at me. Bajram had buried his face in his hands. *What's happening,* she asked, her voice trembling.

"I don't know. Sit down," I said.

And she obeyed me. She sat down next to her brother and took him by the hand. Ten minutes later the shuddering stopped. The yellow lights were switched off and the other passengers continued to look exactly the same, continued to leaf through their newspapers and sip the drinks the stewardesses had served them.

"Don't speak to them like that," Bajram snapped. His eyes had opened and his fingers clenched round the armrests.

When we arrived we were driven to a reception center, a building that looked like a hospital for forgotten patients. I can remember almost nothing about that trip, though one would think it impossible to forget even a moment of such a journey, of the surprise at how different everything looked, the lights, the houses, how differently people walked along the pavement, the way they dressed, the smell of the air. And what a shock it was to discover that all the buildings were low, not high-rise, and looked cheap. That there was so much water and forest.

Before long we were on the fourth floor of a large building, sitting in a deserted corridor with gray walls. We were waiting for Bajram. His voice could be heard from the room opposite. The reception center official was speaking English, but Bajram spoke only a few words of that language. I had expected we would wait until the interpreter arrived, at least that's what we had understood from the official who had driven us here, but Bajram gesticulated impatiently and raised his voice to the blond-haired woman who seemed to be repeating the same couple of words to Bajram over and over.

Finnish sounded like a colorless, inexpressive language. The words seemed to crack like brittle, unhealthy bones.

We remained at the reception center. We had imagined we would be given our own apartment with our own kitchen and bathroom. Along one of the walls in our room were three bunk beds, all painted red, and along the other wall a row of wardrobes for our clothes. The beds were metallic and badly made and they gave a shrill creak every time you moved. The creaking beds all but drove me and Bajram to distraction, and eventually we took all the mattresses and placed them on the cold floor simply in order to get some sleep.

Bajram had told me that people in Finland lived in enormous detached houses with swimming pools, laminate floors, and large kitchens. He said that all the houses were at least 150 feet apart and that in Finland people respect one another's privacy by placing their houses far apart, unlike in Kosovo, where houses are built in a row, each higher than the next. Imagine, *grua,* it's a completely different world.

One morning I lifted my bare feet from the cold concrete floor and placed them on the armchair, looked out of the window, and wondered at how brazenly he had lied to us.

I was furious. I could think of nothing else for many nights, many weeks, many months, and every time I saw him, every time I spoke to him or smelled him, every time he lit a cigarette, when he snored or ground his teeth, every time I hated him more and hated myself more. I wanted to kill him.

The Finnish houses he had talked about were nowhere to be seen, the swimming pools, the remodeled attics, the bright rooms. Everything we had had before, everything we had owned, had been swapped for these plastic floors and old beds.

There were eight families on our floor, eight apartments and one kitchen. The bathrooms had elevated toilet bowls with dubious-looking stains running down the sides. The greatest shock of all was that Finnish people didn't wash themselves after doing their business but settled for a piece of toilet paper. Paper! That's why there were no jugs or bottles of water in the bathrooms. It was the most repulsive thing I'd ever seen. How could they walk after doing their business?

In the room opposite was a family of eight from Somalia. They made a racket night and day and their language was strange. When I saw my children playing with their dark-skinned children it felt as though something was wrong, something had been turned upside down. We had become just like them; we befriended them because we too were oppressed and disliked. We were as rejected as the Gypsies, another group of people who had come from far away and wound up in this country, a place where the people were so white they might as well have been made of snow. I considered us white too, but in their eyes we weren't white in the same way.

I spent most of my time sitting in our room and thinking. It felt as though the Finns looked at us like animals in a cage. I was ashamed even to go out for a walk because I knew people would spot me simply by the way I carried myself. I was ashamed of taking public transport, of sitting in the park, of looking people in the eye and going into shops other than the supermarket.

And when in one shop I bought five discounted loaves of French bread and five cans of chopped tomatoes without separating my purchases with the divider, I could have died of shame when the cashier began angrily speaking Finnish to me, lifted the divider into the air, and showed me how to put it on the conveyor belt after my own shopping because now she had almost charged me for the next customer's shopping too. I didn't understand a word. I handed her a banknote, left without waiting for my change, and never went back to that shop again.

I admired how organized everything was. Imagine, in Finnish supermarkets you could separate your shopping with a divider; they even had their own groove to keep them in a neat row. There were no dividers in Kosovo. I imagined that, when I got back home, my story would start with the dividers.

But when I got back to our room and saw how the staff at the reception center greeted me, how pityingly they smiled at me, I wanted to punch them in the face. And when they spoke to us like children and said you shouldn't eat with your fingers, I wanted to clobber them round the back of the head with the frying pan.

We might eat with our fingers, I thought, but you won't find our men sleeping on park benches and bus shelters in the morning. The Finns drank so much alcohol that they couldn't remember what they had done or where they had been, and when I heard that some people lost everything—their family, their health and work—all because of alcohol, at first I shook my head then doubled over laughing because I'd never heard of something so thoroughly nonsensical.

I've never seen people like this, said Bajram. *They stand around like trees, statues, staring at us.* He gave a mocking laugh. *Let them stare.* He seemed unable to comprehend it when I tried to explain that they were probably staring at us because they didn't want us here in their country.

Look around you, woman, he said and gesticulated wildly. *They have more than enough. Why on earth wouldn't they want us here? What could they need that they don't already have?*

THE TOWN

After living in the reception center for almost a year, we settled in a small Finnish town that went to sleep at eight o'clock in the evening at the very latest. All the other immigrants were placed in the same district.

The immigrants spent time only with one another and didn't care that you were supposed to be quiet in the apartment buildings after 10 p.m., that you were supposed to use the sauna only when it was your turn, that you weren't allowed to leave clothes in the drying room overnight, or that you couldn't just pick any empty parking space outside the building. Such rules seemed incredibly petty, and once they noticed how much breaking them irritated the Finns, they simply laughed.

The other immigrants in the area soon began working at one of the local factories, but Bajram would not accept a job like that. He didn't believe it worthy of him because he had a university degree and had held respected positions in the past. *Nobody here with a university education would take on a job like that,* he said. *Never.*

Bajram learned Finnish better than I did, better than all the other immigrants, and found Finnish friends whom he regaled with stories about his world and his culture and whom he even invited to our house.

He showed me and the children off to these middle-aged men as he would any possessions, and the men sat at our table smiling and peering around. *My son, he is good boy. And my daughter, she make good food,* Bajram boasted.

I prepared food for them, peppers stuffed with ground meat and *mazë*, I baked fresh bread for them and offered them tea, and they ate and patted their bellies in a manner that even I understood. But Bajram wasn't yet full. He picked up his empty plate and held it toward me without saying a word. I had just put food in my mouth and my fingers were covered in the *mazë* into which I had dipped pieces of bread. Bajram saw this.

I took his plate in a panic, tried to swallow my mouthful and surreptitiously wipe my fingers on the table and beneath his plate, but there was too much of it and my fingers were still slippery with grease.

I placed two stuffed peppers on Bajram's plate, though the dish with the peppers was closer to him than to me, and put it in front of him. I tried to continue eating, though I could see immediately that he wasn't moving. I wished he would let the matter pass. When I looked up, he was puffing like a bison. He raised his index finger and tapped his nail against the surface of his plate. *Please don't do this,* I begged him silently.

His unflinching stare felt so crushing that eventually I got up, took a fresh dishcloth out of the drawer, leaned across the table, and wiped the almost imperceptible smear of *mazë* off the side of his plate. After this he began to eat again.

The men sitting round the table gave me a look of pity. I glanced at Bajram, who was concentrating on stuffing his mouth with *mazë,* to make sure that I could look up at them the way I wanted to look at Bajram. All four of them looked down, picked up their cutlery, and began spooning the creamy *mazë* like soup.

Bajram spent all his evenings and weekends with these men. They visited famous places, drove across Finland, and watched sporting and musical events. Bajram missed the children's birthdays, their first day at school, the moment they learned to ride a bike. I had imagined he would start taking an interest in things like this, especially now that he had nothing better to do, now that his children needed him more than ever before, but once Bajram got to know other Albanian immigrants in Finland, with whom he could finally speak Albanian again, we saw even less of him.

Every time he went off somewhere, he left money on the kitchen table. I quickly learned how to gauge from the amount of money when he would be back. He had worked out that one hundred marks per week was plenty. It was always a relief when Bajram went away. I took the money from the table and began budgeting for the following days, and from every sum I counted I put a small amount aside.

Our eldest children started going to school. When it turned out that children in Finland are entitled to preschool education even before they start school, I was so happy that I could hardly believe it was true. I was afraid they might send the children back home and say there was no good reason why my children should be at preschool.

Because Finnish women had jobs, they didn't have time to stay at home with their children, and so they let other people take care of them. When I heard that children as young as eighteen can move away from home, I was shocked. What kind of person is an eighteen-year-old? What does an eighteen-year-old know about life? Nothing whatsoever.

Every day I sent my children to school and preschool slightly early and collected them late in the afternoon. All my spare time I spent sleeping. I couldn't get enough of it. It was as though I was addicted to killing time: the time until my husband would come home again and leave again.

11

When I arrived in Prishtina for the first time in eight years, everything had changed from the images in which the city had remained in my mind. Dust floated down from the sky like slow rain and rose up through the drains like fog and mixed with the gasoline and sweat hanging in the air.

A long line of taxis was waiting outside the terminal for all the Kosovans who had moved abroad and who flew back to their homeland for the summer.

The taxi driver was holding a cigarette smoked right down to the filter in his thick, brown, weather-beaten fingers, and his expression didn't so much as flicker when I responded to his attempt at conversation by telling him to drive forward. He looked around himself, regularly wiping his sweaty brow with his yellowed shirtsleeve.

I turned and looked out of the window at the view in which the advertisements, shops, and cafés of the airport quickly changed into an attractive panorama of trees and mountains that looked like a row of hats. An unrelenting heat parched the terrain like a fluttering sheet.

The closer to the city center we drove, the more crammed

the streets became with orange, yellow, green, red, and blue bill-boards, each of them shouting to be noticed. The streets were crowded, the heat was unyielding, and the smell of sweat clawed at me everywhere, and all around there were orange-bricked houses, most of them only half finished, nothing but black holes where there should have been doors and windows. There was rubbish everywhere, between the houses and at the side of the pavement. Through the doors of the shops spilled the wares that people were desperately trying to sell inside—fruit, appliances, and toys—as the traffic tried to negotiate its way around them.

I arrived at my hotel room and put my suitcases on the bed. The Grand Hotel was situated near Bill Klinton Boulevard at the northern end of a street named after Xhorxh Bush and just south of the Skanderbeg statue. The central pedestrian street was full of people, clothing shops, cafés with music blaring inside where people had to speak all the louder to make themselves heard.

I walked around aimlessly, my hands in my pockets, and eventually decided to sit down at a café where people were sitting outside talking about literature, education, and equality. I'd expected to see people licking their wounds and shutting themselves away in their homes, but I soon came to understand quite how much those who had moved away from Kosovo, the *shqip-tarët e diasporës,* had fallen behind. People's attitudes and values seemed to have remained unchanged from the time when they left the country, and they were preserved in tight-knit communities in overcrowded European apartment buildings in disreputable parts of town, places where the homeland was only present through radio and television.

A handsome waiter brought me a fifty-cent macchiato, and I sat quietly listening to the people around me. Right then I realized that I could no longer speak properly; my Albanian was clumsy, slow, and unsure. I didn't recognize all the words they were using because the language had changed. Still, all the smells and tastes, the soft aroma of the macchiato, the thick, wooden tobacco smoke, and the smell from the stalls selling roasted corn on the cob were all familiar.

I was worried that somebody might come and start chatting to me, because then I would be caught out. I knew how shameful it was to be an Albanian who had forgotten his mother tongue. I turned the coffee cup in my fingers, stirred the two-colored foam with a red plastic stick until it was a single-colored mixture, and ordered all manner of different coffees that I only tasted, desserts that I didn't touch.

I felt guilty for being so tired and for thinking about the wrong things, for the fact that returning to this city after all these years didn't feel any more special than this. It should have felt as though I had come home, that I had come back here to die. I should have been making plans, should have written out a list, Muzeu i Kosovës, Muzeu Etnologjik, Varrezat e Dëshmorëve, and Galeria e Arteve, and visited photography exhibitions with photographs of mass graves, visited cemeteries, talked to people who had survived and told their story for future generations.

Perhaps I should have thought of all those dead people, those who had killed others or who had themselves died. Tiredness was nothing compared to spending months in a wintry forest, your fingers and toes freezing and eventually falling off. Nothing compared to children being born already dead and buried in a pile of snow.

The first time I heard the cat's plaintive meowing was on the way from the café back to the hotel. It was coming from a car wash near the hotel. Needless to say, I had to step inside and ask where the sound was coming from. After recovering from the shock of a complete stranger starting up a conversation by asking about a cat, the owner explained that a cat had turned up behind the building a few days earlier and wouldn't stop meowing.

Wiping his hands on his dirty sleeveless shirt and stained blue jeans, the man asked me over the rush of the pressure washer why I wanted to know. After all, it was only a cat, *vetëm një macë*. I was so agitated that I didn't hear his question but asked what kind of cat it was. The man told me he had never gone behind the building to see what kind of cat it was because it was only a cat.

Shut up, you fat idiot, I felt like shouting at him, but before I could do so I snuck behind the building, as slippery as a herring, as agile as a squirrel. It was an old house, traditional and built in three stories. The owners of the car wash lived above the garage, situated on one of the busiest streets in Prishtina.

As I arrived in the backyard I saw a wooden ladder propped against the wall and, a meter from the house, another tall wall separating this plot from the next. The wall seemed to stand there so lazily that it looked as though it might come crashing down on the house at any moment.

The backyard was a mess of plastic bottles, old food, and scraps of paper. And standing on all the litter was a small orange-and-white cat digging for something to eat.

The cat had slender paws and a frail-looking body. Its orange coat was dappled with irregular white spots, and the cat looked extremely unwell, as though it had taken a mud bath and then gone through the dryer.

When I took a step toward the cat, it stopped digging for food and turned to give me an accusatory look in the eyes, as though my step had put its life in danger.

As I took another step, the cat got itself ready to retreat. Its backside rose up tall and its paws tensed, its yellow claws protruded.

Then I began calling to it. I crouched down to its level and held out my hand, clenched in a fist. At first the cat looked at it, curious, then a moment later took its first step toward my fist, toward this strange person smiling and speaking to it, a thing the cat had probably never seen before.

It took almost an hour for the cat to start trusting me. Every now and then it took a cautious step toward me only to leap suddenly back onto the pile of rubbish upon hearing a single uneven breath.

I let the cat watch me and smell me in peace and quiet, and only once it touched me did I finally touch it. I stroked its small head and tail, its back and tummy, and eventually it climbed into my arms.

I decided to take it back to my hotel room. It didn't have a home, I thought. What a shame that nobody wanted to take the cat in, and such a beautiful cat too. Under no circumstances could it be left at the mercy of a man for whom this adorable creature was *just a cat*.

With the cat in my arms I walked back to the front of the building and turned furtively to see if anyone was watching me. I almost collided with the car wash owner's enormous stomach as he shouted at me, asking what I was doing with a stray cat.

"Macë e rrugës!" he kept repeating, shaking his head and laughing. *"O budallë!"*

A cigarette wet with spittle dropped from the corner of his mouth.

I gave him a murderous look and hid the cat under my shirt. If everybody around here was as disparaging about cats as this man, I thought, it was best to keep it hidden.

Once back in the hotel room I put the cat in the bathtub and took off my shirt, which had started to smell sour. It was covered in dark spots, grease from the cat's fur.

To my surprise, the cat turned out to be one of the gentlest cats I'd ever encountered. It was a real charmer. When I started running water into the tub, it looked up at me with its bright glowing eyes and didn't seem to care a jot about the water flowing over its body. Instead it started to wiggle its bottom. If it had behaved differently I would have understood; if it had scratched or bitten me, I would have assumed that must be because it had been pelted with stones, taunted, and beaten simply for being a cat.

Because its fur was so terribly tangled, I pampered the cat with fruit-smelling shampoo. *Soon you'll be clean, clean and happy, and you can eat as much food as you can manage,* I said as I ran my fingers deep through its rough coat.

As I fluffed its fur, the scratches and bruises, the wounds and scars were revealed one after the other. Of course, this cat had been through a lot, it had fought with other cats and gone without food for so long that it had shrunk to half its normal size. What a heartless and unpleasant thought. Yet this made it all the more extraordinary that the cat didn't make the slightest fuss about its bruises. Instead it lowered its head, closed its eyes, and retreated to the far end of the tub as though it were ashamed of them.

I dried the cat carefully and lifted it back into my arms. From now on your life will be different, I said. It will be a good life; I will make sure of that. *You won't have to go out into the streets or suffer ever again. I promise you that.*

Then I called room service and ordered some food for the cat, and the cat ate heartily. Lettuce, tomatoes, cucumber, French fries and beef, creamy gravy and fresh white bread—everything I took from the tray and put on its plate, it ate.

"Well," I said.

I smiled. I watched it and waited at the other end of the table to see whether it might smile back at me, but it was still eating, eating ravenously. Once it had finished its meal, it meticulously licked the plate and meowed for more.

"You can't eat everything at once," I chided it in a fatherly tone.

I stood up and went over to the bed to lie down. The cat hopped down from the table, ran across the room, and jumped up onto the bed. It climbed on my stomach and paced back and forth until it found a position that was so comfortable that it started breathing contentedly, as calm and relaxed as someone on holiday.

Once both of us were on the verge of falling asleep and the cat luxuriously stretched its limbs and rolled on its side, almost from force of habit I placed my hand on its little head. The cat twitched as though it had flinched at its own dreams, and I began to stroke it. My hand first stroked its head and neck, then its soft, long-clawed paws and thighs, its stomach and back, and finally its tail and hind legs, and it purred next to me in such a way that I knew it was overjoyed.

THE SNAKES

One night my younger son Bekim started having nightmares that wouldn't go away. He came into my bedroom shouting and holding a rolling pin with such force that his knuckles were white. A blood-red glow had risen to his cheeks. I grabbed him by the shoulders and asked what was wrong.

He began telling me about his nightmare, about the snake dangling from the light fixture on the ceiling that was so long and powerful it only had to wrap itself round the lampshade once, then it could stretch out the rest of its body to reach him.

"Shh," I said. "There's no such thing." I tried to reassure him and send him back to his bedroom though he had his hands between his legs, which were tense and stiff.

But he shouted again, and this time he shouted as though he was going to die. I ran to him and turned on the lights, took him in my arms, and told him there were no snakes in the room, not under the bed and not under the blankets. It hides when it hears footsteps, he told me.

I couldn't understand him. The dreams he told me about were terrifying. They featured cobras, their flared heads hooded, and giant boa constrictors that could crush entire buildings, and small black snakes with red eyes that could talk and threaten him. They wriggled around one another in such a tight ball that their skins creaked like wet rubber. *Open your mouth and I'll kill you. Go on, open it if you dare.* These were the kinds of things the snakes said to him.

"Shh," I said once again, though I shuddered.

I sat next to him almost all night. He slept quietly against the wall, his legs crossed, continuously flinching at his dreams. While he was asleep he ran his hand across the wall, touching its rough surface, and pressed his other hand against his face.

A few evenings later I tried to get him to sleep by taking him into my bed, but all he did was howl. He clenched his teeth together and wouldn't stop kicking. It was as though there was something right in front of him.

"What's the matter?" I cried.

Eventually his shouting drove me into such a rage that I slapped him. I slapped him so that he would answer me. Or at least so that he might be quiet so that everyone else, his siblings and I, might get some sleep. But that didn't stop him either. He didn't feel a thing.

The door opened and closed. Bajram walked along the hallway and into the bedroom, sat on the bed, took off his shoes, his socks and other clothes, threw them into the corner, lay down, and sighed with exhaustion.

"Is he sick?" he asked.

I told him the boy was having nightmares, violent nightmares about snakes.

"It'll pass," he said dismissively.

"And what if it doesn't?"

The desperation in my voice made him sit up from the sleeping position he had just assumed. *Shut your mouth, of course it'll pass.* Bajram pressed his hand against the boy's red, sweaty forehead.

"Shh," he said, trying to comfort the boy, but the crying wouldn't stop. "They don't exist," he continued. "I'll kill them if they come here. I'll kill them all with my bare hands. I'll tear them to pieces."

I wanted to stop him saying another word. The confidence in his voice made me wish he wouldn't touch the boy. I wanted to crack him over the head with a chair, shout right into his ear, tell him that's no way to comfort a small child. These were nightmares, not an ice-cream cone he'd dropped on the floor.

"Shh now, shh now," he repeated as though he had finally found a solution. The boy was kicking and screaming, his face was taut, and for a moment it looked as though he had stopped breathing altogether. I shook him, but this only caused more wheezing and crying.

Bajram stood up angrily and knelt down in front of the boy, took him firmly by the shoulders.

"What do you want?" he shouted, shaking the boy. Louder, louder, each time tightening his grip. I began to pity him. Bajram was shouting at him and I was shouting at Bajram, our selfish egos preventing us from understanding why one nightmare could be such a big deal. Why couldn't he just go to sleep again once he realized it was only a dream?

Finally Bajram moved his hands beneath the boy's arms, took him even more firmly, and shook him so hard and so long that the crying finally stopped—because he had lost consciousness.

"Don't ever do that again," I seethed once we had carried the boy back to his own bed and returned to our room.

"Are you going to tell me how to raise my children?" he shouted and punched me in the chest with such force that it felt as though someone had dropped a bowling ball in a pool of water. *One more time,* he said. *Do that one more time. It'll be the last thing you ever do.*

As I lay beside Bajram and listened to his loud snoring, I

sensed the sweat tingling on my forehead, the hairs stuck to my neck, my cold shallow breath that barely made it in and out of my mouth. How could he fall asleep so easily? At a moment like this?

We took the boy to the doctor. During the therapy sessions Bajram sat in the cafeteria. He was ashamed of having to talk about matters like this through an interpreter. He couldn't bear one of his compatriots seeing him in a situation in which he was unable to cope by himself.

The hospital smelled of metal and disinfectant. The boy chatted with the female psychologist in a room that was brightly lit and almost devoid of furniture. At the beginning of the sessions they talked in general about animals. The psychologist drew up two lists: the first of animals the boy liked and the second of animals he didn't like.

Later on the psychologist showed me the lists. The first one included dogs, birds, fish, dolphins, and monkeys, and the second featured sharks, crocodiles, lions, tigers, and cats. She explained that children like animals with which they associate safe, positive images.

"And they reject animals with negative associations," she stressed. "Animals that they consider threatening and dangerous."

She placed a finger on the second list. *Can you explain why he might have put cats on this list and not the other one?* I couldn't answer because I didn't understand the point of the question. We hadn't come here to talk about cats but about my son's nightmares. On our next visit she asked the boy the same question. *Don't know,* he answered.

I told the woman that I didn't particularly care for cats either, I am like my son. They are too erratic, too quiet. I said I couldn't understand why Finnish people kept them as pets because in Kosovo the cat is considered a dirty animal. I expressed surprise that she was asking so many questions about cats and none what-soever about snakes.

The following week the psychologist showed me a picture of a tree with two thick branches: one represented the journey into my son's mind and the other our journey out on the other side once we'd dealt with the root of the problem. The idea of this therapy was for us to gradually shed our emotional baggage—in this case the snakes—by looking into the mind.

It was only after several months of therapy that the psychologist first mentioned snakes to the boy, though his symptoms hadn't subsided. Most nights we had to listen to his cries, and we pitied him so much that we devoted all our spare time to him. We bought him what he wanted, we watched all his favorite TV shows, and on quiet nights we prayed that the nightmares might finally be gone for good.

They drew pictures of the animals on the second list, talked about them and their role in nature, looked at photographs and later on even watched videos of them. The psychologist told him normal facts about these animals: how they behave in their natural environments, what they eat, and how they spend the winter.

With each animal the psychologist asked him whether he found the photographs frightening or whether he might do something as brave as stroke the animal in the picture if he had the chance to do so. One by one, none of the animals seemed threatening any longer, and only then did the psychologist talk about snakes.

According to the psychologist, nightmares like this can be caused by almost anything at all. *The human mind is as fragile as paper, and it can tear at any time*. Nightmares can be set off by a scary film or a horror story, an event that shocks the mind.

She was convinced that this was not about a fear of actual snakes but about things the boy associated with snakes, the images and memories he had of them.

Eventually I suggested to Bajram that we move somewhere else, as we hadn't yet properly settled in Finland. *It would do him good, the light, it's so dark here all the time,* I said. But then Bajram secured a job in Finland.

He started teaching Balkan languages in different towns, places that during the 1990s saw an increase in immigrants, notably from the former Yugoslavia.

He left early in the morning and came home late at night, but still it seemed as though Bajram was with us all the time. We couldn't have our own space, because he had always reserved the bathroom. Or he was in the living room watching television, snoring on his bed, or wanted his dinner.

The children began to grow and started to make different demands on us, asking for things, time, clothes, toys, makeup, sanitary products, and more space, because there was no room in their bedroom for anything except their beds. Their possessions couldn't fit in the wardrobe.

A small apartment like this isn't designed for such a large family, I complained to Bajram, and when he said we couldn't afford anything else I suggested we sleep in the living room and give the girls a separate bedroom. He answered by muttering that when you are the one paying for all this, you can make the decisions.

Bajram stood up and went into the children's bedroom.

"Who do you think you are?" he asked them and kicked our middle daughter with his heel as she sat on the floor, making her crawl to the other side of the room.

And her expression. I'll never forget what my daughter looked like at that moment: her lower lip drooped down to her chin, and she scratched her side and turned to watch the television as though she wanted to hide how terrified she was. *I haven't brought you up to behave like that. You're prepared to have your mother and father sleep in the living room, is that it?*

I watched as the children gradually began to avoid him more

and more. Soon I was the only one to know about it when their shoes wore out or when they needed a new toothbrush. *Why don't you ask your father?* I once asked my eldest daughter. *He could buy you a new pair of mittens to replace the lost ones.* She looked at me dumbfounded, leaned her head to one side, furrowed her brow, and said she would rather go without mittens than ask her father for anything.

I swore to myself that when Bajram came home that evening I would ask him. When did you turn into this kind of man? Your children are afraid of you. But when Bajram came home he wrenched the door open and slammed it shut again and tore the shoes from his feet so that they struck the wall like stones.

His heels battered against the linoleum floor as though someone were beating it, and he yanked the refrigerator door open so violently that the milk carton almost toppled out and fell on the floor, and he slammed his glass down on the kitchen counter so hard that it almost smashed, poured the last of the milk into the glass and drank it, and once the apartment was filled with the hoarse up-and-down gulps of his throat, I rubbed my earlobe and asked him whether he would like to eat now or rest first.

12

When people ask my name I sometimes give them an honest answer, but just as often I say it's Michael or John, Albert or Henry, because that way I avoid the next question, which is, *Where are you from?*

I always wonder why people want to know that. Are they asking me because they are genuinely interested in my home country or in order to make judgments about me? Because it's one thing to tell someone you are Swedish, German, or English and quite another thing to say you are Turkish or Iranian. It's only very rarely that someone's home country is of no significance at all. When I invite people to my apartment they generally accept, because they are fascinated by the fact that I own a snake. They take off their shoes, step inside, and see the terrarium with no snake inside it. *Oh.*

When I tell them it's probably under the sofa they stop at the living-room door and ask why I decided to have an animal like this as a pet. Before answering I always have to correct them. *This isn't any old snake; this is a boa constrictor.*

On a few occasions I've told them the truth and said I don't know, because I'm actually afraid of snakes. Still, most of the time I simply say that I got it because I know a lot about snakes, because they are calm creatures, suitably independent, and don't need much looking after. A snake is the perfect pet for someone living alone.

When I start pulling it out from under the sofa, my guests suddenly need to go to the toilet, and when they come back they have to leave, they back off and start putting on their coats. It's too big and terrifying as I wrap the length of its body round my shoulders, and its skin isn't slimy, as they'd thought, but dry like soft plastic, like shining silicone.

A giant thing like that, wow, they gasp as they open the door. *Aren't you afraid? What if it gets into the toilet and slithers down the drain?* They close the door after them, and I wonder why they ask things like that about the snake. It could just as well learn to moisten its skin in the toilet and slither out again. Or learn to do its business there just like everybody else. Is it really the case, I wonder as I stroke its coarse head, that people expect the worst of it simply because it is a snake?

THE IMAM

B ajram had heard of a Turkish imam living in Helsinki who had the power to exorcise evil spirits from the body. Three days later he knocked at our door. He had a congregation of more than a hundred members in Helsinki.

When the imam stepped into our house, there couldn't be any crosses on display. If the remote controls had accidentally been left across each other they needed to be moved and placed adjacent to each other, because otherwise the exorcism wouldn't work. We took all of the cotton swabs out of the bathroom cabinet and placed them in a row on the floor, we emptied all possible cupboards and drawers and placed their contents in similar fashion on the chest of drawers, on the floor, and on the beds. Worst of all were the clothes in the cupboards because their sleeves might have accidentally folded in a cross. Then there was all the cutlery in the kitchen drawers, the forks, the knives. Eventually we stuffed all our clothes, cutlery, and food into enormous black garbage bags and took them out to the car.

"Only God can help him," said Bajram. "God will judge every dead Muslim, and he will torture any who have lied and who do not pray. All those who have been unfaithful. All those who have sex out of wedlock and who drink alcohol."

The list of transgressions and those who would be tortured was so long that there was surely no Muslim who had not lapsed at some point. Even Bajram himself used to say so.

The imam hadn't come dressed in religious attire, as I had imagined. He was wearing a dark-gray bespoke suit. He had two handsome thick golden rings on his fingers and a matching, suitably thick golden pendant round his neck and a steel watch on his wrist. The top two buttons of his shirt were open. White chest hairs spilled from beneath his shirt, his heavy pendant pressing them down against his sweaty skin. The imam shook Bajram's hand firmly, only gave me a cursory look in the eyes, and asked Bajram in Finnish where the child was.

Bajram showed the imam into the apartment and the imam followed him after taking off his snakeskin shoes and leaving them in the hall. His socks, the same color as his suit, were damp at the toes.

Bajram and the imam stepped into the children's room. The boy was lying on his bed staring fixedly at the lampshade above, as though the light didn't dazzle him at all. The boy had developed a penchant for light and he'd started asking us to leave the lights on at night too. There were dried tears on his cheeks. Bajram took a handkerchief from his pocket and gently wiped the boy's cheeks, then gave him a soft pat on the forehead.

The imam sat down next to him on the bed and said he was ready to begin. The boy blinked for the first time since we had entered the room. He turned and looked anxiously first at the strange man then at me.

"Everything is fine," I said and walked to the other side of the bed to stroke him.

"This man has come to make you better," said Bajram.

The imam looked around him cautiously.

"What's the matter?" he then asked the boy.

The question made the boy move. He turned his back on the

imam and said he was frightened. I tried to calm him and continued to stroke his thick hair, which had stuck to his forehead.

"I will only be here a moment," the imam added and stroked the boy's head as though he had just learned from me the proper way to calm a child.

He told Bajram that the room had to be absolutely dark throughout the procedure because the evil spirits will not appear if it is light. And there must be nobody in the room but him and the boy.

"Very well," said Bajram.

"Why?"

The question leaped out of my mouth as though someone had squeezed it out, as though it had been wrapped in a small bag filled with air and popped free.

The imam looked first at me, then turned to look at Bajram and said that when the evil spirit leaves the body it will immediately try to find another body, and without that it will die.

"I will grab it as soon as it appears . . ." He paused for a moment. "And I will destroy it. I am immune to it."

Bajram smiled contentedly. *Thank you,* he said. And he said it with that same carefree note in his voice that was always there when something that had been plaguing him for a long time was nearing a resolution.

I didn't trust the imam and the imam didn't trust me. I didn't want to leave the boy in the room with him, but Bajram dragged me outside, leaving the boy alone in the darkened room with that strange man who could do anything to him. The imam looked at Bajram with an air of self-righteousness, winked, and closed the door.

The boy hollered for many minutes. At times it sounded as though he was being hit, at others as though he was beside himself with fear. Our other children asked what was going on, when he was going to be cured. *He'll be fine in just a minute,* said Bajram. *It shouldn't take very long now.*

We had gathered next to one another on the sofa. Bajram sat on the armrest and I sat next to him, and beside me our four other children sat in a row from oldest to youngest. I couldn't remember us ever sitting like this before. There were no pictures of us sitting next to one another or doing things together, and I realized this was because we never did anything that anyone might want to photograph. Slowly I began to sense something powerful, something rising up from my stomach, and it felt good. Just sitting with them. We were together now, sitting here on the sofa. We all wanted one and the same thing, and we all sensed it from one another.

No matter how much I wanted to stay sitting there, to bathe in the notion of better times, I opened my mouth. *I don't believe in this. I don't believe this will cure him. I don't want to lie to you.*

And at that moment Bajram looked at me the way he always looks at me when I am not quiet when I am supposed to be. Bajram had reserved a look specifically for this occasion, and he used it now: lips tightening, mouth slightly open, both his upper and lower teeth coming into view like a beaver, his mustache rising up to his nose, tightening the skin across his face. He turned to look at me, and at that I knew what would happen once the imam had left.

After a few minutes the imam opened the door, walked briskly into the hall, and crouched down to fetch his snakeskin shoes. The boy got up from the bed, terrified, and switched on the lights. On the way back to his bed he stepped quickly across the floor as though he was only able to touch certain spots.

He lay on the bed panting with relief, pulled the duvet over himself, and lay there staring at the lights on the ceiling just as he had before the imam had arrived. Bajram asked the imam what had happened in the room.

"Everything is fine. When he wakes up in the morning, he will be normal again," the imam declared, opened the front door, and made to leave.

"Really?"

The sorrow of Bajram's question embraced the walls like thick velvet curtains.

"Yes. The evil spirits have gone," said the imam. "They have been destroyed," he explained, lifted his hand toward the ceiling, and said there was no need to worry. *God is great and God is good.*

Bajram reached out to the imam, gripped his hand, and pulled him toward himself as if to embrace him.

The imam left our home showered with thanks after only half an hour's visit. He slipped the wad of banknotes Bajram had given him into his left jacket pocket, the one nearest his own heart. He shrugged on his coat, slipped on his shoes, and said, *God's blessing. He has given us everything we need. All questions and all answers, he shall give.*

When I awoke to a new morning, I turned to look at the boy, who had been sleeping between us for several months. Bajram had already gotten up and gone to the shower. From the bathroom came the sound of splashing as drops of water fell onto the hard tiled floor.

"Good morning."

I reached across the boy and pulled him closer to me.

"Be quiet," he said and placed his hand over his eyes to close them.

Then he clenched his eyes shut and muttered something to himself. His eyelashes twitched and his cheeks quivered, his breathing was fast and frozen, as though his mouth were stuffed full of ice.

13

When I stepped out of the bathroom the next morning the cat had woken up. It was meowing contentedly, its stomach still full from the meal the previous night.

I asked it whether it would like to go on a trip with me. For a moment the cat looked at me in bewilderment, then hopped from the bed onto the floor and rubbed itself against my trouser leg. Yes, it would go anywhere with me.

I closed the hotel door behind me and wrapped the cat once again beneath my shirt so that nobody would see it. With the cat in my arms I jumped into a taxi waiting outside the hotel. I chose an orange Volkswagen to please my orange-and-white cat.

When I released the cat from beneath my shirt, I could see immediately how much it liked my choice because as soon as the car started up it raised its front paws to the window and craned its neck to watch the landscape opening up behind the window, a landscape that in only a few minutes turned from a restless urban jungle to a cluster of peaceful mountains. Soon they too disappeared behind us and the hot asphalt sank beneath the tires like black lava.

. . .

The village was on one of the mountainsides. The sandy road leading up there first wound its way up along one side of the mountain and went down along the steep opposite side.

"Stop," I said to the driver as we approached the village shop.

"What, here? Is it one of those houses?"

The driver pointed at a group of redbrick houses farther off, a neat row of pear trees standing in front of them. On the other side of the street Mehmet was still running the shop that had been there for as long as I could remember.

"I'll get out here," I said, paid him, and stepped out of the car.

I looked at the village as though I weren't really there at all, as though everything around me was nothing but a dream, a mirage blown in on the wind. I sighed and breathed in the heavy, dusty air—I couldn't bring myself to believe that I had come here, that I was standing on this sand after all these years, how familiar the sound of the earth was as I placed my foot on its surface. It was a soft sound, the same sound as waves and leaves caressing the earth. The mind always tends to forget these things, I thought, but the body never forgets.

I stood there with my cat outside the village shop and looked at the sandy road winding its way between the mountains and far beyond them. Several hundred feet away the road split in two; from the main road emerged a narrower, dusty track leading to a cluster of a few unassuming houses.

I walked into the shop to buy breakfast for me and my cat. I took a packet of cookies from the shelf, some water, juice, chewing gum, and for the cat a few pieces of dried beef. I placed my shopping on the counter, and the idle hands of the man behind it made me look up at him. I recognized that face instantly, his broad smile, his bad teeth. Nothing had changed.

"Is it really you?" asked Mehmet.

The wrinkles in his face deepened as his smile widened.

"Yes, it's me," I mumbled and glanced at him furtively.

"*O Zot i madhë,* how are you, boy?" Mehmet asked in disbelief. "I haven't seen you in years."

Mehmet wiped his face with a trembling hand. He rubbed his damp eyes and didn't know where to put his hands. His voice quavered as he tried to say several words at once.

I responded briefly and hoped he would stop asking me things.

He wanted to know how my mother and my siblings were doing. And I told him the truth, for I had nothing to hide. When I told him there was no point asking me that sort of question, as I hadn't seen my mother for some time and we weren't really on speaking terms, he cleared his throat and wiped his brow.

"But . . . well, then," he said from behind the counter as though he had to force himself to ask the next question. His stern expression had seemed to paralyze his face.

"Is that a cat you've got wrapped beneath your shirt?" he asked and pointed at the cat, his finger crooked, as though he wanted to keep his distance from it.

"Yes it is, but you can't touch it," I said and quickly packed my groceries into a white plastic bag, hoping that Mehmet might take the hint and stop trying to make conversation.

"Are you going to visit your grandfather and your cousins?"

"I don't know."

"You should. They will surely be thrilled to see you, especially your grandfather. He speaks about you often. He thinks about you a lot."

As I left the shop Mehmet shook his head as though he had seen a ghost. I could see from his lips that he was muttering that familiar mantra whereby we invoke God twice, *O Zot, o Zot,* and shake our heads, so full of emotion. This is an answer to anything for which we cannot find words or for which words do not exist.

I walked toward the houses until my heart began to beat so hard that my entire chest seemed to move in time with it. My neck and hands felt clammy, and my throat clenched shut and tingled as though it had been filled with sand.

Almost without my noticing, my hands had slipped beneath my shirt and my fingers were gripping the cat by the neck. When I let go of it, the cat let out a pained meow. I took hold of the cat with both hands and lifted it above my head so that the sun lit up its ginger stripes, and it looked at me, almost smiling, and its tail and legs dangled like socks on a washing line, and I asked it for forgiveness—*Please forgive me,* I said—and lowered it once again to kiss it right in the middle of its tiny head.

I started to feel ill. The heat was unbearable, and eventually we turned in another direction, the cat and I, and began walking up the mountainside.

Halfway up, thirty or so yards from the dirt track, was a large, tall boulder from which you could look out across the entire village, every house, every path leading into the village and leading out again. The boulder that my mother had always spoken about and that she had loved. Whenever we visited Kosovo, she climbed on this boulder almost every night and looked out at the world she had left thousands of miles behind. *Nothing beats this landscape,* she said. *I love this.* The red sun shone across her face, she held a hand up to her forehead, and she stood there proud as a deer and tall as the mountains behind her.

I turned from the path and walked toward the boulder, climbed on top of it, and sat down with my cat at its highest and most beautiful point. I placed the cat next to me and it relaxed, then I took the cookies and dried beef from the plastic bag and laid them out in front of us. As I watched the cat eating, I took a cigarette from my pocket, placed it between my lips, and lit it, and the smoke didn't seem to disturb the cat in the slightest.

The smoke whirled round the mountain, the cat, and the boulder, the world felt smaller than a fingernail, and the whole village rose up before us like a ruptured blister oozing the scentless liquid of houses and cars and people.

OPTIONS

If we had given him poison to drink or mixed strong sleeping pills into his food, buried him in the woods in the middle of the night and told the police and everyone else that he had run away or that he had been kidnapped, snatched right out of our backyard, it would all have been over. In Kosovo people disappeared all the time, young girls were abducted at the bazaar, small children stolen from their mother's arms and driven away. The boy's death was one option among many, a very good option too, because I was convinced he would be unable to live a life worth living, a life of any degree of human dignity. This would end his suffering and we would cease to be a part of that suffering.

Living with him was like being caught in fog; we sank into it, disappeared, we had sunk into a grave in the deepest recesses of the ocean, a place nobody had ever been before. The pressure of the water howled around us like frozen steel, and we could see neither the surface nor the bottom, for there was only black. That's what he had become, that's what his desperation had caused; it was like walking from one destination to another deaf, dumb, and blind.

Nobody seemed able to help him, least of all us, though the

boy was our own flesh and blood. Should we have done more? I wondered. Was it a parent's duty to do for her child what she deemed sensible, then wait and see what happened, or to do everything possible all of the time? Because there was plenty more we could have done. I could have spent more time with him, and so could Bajram. He could have been at home more often, bought the boy something, talked to him.

I don't know why I began thinking we should take him to a better place. Just as suddenly I became fascinated by something as mundane and trivial as counting—how many times I swallowed in an hour, how many steps it took from one place to another. Was I desperate or insane for letting such thoughts take over my mind? Both perhaps? At one point I began watching the clock and timing myself to see how quickly I could clean the bathroom, iron Bajram's shirts, or vacuum the apartment.

When I mentioned this to Bajram as I prepared dinner, he was silent for a moment and didn't answer me. Then he picked up the flour-coated rolling pin in his right hand and threw his cigarette into the sink, as though he couldn't hold it while hitting me on the back with the rolling pin.

"Have you gone mad? *Oj budallaqe,* you stupid, careless woman," he said and hurled the rolling pin back onto the table.

The thump was followed by the sound of hurried footsteps. The boy appeared in the kitchen. We had had to take him out of preschool because the staff hadn't even been able to force-feed him. He had clenched his teeth together so hard that they cracked.

"Don't touch her," he said, his voice tight. "Or I'll kill you."

The boy sounded at once fearful and fearless. I took my hand away from my hip so that he would see I was fine, and I walked him back into his room, where Bajram then disciplined him. *Who do you think you're talking to?* he said and thrashed him with a belt.

Bajram was right to hit me. Did I want what was best for the child and what was right in God's eyes, or did I simply want the gloom to end? I couldn't even bring myself to say the boy's name or answer when Bajram came home from work and asked how the boy had behaved. He was on my mind all day; he filled every conversation. I deserved to be hit because no sane person would ever seriously think things like that, not even half seriously, not even in jest. And she certainly wouldn't say such things out loud even if that's what she was planning.

The day after the beating the boy got up after a long night's sleep. He had slept very well without a single nightmare. When he walked into the kitchen the color had returned to his cheeks, and he sat down next to his father at the table and smiled. *Good morning,* he said and looked at his father, and he never again spoke to us about nightmares or snakes. Or indeed about his life.

Bajram said his recovery was a miracle, and that's what I thought too. Nobody could recover from something like that overnight, not even a child. I began to wonder whether all this time he had been pulling the wool over our eyes and claiming to have nightmares in order to get our attention. *Don't be stupid,* said Bajram. *Children are children, first they think one thing then they think another.*

Only once he had said that did I realize quite how carelessly Bajram thought about his future. He was certain that his children would look after him when he became old and the children grew up—this despite the fact that the children were still small when we moved to this "godforsaken country," as Bajram called it.

I knew that the unrest in Kosovo was only going to get worse, so it was unlikely that we would be able to move back in the near future. I knew that in that time the children would become more like *them* and less like us. I knew that what always happens was bound to happen to us too: they would begin to despise people who were not like them. It was inevitable, that's what always happens. After all, Bajram disliked everyone except other Albanians.

Once the situation with the boy calmed down, I began to wonder how Bajram felt about the course of his life. Was it selfish of me not to ask him how things were going at work? Or how much money he had left when I asked for some? What did it feel like for a man to fail in his most important task? It had never occurred to me what it must feel like for a man who doesn't have enough money to buy his children clothes or what it feels like to look at a dining table with nothing more than a pot of soup. What did it feel like to give his children slices of *pite* with nothing between them but pieces of onion and leek?

I noticed that it was hard for us to form any kind of relationship with our children, hard to fathom them. They didn't like talking about their lives, and we didn't go out of our way to ask them how they were getting on at school. We behaved like idiots; the children were allowed to come and go as they pleased. They had no boundaries.

Our elder son began spending the night with his friends. Every now and then, almost as a formality, he asked us if it was all right for him to be away for a while. Of course it is, I said. And Bajram said the same thing. We allowed them to be raised by their teachers, we trusted the system lauded as the best in the world.

Bajram rarely spoke with them. And when he did, he raved on about Islam and the situation in Kosovo. About wars and prophets, about the Battle of Kosovo at Kosovo Polje, the Ottoman Empire, Skanderbeg, and Enver Hoxha, about people who had already fled the situation in Kosovo but who now wanted to return and join the ranks of the Kosovo Liberation Army. *They are heroes,* said Bajram. *Only God knows whether they will ever return to their families.*

Presumably Bajram expected them to understand that he too might become one of these men who leave their wife and children to fight for their freedom. But they never asked him anything. I imagined Bajram might disapprove and blame me for bringing them up badly, *but,* he said, *the fact that they don't feel they need us is a good sign. The best sign.*

My younger son started school and learned to speak and write Finnish in a couple of weeks. According to the teacher at first he didn't understand all Finnish words but he knew to ask about them—and he asked a lot.

His teacher showed me pictures with three knives and four cars or six houses and five apples, which the pupils were supposed to draw on their own sheets of paper after seeing the picture only once. My son's drawings were incredibly precise, the pictures had shadows and he remembered lots of details about them, things even his teacher hadn't noticed.

Apparently he always wanted to stay in school longer and resisted having to go home. In the afternoons he nervously stared at the clock ticking on the wall, packed up his things very slowly, and loitered around the school corridors for a long time.

The teacher asked how things were at home.

"Fine," I said. "Everything is fine."

Given the silence that followed my answer, I imagined that would be the end of the conversation.

I looked around for a moment, looked for something to focus on, an item to pick up, something to help me find the right words before finally looking at the teacher again. Then I asked the interpreter to tell him I understood and that I would tell the school immediately if we had any problems.

I noticed that the teacher was clearly still waiting for some kind of answer. What could I have said? That it was difficult for me to adjust to being in Finland and that my husband found it hard to process events in Kosovo, that this situation was difficult for the whole family? How would this have helped? Even if I had explained that a war was about to break out in my homeland, I could sense it, sense it so viscerally that I felt faint and that sometimes I forgot to spit the toothpaste out when I was brushing my teeth. What could he have done?

I held my son's hand all the way home and didn't want to let go of him, because I was thinking of everything he could one day become. A doctor, a lawyer, the CEO of a large company, a banker. Anything at all. How wonderful it would feel to be complimented, to be his mother at a time like that. My child would become something greater than me; he would know things I could never learn. Perhaps, I thought, this feeling was the very reason why people decide to become parents in the first place.

I squeezed his hand more tightly because I could feel myself drowning into the gray of the endless pavement.

The following morning, I was sitting opposite Bajram at the kitchen table, though I normally let him eat undisturbed because the children and I generally ate after him. Bajram looked content as he sipped his coffee. I could tell from his expression how perfectly the coffee had been brewed, and the autumnal sunshine warming his wrist made a small, modest smile spread across his face. The boy hadn't displayed any symptoms in a long time. Finally we could sleep and live in peace.

Bajram's life had taken a turn for the better, and that morning he looked so open and receptive that I began speaking to him. I told him of the meal I had planned for dinner, talked about our old set of china, our upcoming trip to Kosovo, and listed all the people whose houses we would visit. I told him what the teacher had told me at school the day before, spoke of how much the children enjoyed being at school, that they studied music, mathematics, literature, and world religions.

"They could be on their way to something decent and worthwhile, something different from this," I said and looked at the kitchen cupboards and stared out of the window as a harsh autumn wind blew across the yard.

"What? What did you say about religions?" he interrupted me angrily and slammed his coffee cup on the table.

"Yes, at school the children learn about all different religions," I said warily and breathed out as calmly as I could.

Bajram hit the table with his fist so hard that coffee spilled from the cup. He stood up and walked over to me. I didn't dare look at him because I could feel his expression without looking. It was red-hot, like a ceramic burner turned on full.

"Why have you sent our children to a Sunday school?" he asked and hauled me to my feet.

"I haven't done that," I tried to assure him. "In schools here they teach children about all religions."

I tried with all my might to calm him down, to escape the ensuing conversation. "It's part of their basic education, part of their curriculum," I said and tried to slip free from his hand.

Bajram looked at me for a moment with that same expression on his face, that bloodthirsty expression, the kind of expression you see only on the face of one who is about to exact the final, ultimate revenge. He held my shoulders with both hands, moved his right arm round my neck, and began to squeeze.

The very next day Bajram marched into the children's school and forbade the teachers to teach them about religion. According to Bajram, the teachers had stammered in response, trying to lie to him, and said that this was an optional course about life philosophy in which the students were encouraged to think about the world and its various phenomena, including religion. At first Bajram had scoffed at them, dug his fingers into his forehead, and shaken his head as though he had a headache. Then he asked them why he hadn't been told about this. *It's as if you're trying to steal my children from me,* he said.

When he came home he told me how he had shown them what's what. I couldn't understand how he seriously imagined he would be able to change their ideas of life by talking to them about Islam. On some level I admired his determination and resolve. He blindly believed in his own world and trusted that his own faith would save him from all imaginable sins for which he feared divine retribution. It wasn't a bad way to live your life.

The following month Bajram lost his job. He was genuinely shocked at this—despite the fact that he knew his employers had found out that he had been deviating from the prescribed syllabus. He had been talking to the students about Islam and told them their life philosophy classes were a pack of lies.

He had been given two options: he could either resign or he would be fired. Upon realizing the difference between the two and the implications they might have, he took the former option. After this he seemed depressed for a long time because he truly loved his job and had wanted to do it full-time, not just in the afternoons and evenings.

His employment record arrived in the post. Bajram looked at it for a while and slipped it into his desk drawer. He took it out again, read it for a moment, then put it back in the drawer. He did this so often that one day, when he had gone out for a walk, I took out the sheet of paper and read it for myself.

Employment terminated at the employee's behest due to disagreement over interpretation of the school's aims and values regarding equality.

That's what it said.

14

Everything looked smaller from high up on the mountainside. The trees had no shadows, the fields looked like mirrors that drowned the roads in their reflected brightness. The houses were nothing but short strokes of a paintbrush, lacking clear contours.

All at once my cat started hissing. It had walked to the edge of the boulder, its teeth bared, and began to hiss at something moving around in the long grass below us. The cat was leaning forward—it looked almost as though it might topple off the edge of the boulder. Its fur had become bristled and restless, and its sharp shoulders stood unnaturally high and its mouth opened and now looked extraordinarily large compared to the rest of its body.

Down in the grass I could just make out a series of clear, black curved patterns that formed a long line, metallic, greasy-looking patterns that for some reason had perturbed the cat greatly. At one end of the line, the patterns merged into a slightly raised head with a pair of black eyes and a mouth stretched and ready to attack, a set of sharp fangs exposed.

The snake was plump and must have been about a yard long. It was clearly a sand viper, *Vipera ammodytes,* the most poisonous viper in Europe. Its silvery gray body was covered with narrow black diamonds the shape of licorice caramels. The middle of its body was many times thicker than the head and its jaws were gaping wide. Judging by the bump in its stomach it must have eaten something very recently, gobbled a bird or a vertebrate, a lizard or a rodent.

I lifted my cat away from the edge of the boulder, though the sight beneath us was captivating. The snake retreated and wrapped itself into an even tighter coil. From above it looked like a spinning top whirling very slowly on the spot, its black scales gleaming like a sweaty forehead.

The cat and I backed off to the other edge of the boulder, but the viper sensed us nonetheless, and we could hear its hissing all the while.

I still had Mehmet's plastic bag, and I had all the knowledge about snakes I needed. I knew that snakes can't hear but that instead they form their understanding of the world using their senses of smell and touch. They don't need ears and that's why they don't have any. They feel vibrations in the earth instantly, but because there was a boulder between us that must have weighed tens of thousands of tons, stamping on the ground wasn't going to help.

The cat prowled round the boulder and wouldn't sit still. It wanted to walk to the other side of the boulder where it could climb down, jump to the ground, and run away, but it didn't dare. Perhaps it thought the snake would be waiting for it down there, would attack it, sink its teeth into the cat's neck, and eventually paralyze its central nervous system. After that the viper would slither round and eat it, and the cat would melt in the snake's stomach for weeks. It was hard to imagine a fate worse for the cat than being swallowed by a snake.

To attract the snake I put a piece of dried meat in the plastic bag and went back to the snake's side of the boulder. The cat came and stood beside me and started hissing again, even though I'd told it to wait at the other side of the boulder and keep still.

"Are you crazy? Get back!"

The snake was in an aggressive mood, and out of sheer thoughtlessness the cat and I had disturbed it. It must have been sleeping in the shade of the boulder and our picnic had woken it from its siesta. But you couldn't blame the cat for being curious. It wasn't the cat's fault.

I dangled the plastic bag in my hands for a moment. I watched the snake, watched its narrow mouth open even wider than before, watched its teeth grow larger and more grotesque, watched its entire body start to tremble, its scaly skin begin to moisten as its hissing became grating.

And then I dropped the bag.

It fell through the air as slowly as a feather. When it was about three feet from the ground, the snake leaped up toward it, its fangs bared, writhed in the air, and eventually fell back to the ground with a thump like a stone dropped on the grass. I jumped backward and gasped with relief, for the snake was far longer and heavier than the cat and I had initially guessed.

We could hear the snake wrestling with the bag. When, a moment later, we looked over the edge of the boulder, we saw the viper writhing inside the bag as though it were about to suffocate. It was wriggling and thrashing, twisting and turning, the plastic was confusing its sense of touch and smell. Its hissing was filtered through the bag and sounded almost catlike, and before long it was so exhausted that its movements became more stiff, more tired.

I picked up the cat and we looked at the snake together— how slowly it was moving, like an elderly man about to faint, how it was constantly gasping for breath with the desperation of someone buried alive.

After struggling inside the plastic bag a moment longer, the viper finally gave in. It no longer had the energy to move. Once it had gone without oxygen for a while, it fainted. Its muscles went limp and shrank slowly like a burst bicycle tire.

The snake's frantic writhing had pulled the bag tight and constricting around it, so that both ends of the snake were inside the bag and only a small section of its black-and-gray side was visible from one end of the bag.

The cat and I slowly made our way down from the boulder. I snapped a thick branch from a nearby tree and walked round the boulder to where the snake was. I stepped over the piles of twigs and through the long grass, deliberately making noise, stamping on the ground and snapping twigs to test the snake's senses.

The hissing had stopped some time ago, and now the snake was lying inside the bag, motionless. The cat sniffed the snake as though the smell was not to its liking. I began to poke the viper with the branch, and when it didn't even react to forceful prodding I crouched down to its level and put my fingers on its skin. Its tight-fitted scales were hard and rough like a wire fence.

I then picked up the snake with my bare hands. I pushed its heavy, limp body inside the plastic bag and twisted the top of the bag so that it became almost like a balloon from which the snake had no way out.

After that I began striding back down the mountainside— a ginger-and-white cat on my shoulder and a black-and-gray viper wrapped in a plastic bag dangling from my right hand.

MY YUGOSLAVIA

It was clear that there was no way we would be able to save enough money to take the family to Kosovo the following summer. When he realized this, Bajram was utterly crushed. He sat on the sofa with the money he had saved and counted it out again and again. He said it would be too late to go to Kosovo the summer after next. By then there might not be anything left.

He placed the money back on the table, defeated. His steps were slow. He lay down on the sofa and turned to face the backrest. And right then, for the first time ever, I saw Bajram weep.

At first he started to whimper, quietly, as though he was trying to unblock his sinuses. Then he started to howl like a dog that had been kicked.

It wasn't long thereafter that I saw him weep again.

Bajram and I were watching a news item in which it was reported that the KLA had admitted to murdering Serbian policemen. The KLA had given a statement claiming the attacks were retribution for the Serbs' dominance, the oppression of the Kosovan Albanians, and the new direction of social policy, which the Albanians could not accept under any circumstances. Language and education policy must be changed and returned to the way they had been in the past: Kosovo should be allowed to take care of its own affairs.

The camera swerved and showed a man fighting with the KLA. He proudly slung a rifle across his shoulder, pulled up his chin, clenched his teeth, and fixed his face in an expression that was merciless and unyielding. I found the man on the screen frightening, though I respected him and the values that he was prepared to defend to the death.

"That's a brave man," said Bajram, his voice heavy with emotion, almost a whisper, and hid his face behind his hands, now clasped into a single large fist.

Tito had ruled Yugoslavia for almost thirty years. During his time in office we blossomed. We were independent in all but name. We had our own university, our own radio and television station, though we Kosovan Albanians weren't considered a people in our own right. But Tito liked us, and for that we received wealth from the rest of Yugoslavia, because Tito knew that we needed it the most. He managed to keep the worst of the conflicts and differences of opinion within Yugoslavia at bay by favoring both the poor and the wealthy, both Muslims and Christians. In that way he gained respect from everyone.

But then those who already had plenty decided that was unfair. The rich should be allowed to keep all their wealth for themselves. And once Tito was gone, nobody else was able to argue the case against these people convincingly.

Bajram knew that full-out war was round the corner. Worse still, he knew he wouldn't be able to get back to Kosovo before it started or while it was going on.

It was then that I began to pity Bajram for the very first time. His melancholy and annoyance affected us too, the walls seemed to sneeze at his despair, and the constant sweat on his brow was the result of a deep-set rage. Many times I thought of going to him, stroking his hair, and comforting him by saying everything would be all right because things had a habit of working out.

But is it appropriate to comfort someone whose homeland is riven with war and whose entire family is in danger? Can people in the same situation really comfort each other? It was as though my mouth were bricked up. I couldn't say anything to Bajram without my words sounding silly.

Instead I concentrated on keeping our apartment clean. I washed the windows three times a week, changed our sheets every evening, carried brushes and detergents back from the supermarket and vacuumed every single day.

For the next few years Bajram was glued to the television. Nothing was allowed to interrupt him during the news.

I often left him at the kitchen table swirling the spoon in his coffee cup, only to return hours later to see that he hadn't touched his coffee. *It's impossible to enjoy anything,* he sighed repeatedly. It was then that he mentioned he'd started thinking about death. After each battle claiming the lives of scores of people, he said he tried to imagine how those people had died.

When war finally broke out, the television was our only source of information. Phone lines were down and we couldn't contact anyone. We hoped we might catch a glimpse of our relatives on the news, that we'd recognize members of our families when the television showed footage from a protest march.

Bajram heard from an old friend who had fled to Greece that his sister had been killed. The Serbs had burned the village where she had lived to the ground. Bajram grieved for his sister and her children. They were dead for a month until, suddenly, he received word that they were alive after all. And he could hardly believe it. When his sister telephoned him to say she had fled to the woods and managed to survive, he slowly slid from the sofa and onto the floor, all the while rubbing his chest, and asked me to call an ambulance. That evening Bajram had a heart attack.

Those were the quickest years of my life. I forgot them almost instantly, I couldn't keep up. On the news we saw images of burning buildings and dead civilians, women and children. Nobody should have to see images like that, images in which bodies were no longer bodies because parts of them were missing and the skin was no longer skin colored but a mass of bright red and dark red, images in which the roads were no longer roads but mass graves. How was it possible for people to get into a situation like this? Massacres, bloodbaths, explosions, voting fraud, collateral damage, fires. Listening to news like this was an everyday occurrence.

At times it seemed as though what we saw on television couldn't really be happening. It was a mirage, an unreal reflection of unreal events. But it was all truly happening, the lives of every single one of those people had ended, and I felt like a coward for refusing to die in the conflict. We will all die one day, I thought, and there will be nothing left of us. Wouldn't it be nobler to die back home rather than to run away? To die in battle rather than of old age?

When the news reported the events in Račak on January 15, 1999, we began to question the existence of God. What had that woman, gunned down, ever done to the Serbs? What had that child done, what had those desperate men done, men who realized their village was surrounded by Serb troops? And when those men saw the soldiers shooting randomly at innocent people, where was God then? Where was he? When men who had been captured were suddenly told, *Run away,* and when those men ran away up the hill only to be cut down halfway there, where was he? And when after this skirmish they showed video footage of an orphaned little boy weeping, what did God do with that child?

God did nothing with that child because there was no God. There was war, and war was a row of tornadoes tearing up the ground one after the other, and war was a set of tidal waves swallowing up buildings, villages, towns, a tsunami of water kneading them into a paste before finally spitting them out.

I ran faster than I'd ever run before, past Mehmet's shop, past the red-roofed houses with their whitewashed walls, past the unpaved roads, past the whole village.

I arrived at the boulder, and despite the clammy heat its surface was cool, forbidding, and bare, and I felt as though no amount of oxygen would satisfy my need to breathe. I rubbed my chest, felt the rocking as it swelled and relaxed, and wiped beads of sweat from my forehead. I breathed heavily, closed my eyes and opened them again, and my dizzy head seemed to sway in the heavy flow of air around me.

I leaned both hands against my knees and my ginger-and-white cat was nowhere to be seen, though only a moment ago its long body had been dangling round my neck. There was no snake either. No sand viper and no cat. I straightened my legs and stood upright and looked around for my cat and my snake, because I wasn't supposed to misplace them but they were nowhere in sight.

My cat and my snake.

I lost them.

I spent another week in Prishtina. The hotel window looked out onto the main street through the city. People arrived in this city the same way as they arrived in all cities: their chest and head full of dreams that could come true at any moment. One day you could be sitting in a café or walking along the street, in the right place at the right time, then a bell rings and nothing is quite the same again. An unfamiliar person walks toward me and realizes that I have the looks of a model, the intelligence of a doctor of psychology, good motor and language skills, the largest shoulder muscles in the world or the smoothest hands, something that nobody has ever noticed about me before.

And this unfamiliar person, I thought as I stood smoking a cigarette out of the hotel window, will love me as unconditionally as a dog loves its master, and he will buy me a plane ticket into a world of enormous sets and spotlights, amid crowds of people, but I will deliberately keep him at arm's length because I want to remain a mystery to him. I will enjoy how intoxicated he is with my uniqueness, and I will wake up every morning in a bed with expensive sheets and look out of the window, and for a moment I will doubt it all—can all this really be for me? Then I will realize that of course it is for me. Finally. For me.

My father used to say there was no evil in the world in the form in which we imagine evil to exist. As he watched news of the unfolding conflict in Kosovo he said we should come up with another word for evil, and that name should be laziness.

Because nobody is born into this world evil, he argued. *There is no genetic distortion that predisposes people to committing evil deeds or that can explain warfare, inequality, poverty, and famine. A man cannot harm another man without feeling guilt, and nobody can sell himself for money or take another life instead of his own. There is only laziness; it comes creeping through the shallow waters and fills people's mouths and brains with shit. It has become a parasite whose hosts are without exception in the depths of despair, and so the cycle continues. That's the problem with this world.*

I thought of his words as I watched the people in the city, and I almost missed him, so precisely did we agree on the matter. Sometimes I felt as though nobody was able to speak about people and matters as incisively as he had.

I switched on my computer and Ardi sent me a message. *Hey, sexy,* it read as it clinked into my profile with the picture of my shirtless upper body aimed at getting as many clicks as possible, to be as desirable as possible.

Ardi took the bait, complimented my profile picture, and asked me where I was right now. *Prishtina?*

Prishtina, I responded and wriggled my way into Ardi's profile. I looked at his profile pictures. In one of them Ardi was lying on a deck chair in the seaside resort of Sarandë in Albania. His dark leg hairs straggled like an unwieldy coat despite the glare of the sun, though the bright white light seemed almost to swallow up part of Ardi's legs. He was leaning on his elbow, he was doing everything he could to tense his stomach muscles for the camera and was clumsily holding his arms unnaturally far away from each other in an attempt to trick the viewer.

In another picture a trouserless Ardi was sitting on a chair. His backside was pressed against the chair's surface, and beneath his legs was a glimpse of the jeans he'd pulled down only a moment ago and the white, triple-striped socks on his feet.

D'you want to hook up? he asked. *Coffee? Meet at the café beneath the Grand Hotel. You know the place?*

I know the place, I replied. *See you there in half an hour.*

Sitting at the terrace café outside the Grand Hotel Ardi looked as natural and carefree as a thirty-one-year-old Kosovan man can be. The tables were full of people, and the area was edged with rows of tall bushes with gateways leading out into the busy street while the Grand Hotel itself blocked the afternoon sun, casting a shadow across us like a cold blanket.

Ardi didn't draw out his words by effeminately lengthening the vowels, didn't pronounce his consonants lazily, didn't wave his head as he spoke—all mannerisms he would have picked up in the West by watching others of his kind. Rather he looked and sounded like a man who could claim to be anything at all.

He was wearing a pair of tight, light-blue denim shorts that came down to the knee, flip-flops that bore the impression of the sole of his foot, and a thin blue stripy T-shirt that revealed the few beads of sweat that had exuded from his tanned skin.

Nobody batted an eyelid at us, wondered why two men were sitting together enjoying their fifty-cent macchiatos, why we were chatting like best friends and looking at each other the way a man looks at a woman he desires, the way a woman looks at a man she desires.

He chain-smoked cigarettes, seemed relaxed as he talked about cars, his work as a builder, and his dream of making it to the West. He wasn't concerned with what I thought about his dreams, whether or not I found them credible or worthwhile.

He laid his hand along the backrest of the chair next to him and revealed a sweaty armpit to which the thin cotton fabric of his T-shirt had stuck. He talked away for a while, occasionally waved a hand to emphasize his words, told me more about himself, and interrupted himself all of a sudden.

"Tell me something about yourself," he said.

"Like what?"

"What do you do?" asked Ardi. "People always have something to tell. What job do you do? Are you at university? Tell me your dreams."

"Hard questions," I said, finished the remains of my coffee, and stared at him. His easy social nature and genuine curiosity were mesmerizing. I couldn't stop looking at him, but I had to say something. I started to laugh and assumed the same position. I slipped my arm along the backrest of the chair next to me, tensed my biceps so that it swelled to twice its size, and waited for his gaze, which would only move toward my biceps on one condition: Ardi would only look at it if he really wanted to. If not, it would be best to run. Fast.

But his eyes fixed on my biceps like a laser locating a target.

"Do you want to come upstairs?" I asked and stubbed out my final cigarette. "I need some more cigarettes too."

"Yes," Ardi replied instantly, though he still seemed hesitant. "Aren't you afraid?"

"No," I said. "What is there to be afraid of?"

"Well . . ." He thought, stood there tasting his words, wondering how to say them out loud, whether to say them at all. "It's dangerous round here. Anything could happen."

"I'm not worried," I said and looked at Ardi, who suddenly seemed agitated.

"You're brave," he said and pulled himself together as we walked past the row of tables bubbling with conversation. "If only I could be like that," he eventually said over his shoulder.

I laid my hand on his lower back, and when we'd walked side by side across the hotel foyer, past the reception desk, and reached the elevators, where there was nobody around, I pulled his clammy T-shirt up, pressed a finger against his skin, and with my other hand stroked his smooth, muscular wrist, and kissed him.

He wanted to make love for a long time, to start as the door closed behind us. He couldn't get enough of it.

He panted beside me, touching his muscular stomach, until he stood up from the bed, wiped his lower back and groin on the end of the sheet, and swung into the bathroom and closed the door so carefully that its sound inevitably reminded me of Finnish bathrooms, their perpetual openness, the ostensible naturalness they had. Finns always left the door open when they went into the bathroom to do their business, rinsed their groin in the sink, and peed right into the center of the toilet bowl so that even the neighbors could hear the splashing.

Ardi suddenly opened the door.

"There's fur all over the place," he said, somewhat bewildered, in the doorway.

"I know," I replied.

I thought of getting out of bed, coming up with an excuse. I thought of telling him to leave, but I couldn't get a word out of my mouth.

"Why?" he asked, because for him no question was inappropriate or too embarrassing.

"Because I washed a cat in there," I replied from the bed, pulled the duvet farther up my body, and waited for his reaction.

"A cat?"

"Yes."

"You're really weird," he said and closed the bathroom door again.

He turned the shower on. From the bed I could hear his vertebrae cracking as he stepped over the edge of the bathtub. I started to get dressed.

"I have to go," he said as he stepped out of the bathroom and almost stumbled on his flip-flops, which he'd left just in front of the door.

Ardi had wrapped a white towel round his waist and dried his hair so carelessly that droplets of water were still trickling down his stomach. His black leg hairs twined wet against one another; it looked as though someone had taken a felt-tip pen and scribbled across his shins.

"Well go then," I said. "I've got to go too."

"I've got to pick up the kids," he said a moment later.

When I turned to look at him he was already dressed, he had picked up his sandals, dried his short hair, found his T-shirt and denim shorts. And now a golden ring had appeared on his right ring finger.

"You're married," I said, almost a question, and stood there gazing at his right hand, which was now fumbling with the zipper on his shorts.

"Of course I'm married," he said dismissively. "I'm thirty-one. I've got two daughters," he continued and adjusted his belt until it was tight enough.

He tugged at his T-shirt a few times to air his damp body, pulled it down slightly, and turned to look at me.

"Thanks," he said.

I got up from the bed and went to him. On the way I looked at everything: the crusted corner of the sheets, the steam billowing from the bathroom, the open suitcase in the corner of the room, the clothes inside it neatly folded.

"Thank you," I said, closed my eyes, and tried to kiss him, but my lips touched only his cheek.

Then I tried to hug him. Again I closed my eyes; I wanted to feel his soft cheek but I didn't want to see him, his discomfort, the disgust he felt toward himself and toward me.

"Hey," he stammered, startled, shoved me firmly backward, and assumed a threatening boxer's pose: his hands clenched into fists, risen up to protect his chest, one leg farther back in case he might soon have to launch himself at me.

"Money," he said.

"What?"

"Money. Have you got any?"

"Sure, I've got money," I said and peered at my suitcase.

From the side pocket I dug out the small wallet where I had kept all the money I would need for this trip. I counted my money for a moment and wondered how much to give him, how much of the money I had saved up, how much of this I could give him.

"Are you rich?" he asked.

I wanted to tell him I was made of money. Instead I closed the wallet, turned to face him, gripped his wrist, and closed the wallet into his hand.

He opened it instantly, pulled the bunch of notes into his fist, and started counting them in astonishment.

"Are you giving all this away?"

"Yes. Take it."

"This is unreal. Thanks. Thank you," he repeated, hugged me, and kissed me on the cheek.

The door closed, I threw myself on the bed and lay there. What if I had a child, I wondered, a five-year-old daughter waiting at home? She would be there waiting for me while I met up with strange men in hotels. What if my life was like this, I wondered, hotel rooms, dark alleyways, an online world where you always had to remember to delete your browsing history. Paranoia and suspicion, fear that someone might send me a message and that he might be perfect, a man with thick blond hair and a tall, sinewy body, and he might ask me to meet up at the beautiful peak of summer.

He would tell me about the life he dreamed of, a life he wanted to share with me, about his little house by the sea. There would be a garden at the back with trees and enough room for a couple of dogs, and the sun would always be shining—not a harsh sun but a carefree sun that doesn't lick your body moist but that embraces it. *We could escape to a place like this, you and me, and we'd live the rest of our lives like that,* that's what he'd tell me and say, *I'm leaving now but I hope you meet me at Skanderbeg's statue, I'll be wearing a white shirt, blue jeans, and red shoes, tell me what you'll be wearing so we can recognize each other and run away together.*

And I would want what he promised me so fervently that I'd tell him what I would be wearing when we met at the foot of the statue, a black sleeveless shirt, white jeans, and blue shoes, see you there, of course I'll see you there, I'm almost in love with you already, do you hear? In love with you.

And I would think of everything we could become together, the two of us, and how happy we would be.

But it wouldn't be him at the statue but someone else, a crowd of people. They would have baseball bats and everything. They would grab me violently and force me into the trunk of their car. They would drive out to the middle of nowhere, throw me to the ground, stub out their cigarettes on my skin, spit on me, urinate and defecate on me, then they would grab their bats and shove them inside me, then into my mouth, and they would force me to say, *Yes, what I do is wrong and disgusting and I deserve to die, please, do it now.*

I watched him from my hotel window, watched the way he walked off down the pedestrian street running through Prishtina, past the small square, how he placed the temples of his sunglasses over his ears and returned to his other life, and I scratched first my shoulder, then my knee and my chin, for every bit of me itched, and I sat on the bed for a moment because it felt as though someone had drawn a cheese grater across my skin.

SALVATION

NATO began airstrikes on Belgrade on March 24, 1999. In June that year the war came to an end and in July that year Bajram and a friend robbed a supermarket.

"It was perfect," he said and flexed his hands.

Then he told me what had happened from beginning to end.

A friend of Bajram's who lived in Helsinki had visited a number of supermarkets and asked one of the security guards in passing about his work, ostensibly because he was interested in getting into the profession himself.

At first the security guard described his work only superficially, but after a while he took Bajram's friend to one side. When the friend continued talking about his terrible experiences as an imaginary security guard in Kosovo, the guard began talking to him like a brother. Here in Finland, he explained, the profession is plagued by a lack of resources. Bajram's friend told him about security work in Kosovo. *In Prishtina a group of men once robbed a convenience store. In a situation like that the security guard can only apprehend one of the thieves, if that.*

If only that were the case here, the guard had said. He explained that he was responsible for a number of shops over a large area, and he was expected to look after them all at once. If there was a robbery in two shops at the same time he would only be able to deal with one of them. *It's the same story across the country, especially in smaller towns.*

A week later Bajram and his friend bought themselves a couple of fifty-mark airsoft guns that looked and felt like real firearms. They cut holes for the eyes and mouth in their gray balaclavas as though they had taken inspiration from a cheap movie. The sight of them in front of the mirror with balaclavas pulled over their heads and fake guns in their pockets was more ridiculous than frightening. They truly had decided to do something so utterly absurd. I tried to tell them if they got caught they would go to prison. *You won't see your children for years. You'll never get back to Kosovo. You'll spend so much time in a tiny cell that you'll pray for death.*

Bajram and his friend looked at each other for a moment. I thought they might still consider backing out of the plan, but they closed the door behind them with a chuckle.

Bajram and his friend drove to another town. They left the car in the parking lot outside a cluster of high-rise buildings, separated from the rest of the town by a few miles of woodland. They walked through the forest for hours planning their escape route back to the car until they were sure of their plan. They watched to see when the security guard drove away from the back of the lot and waited for another fifteen minutes until they were sure the car had reached its next destination.

Then they charged inside the shop and told everyone to put his hands up. People lining up at the counter dropped their shopping to the floor and looked at them terrified, as terrified as Kosovans looking at Serb soldiers, as terrified as Serbs looking at American troops.

The assistant emptied the cash register and handed Bajram a bunch of banknotes. Just then Bajram noticed a customer peering between the shelves, holding a mobile phone to her ear.

Then Bajram and his friend ran back to the woods as fast as their legs could carry them. At some point Bajram thought he heard the wail of a siren, just like in the movies when the police officer investigating a murder or the police dog finds a clue and sets off in pursuit of the suspect.

They reached the car in less than half an hour and drove home without anybody noticing a thing. When Bajram returned home with his loot, he was trembling from top to toe, frightened and paranoid.

"I didn't hear any sirens," said his friend calmly. "Can we count out the money now? I've got to get home for the night."

Bajram calmed down, let go of the curtains, which he had been holding open with his forefinger, and stopped staring out of the window.

Bajram was still convinced that police would swerve into the parking lot at any moment and take him away. He took a deep breath and told me to make some coffee.

There was a total of 24,200 marks in the cash register; 12,100 marks each. Bajram's friend took his own share and left in the same car they had been using throughout. Once the car had gone the only evidence of guilt was the large pile of cash. Bajram hid the money in a briefcase kept in one of the higher kitchen cupboards, the same place he kept all our savings, university certificates, the children's birth certificates, and an Albanian flag.

"Don't worry, we'll soon be on our way to Kosovo," he said with a furtive look on his face.

And I looked at Bajram as he drank his coffee, his hands steady, and admired his ability to move so swiftly from one emotional state to the next.

The following week we were watching *Police-TV,* and when security-camera footage of the incident appeared on the screen Bajram jumped to his feet and turned up the volume.

Police are looking for the two Russian men in this footage. As yet there have not been any sightings of the suspects. Police urge the public to report any sightings or possible information to the telephone number at the bottom of the screen.

And then he laughed.

17

I met him on an airplane, and his name was Sami. I put my hand luggage under the seat in front of me and swung down into my own seat. When I noticed that I couldn't fit my legs properly I began to calm my growing sense of panic by checking for the emergency exits, how many steps it would take to get there, and what kind of expressions were on the cabin crew's faces.

I was afraid of airplanes, afraid that the engines might suddenly stall and the metal receptacle weighing hundreds of thousands of tons would start gently gliding toward the earth. The air would be soft as guitar music, and the airplane would slowly turn in the sky like a whale, and nobody would hear it. There would be unprecedented panic inside the plane, some people would die of the sheer shock, and the plane would reach the ground as nothing more than a capsule, its wings having come loose during the descent, and it would explode like an atom bomb, sending red-hot metallic debris flying across the crash site, fragments of plane carrying pieces of burnt flesh and small hands, a sole survivor would scream only to be drowned out and engulfed by the roaring flames.

I took the laminated safety instructions from the pocket on the back of the seat in front of me and started fanning myself.

Sami had already installed himself in the seat next to me and was reading the *Times*. I didn't pay any attention to him; I could barely see his face behind the newspaper, only a small section of a gleaming bald patch on his head.

I fastened my seat belt as the captain switched on the little light. Then the plane jolted into life, eventually achieved the necessary speed, and rose into the air. Sami was still reading his paper and I was gripping the armrests, because in my stomach it felt as though the plane were falling until we arrived above the clouds and the world opened out beneath us like a soft bed. The clouds under the airplane looked like downy feathers. When the seat-belt light went out I stood up, pulled out a book, and started to read.

At one point he folded his newspaper and turned to look at me. Though I was engrossed in my book, I could sense him watching my every move over the newspaper folded in his lap. He wasn't even trying to be subtle.

It was only when he pushed his paper to one side that I saw he was wearing a suit and that his legs were crossed. One of his feet had transgressed the invisible boundary between us and jutted into my side of the space. Between his black shoe and trouser leg was a strip of tanned skin and, to my surprise, a red sock. I burst into laughter. By turns chuckling and serious I stared at his foot and the red sock he was wearing.

He twirled his shiny shoe in front of my eyes.

"I was out of black socks," he began in English. "So I had to wear these," he continued in a pronounced Finnish accent.

It was only now that I plucked up the courage to look him in the eye. The small bald patch above his forehead gradually grew into a head of cropped hair, his trim body swelled with imposing muscles, and his modest, handsome face remained somehow distant. His wide, greenish, curious eyes were stunning. He glanced at his smartphone, whose language was set to Finnish, and put it back in his pocket.

"That's very funny," I continued in English. "I must say, they look pretty good on you."

At that, he too began to laugh, and when I asked whether he happened to speak Finnish his eyes brightened all the more.

"Yes, I do!" he replied almost too eagerly and adjusted his position in the chair: took his red-socked foot out of my space, lifted himself on the armrests, and placed his right thumb beneath his chin. His left leg remained casually resting on his thigh.

When I saw he was preparing to ask me a question, I began praying to myself. *Please don't ask me about my homeland, my name, or my mother tongue. Ask me what I want to do or about things I've done, my dreams and fears. Ask me about those things and I'll tell you.*

"How old are you?"

I looked at him, the blood vessel in the middle of his forehead, his full lips and small, wrinkly ears, his head, round like a bowling ball. He was the most beautiful man I'd ever seen.

I told him my age and he smiled.

"Interesting," he said and pulled up his red sock. "What are you reading?"

YEARS AND CIGARETTES

When the war ended, the little sympathy we had received from people here ended as abruptly as if it had been shoved from the roof of the building. *Right, you got what you wanted. When are you going home?* While the war was still raging our presence was somehow justifiable because we were refugees.

Bags of garbage started to appear outside our apartment door, the slightest sound after evening curfew had our downstairs neighbors running up the stairs and shouting in the echoing stairwell: *If you don't know how to behave, go back where you fucking came from!* In the supermarket young men started imitating the way we spoke and placed their hands beneath their armpits like monkeys. *Uu uu uu uuuu, fucking monkeys, shut your fucking mouth.*

We were cut off from two different countries that nonetheless had come to resemble each other more and more, and we no longer belonged in either one. We were vagrants, travelers pushed to the margins of society, people without a homeland, an identity, or a nationality.

Back in Kosovo, people wondered why we could no longer eat white bread and why we wanted to spread our sliced—not torn—pieces of bread with margarine, why we couldn't bear the stench of burning rubbish, and why the hot summer days made us feel like we were suffocating. They didn't understand why we wanted to wash our laundry and dishes in machines and not by hand, why we bought bread from the store when you could bake it yourself. When we picked up a fork, they reminded us that *pite* was supposed to be eaten by hand. *This isn't a restaurant, you know. Do you think you're better than us?*

In Finland we were outcasts. We had no work, no long-term plans, no idea how long we would be allowed to stay. At one point we stopped talking about the subject altogether. We all knew we couldn't carry on living the way we had before.

The situation got worse with every day that passed. We didn't dare speak our mother tongue in public and we couldn't use the laundry room in the apartment building because someone always rubbed out our apartment number in the reservation book and wrote, *Fuck off! Wogs can wash their clothes SOME-WHERE ELSE.* Our children came back from school covered in bruises, other kids spat at them, laughed at them because they didn't have skates and skis on winter sports days, because they didn't have gym shoes or tracksuits, because we had nothing to give to the school raffle. Bajram and I never showed up at the children's school because they didn't want to be seen with us.

It felt as though we'd gone back in time ten years, and once again we started feeling ashamed of our nationality. Bajram told people he was from Bulgaria or Russia—anywhere that didn't have the same associations as Kosovo, because those associations were always negative. There was unrest in Kosovo, the people were disenfranchised and didn't know how to behave. I felt that their newspapers were slandering our homeland.

We were stuck between the truth and the lies. We no longer knew what was real. Our children started speaking Finnish to us in public, though they knew if they did that at home Bajram would punish them.

Bajram started to have brutal, violent dreams in which he was being hunted, beaten, and tortured. He told me and the children about them. *Last night I had a dream where I was shackled to the table, I was in a hospital somewhere, and they were giving me electric shocks. The night before that I woke up twice. The second time I woke up for real but the first time I woke up in a room that had no walls and was full of water. I almost choked.* His dreams sometimes continued into the mornings, long after he had woken up.

He thought of the phone calls he had received during the war. He said he spent every waking minute thinking about the calls and all the people who had died in Kosovo, he was torturing himself. Sure, I understood him—how could we not think about those people?

Bajram started handling stolen goods and selling them on to Finnish traders. *It's their own fault,* he said. The Finnish people formed a single unit that had become his sworn enemy. *They want us to behave just like them, but at the same time they make doing so impossible.*

It was true because Bajram hadn't been offered work in years. He had undertaken unpaid assistantships in schools, shops, and museums, but once the stint was over they always showed him the door. Some employers even told him to his face that they didn't want to employ an immigrant. *We don't want any problems round here. Why should we take you on when there are unemployed Finns who speak Finnish looking for work?* Bajram was furious. *How well do they expect us to speak this damn language?*

He eventually came to the conclusion that the Finns owed him a sum of money they would never be able to pay. The Finns had changed him, taken his honor, and he would never be the same man again.

Bajram and his friend started driving to the Russian border, which had become a notorious place for doing business for Finns and foreigners alike who wanted to make a little extra cash.

Bajram's job was to transport goods—computers, mobile

phones, clothes, and electrical appliances—from Helsinki to the Russian border. For this he received a small fee, cash in hand, and a small share of the cargo.

He told us the strangest stories of how goods were smuggled across the border, how stupid and gullible the Finnish border guards were, and how easily they gave up in the face of the language barrier. And I laughed, first at Bajram then with him as he played out his stories with his hands, his right hand playing himself and his left hand playing the Finns, and his right hand was so swift, cunning, and self-assured that his left couldn't keep up.

That's what they're like, he said. *Quitters. The situation makes them so greedy,* grua, *you wouldn't credit how low and greedy a man can become when he truly believes himself to be honest.*

I had hope that Bajram would give it up, but when he started buying me and the children expensive gifts and we started celebrating birthdays and he stopped putting money into our savings I realized he was hooked.

But the more money Bajram acquired, the unhappier he became.

18

Three weeks after our first meeting I invited him back to my apartment. That night he fell in love with me and I with him.

He loved my snake. He played with it and suggested suitable names for it. *Autumn,* he suggested; *if you look closely, it's covered in autumnal colors. Or Smack, because its tongue makes a smacking sound.*

To him the snake wasn't a strange pet at all; it was unique, individual. He bravely took it in his arms, stroked it, and cooed at it. *I think you like this. There's a good boy.*

He thought its skin was hard, though on the inside it was soft and gentle; he loved the way it wrapped itself round his neck like a giant necklace, the way it tightened round his neck without choking him. *It knows,* he said. *It can sense me.* He believed that the snake enjoyed human warmth and proximity, though it pretended to reject everything except living by itself.

I had made a pot of coffee and handed him a cup. Our first shared coffee at my apartment was perfect and the coffee so heavenly that his first sip was interrupted by an endearing desire to tell me how good it was.

"I'm glad you like it," I said and sat down next to him, content, and laid my head against his soft shoulder.

Outside the window it was a late summer's day, rays of light filtering into the room through the half-opened venetian blinds as it would through the wall of a barn. After leaning against each other for a while, about halfway through his cup of coffee, he said it. *I think I love you. I don't know if I should say it so soon, but I'll say it anyway. Sorry, I shouldn't have said anything.*

He waited for a moment, and at the base of my ear I sensed that he swallowed just before kissing my hair, and at that I felt my heartbeat pulsing in my jugular. Now that these words had been spoken, spoken to me for the first time, there was no taking them back.

I turned to kiss him, harder and more earnestly and passionately, as though I couldn't get enough of him, as though I would never experience this feeling again.

I stood up and held out my hand. He put his coffee cup on the table and gripped my hand, stood up and wrapped me in his arms, kissed my neck and sniffed my hair. I led him into the bedroom and smiled. I turned so that he too would see it. *What you just said makes me so happy.*

We lay in bed for a long time without saying a word. He was breathing calmly, until I lifted my head from his chest. I concentrated on looking at him, not breathing.

"What?" he asked cautiously.

I wanted to tell him that I was terrified. *What if this comes to an end? What if one day you change your mind, though you say that now? How awful would that be? Have you thought about that? Isn't it terrible that when something good happens, we start worrying about a time when we have to live without it?*

I didn't answer. He glanced quickly out of the window where the evening was beginning to darken and turn red. What if I stopped loving him or what if he could no longer bring himself to say it, or what if he fell in love with someone else or got a job on the other side of the world? Anything could happen. He could die.

He stopped waiting for an answer and wiggled closer to me, pulled the duvet partly over his stomach and his right leg. He exhaled heavily, then rolled onto his side, propped himself on his right arm, and slipped his left arm across my stomach.

"Don't think too much. That's your problem."

He moved his hand on my stomach; his fingertips felt warm and soft and his skin smelled of sliced almonds.

Then I said it too, because it would have been sheer madness not to say those words to a man like that.

MIGRANTS

Our children abandoned us one after the other. They left home and went away to study and work in other cities. At least that's what they told us, though it turned out to be nothing but a pretext. I'd never imagined a child could turn against his parents like that. A child can be angry for a while, but that he should suddenly deny his parents, I hadn't thought that was possible, because somewhere deep inside a child always loves his parents and parents always love their children, in some way they are always united.

But when they never called us to ask how we were or to tell us what they were doing, we accepted the fact that from now on it would just be the two of us. They gave us a cursory farewell though we kept them fed and clothed and had given them a home all these years. *See you*.

Bajram took the fact that his children no longer wanted anything to do with him very hard. He slept badly and no longer seemed to care about money. He tried to telephone them but they didn't answer his calls. They sent him text messages only a few words long. *Everything's fine*.

He drove round the towns where they claimed to live but couldn't find them. He stood guard in squares and parks and waited, said he wanted to talk sense to them, but something about them pushed us farther away and something about us pushed them away too. We were like two identical magnetic poles.

Once it was just the two of us at home, Bajram and I didn't say much to each other, and many years went past without much substance to our conversations. Bajram started drinking lots of alcohol and lost a lot of weight.

Now our entire existence hung on our children who had decided to have nothing to do with us. Their departure was like having stakes driven through our bodies. I was so worried about them and so angry with them that I had dreams in which I slapped their faces, shouted at them, pulled their clothes, and demanded they tell us exactly what they were thinking.

After a while Bajram began talking of returning to Kosovo. He said he wanted to move away from Finland but took it back instantly as though saying those words out loud made him less of a man.

Then he started talking about what people would say if he moved back there, and what people would say if he went back without his children. When he asked what I thought about the matter, I was afraid he might force me to go with him, but he said he could happily go back by himself.

Bajram was restless and agitated; he even wept from time to time. I was constantly on edge because he had an ever shorter temper than before and he had trouble with his heart. I was worried he might have another heart attack.

I packed a suitcase in the middle of the night and left. I opened the upper drawer of the old dresser, the one that always creaked when you opened it, and took out all the banknotes I'd hidden over the years and saved. Bajram muttered in his sleep, turned onto his side, and mistook the suitcase next him for the woman who, almost by accident, he had ended up spending his life with.

Everyone had gone and the walls were bare. Not a single photograph was on display.

I lifted my suitcase from the bed, opened the bedroom door, stepped into the hallway, shrugged on my coat. I opened the front door as quietly as I possibly could. The door's tight hinges creaked as though they had been wrenched out of place. Everything else was perfectly quiet, I was quiet, Bajram was quiet. It was as though nobody had ever uttered a word.

I had thought of saying good-bye to him, saying good-bye to the last twenty years, looking him in the eyes for the last time, looking at the deep wrinkles in his skin, his jutting stubble, and the bald patch on his head. I would kiss him on the forehead, clasp his strong shoulders, lay my head on his chest—but I couldn't touch him.

I pushed the downstairs door open. The cold wind was biting, it scratched my face like tiny needles and howled loudly. As I walked onward it felt as though Bajram had gotten out of bed and walked to the window and stood watching me cross the yard and the parking lot, now covered in soft snow like shredded paper.

A few weeks later Bajram left Finland, moved back into our old apartment in Prishtina, and started making a living as a taxi driver. He did this for a few years, and then he died.

III

When you reach the life you wanted.

19

During the next few months he and I went to restaurants and cinemas and theaters, we went on cruises, visited museums, we were constantly doing something new. He took me riding and we tried out wall climbing, we jumped naked into the sea, laughed at people crawling home on our weekend morning runs, and I loved him and he loved me, and we said this to each other every day.

He gave me time to think, time to talk about things I didn't want to talk about, and he didn't worry about the sleepless nights when I kept him awake out of sheer spite. And he didn't mind my smoking or my tendency to stay up late and wake up early, the fact that I drank coffee all the time—to him these were little things, for in return he received more love than he knew what to do with.

I didn't have time for my studies, but he said it could wait, I would have time later. And I kissed him on the neck and said yes, it can wait, it can so wait, and wrapped my arms round his neck—*you know more about me now than anyone has ever known.*

When he went to work, I instantly felt such terrible longing that I could hardly sit still. I cleaned, sorted, scrubbed, organized, and piled things—I did anything at all to make time go faster. And when we met again in the evening it always seemed as though he had become even more handsome: stuck to his skin, his shirt revealed too much of the contours of his upper body, his black leather belt separated the white shirt from the quality fabric of his trousers, which made his legs look criminally enticing.

He wore a bespoke suit, a tie, and leather shoes, and I felt like asking him to stop so that I could look at him from head to toe and admire myself standing next to him in the mirror. I wanted to be envious of myself, of this moment. Of the fact that I had found a man like this, my very own bank manager with whom I could come to any agreement whatsoever.

On those yearning-filled afternoons I teased and tortured myself by imagining him sitting in our favorite café with someone else. He would be holding that someone else's hand across the table, he'd move the salt and pepper shakers to the edge of the table and out of the way of their hands, their love, he would be sipping coffee even more delicious than the coffee I made him, and his love would be all the more ardent. I imagined this someone else by his side, thought this someone else might be better suited to him. What if this someone else had all the same qualities for which he had fallen in love with me but lacked the things about me that made him think twice?

The words *I, love,* and *you* soon became my favorite words, and I wanted nothing more than to say them over and over. I love you. It's two o'clock, only another three hours and his journey home, then he would be here and I could say it to him again.

He and I were becoming *we* without either of us really noticing it. Soon he began casually asking whether *we* were going to his sister's birthday party on the weekend, because *we* obviously couldn't be apart, as if he would have skipped the party if I hadn't agreed to join him. But I said yes, I always said yes, of course *we* are going to your sister's birthday party. Of course I'll go there with you, you don't have to ask things like that, you can just tell me we're going somewhere on the weekend because I won't have any other plans.

Given my age I could have been his son, and he pondered this fact from one day to the next. He had a habit of asking me if his age bothered me, and I repeated over and over that no, it doesn't bother me, this isn't about numbers.

Things were like this for a long time. Everything was fine.

So fine, in fact, that I started to doubt him, though he gave me no reason to do so. It started with little things. I got angry listening to his constant moaning about how tired he was. Irritated, I asked why he was always yawning. I glowered at him out of the corner of my eye and pretended to be reading a book on the sofa when his strong hand slipped between me and the book and started massaging my chest.

"Don't touch me," I said, clamped my teeth together, and imagined his neck between them.

"Fine then," he said, pulled his hand away, and started looking for his black-and-white stripy shirt.

"I can't bear your moaning. Stop it. Right now," I said.

He tried to defend himself. "I'm allowed to be tired sometimes."

"You can sleep tomorrow. And on the weekend. Whenever you like," I replied.

"That's right, I forgot I'm not supposed to tell you I'm tired because there are people right now dying of hunger, that's it," he muttered. "You can't spend your life thinking about what's right and wrong with the world."

He then picked up a pile of my papers from my desk. He had always wondered why I printed out things like this. An article about the Gitarama prison in Rwanda, for instance, where the inmates were so hungry they had taken to eating one another, where the cells were so crammed the prisoners had to stand up.

Every hour of every day they spent standing in a large cage on a floor of hard, cold cement that was covered in feces. Their feet are covered in sores, they turn gangrenous and eventually fall off.

The slums of India, stretching out as far as the eye can see, huts built of trash. Dharavi, the largest of the slums, home to more than a million people. A million people in an area of only a half square mile with no drainage or sewage system. Children play in the dirt, they fall ill, and doctors refuse to treat them. Insurance companies demand forms, hospitals require birth certificates. If you don't have them, you don't exist.

Chapters of books about people sold into prostitution, slave labor, the organ and drug trades. Girls wait for clients in dark shacks, and the clients can do with them as they please. They are bound, drugged, and unconscious. Or they lie on an operating table, scalpels sink into their tender skin; organ dealers take their kidneys and the rest is nothing but clinical refuse. There are millions of such cases every year, millions of people and destinies like this.

He threw the papers to the floor and kicked them.

"Why do you torture yourself with shit like this?"

"Get out."

It was our first argument. He called me childish and went home.

Didn't he understand that it was his responsibility to think about those prisoners and children? To think about if you were suddenly kidnapped and you didn't know whether you would ever see daylight again? What would it feel like to wake up in a cold, dark basement and scream so long that your throat would no longer make a sound, and on each side there was nothing but damp, icy walls? What must that moment be like, the moment when you realize you are going to die soon but not yet? When you only know it will happen and there is nothing you can do but wait?

Of course he should think about this, everybody should.

Not complain about being tired. Ever. It was nonsensical to claim we have the right to feel sorrow and anxiety and tiredness at the most insignificant things, and even more nonsensical to try to justify it by saying that that sorrow and anxiety and tiredness are the same for everybody the world over.

He drove back to my place in his new Volvo and kissed me at the door. His stubble scratched my face, and I stopped kissing him for a moment and said it again: I love you. Really. I'm sorry. You can say anything you want. *No, you're right. Don't apologize. I'm sorry. I won't say anything like that again.*

And so I loved him even more, more than I loved myself, and he loved me more than he loved himself too. We were perfect for each other, I thought, we will grow old together and I will be with him on the day he dies, I will call his relatives, tell them he has passed away, and make arrangements for his funeral.

Until one day I realized I did nothing but sit in the apartment waiting for him to open the door and come home.

He came out of the shower without drying his feet and left wet footprints on the floor and the rugs. Wherever he went, he made a mess. He never washed up the frying pan but left it on the stove, he never scrubbed the bathroom tiles, he never put his dirty clothes in the laundry basket but left them on the floor, and he had no idea how much dust he created because I always wiped it away. I picked up his clothes and washed his dishes and scrubbed the bathroom tiles, and sometimes I imagined his face on the tiles as I scoured them with a wire brush, washed his clothes at the wrong temperature, and cooked his dinner in a dirty frying pan.

He made passing remarks about my neurotic cleaning, about the fact that I changed the sheets several times a week, and before long I was actively seeking out things about which I could make passing remarks too. It became a competition. I watched him closely, manically following his every move just to catch him out: to see when he made a mistake, when I could stick my bristles into his thick flesh and comment on something I would never have done.

Eventually love was no longer enough, neither my love for him nor his love for me, though I gave him more than enough and he gave me even more in return. He started saying I was sick and wondered whether professional help would be enough to cure me.

"I don't know whether you've noticed, but you're quite arrogant," I said.

"Me, arrogant?" he scoffed. "I might be arrogant, but you sit around here all day and won't go farther than the shop. You wait here for me all day. It's pathetic. Get up and do something for yourself."

"First off, nobody's forcing you to stay. Second, I never stop doing things. I wash your clothes, iron your ties, your socks, your underwear, I cook for you and clean up after you. You never have to do anything."

His brow furrowed. His left eye squinted, half shut. I could see from his expression that he was clenching his teeth. He tightened the towel he'd wrapped round his waist and seemed to be giving his next words careful consideration.

"You're free to go," I said as callously as I could and hopped indifferently onto the sofa to show just how insignificant I found this conversation.

I took my phone out of my pocket and began typing a random flow of letters. "Besides, I've been cheating on you."

"What?"

"Yes, I've been cheating on you. I'm just texting him now. You're too old for me. Did you really think I'd stay with you when you're retired and I'm still young? Think about it."

His hands were gripping the knot in his towel. I couldn't look at him, but I sensed his tears through the thick, stagnant air in the room. I got up to open the window but fell back on the sofa almost instantly. His body slumped, vanquished. He scratched his head, sighed heavily as though the air between us had thickened so much that there was no room for either of us to say a thing. He went into the bedroom to find his clothes. Judging by the rustling from the bedroom he dressed quickly, then walked to the door, said *bye,* and left.

After him I stopped doing things, stopped meeting people, stopped encountering the outside world. This lasted for months, summer turned to autumn, hurried people plodded quickly through the rain and the darkness, opened and closed their umbrellas, shook off the rain and continued on their way. I watched them for a while through the window. It tired me out and I wondered how it didn't tire them in the same way.

I began to wish I'd already lived my life, because I simply couldn't bear living it any longer. I dreamed of being an old man with a hoarse voice, a man who had already seen the world, who had loved, hated, and lost, had children and grandchildren, who had sat clapping at their graduations and weddings.

But that's not how it goes, I told myself when I'd thought about this long enough, so I took my sunglasses out of the drawer, and when I put them on I stepped outside and enrolled in new courses at the university and signed up for membership at a gym. That's how it works, it's all about your attitude, I repeated to myself ad infinitum, attitude, that's what matters, and I told myself it was a beautiful, sunny day, the snow glistening like diamond dust, and I got off the bus not because it was full and I would have to stand up but because I wanted to walk the rest of the journey, and my voice didn't quiver as I took care of matters on the telephone and I didn't even hunch my shoulders when I walked past benches full of people.

So I told the cashier at the supermarket that tonight I was

going to make a meal for my significant other with eggplant and zucchini, and when I came home I threw the eggplants and zucchinis in the garbage can and wept. I fell into bed, exhausted, and when I woke up the next morning I looked out of the window and said out loud: *Today*.

Today is an immeasurably beautiful day.

A NEW LIFE

After leaving I spent several weeks in a women's shelter. Then I got an apartment, a small one-bedroom flat near the center of town.

At first I found being by myself difficult. I needed to do the laundry only once a week, the dishes didn't pile up, nobody else slept in my bed but me. I had never lived alone, though I'd wished I could on numerous occasions, and now I felt vulnerable, naked. I had nothing to do, nowhere I was expected to be at a specific time.

I had too much time to think about things. Could anyone have believed that one day I would be here? Without my children and without my husband. Wouldn't it be better, I wondered, to be with somebody than to live like this? Would life with someone else, anyone else, be better than a life lived alone?

Had my children become too Finnish? I wondered. Had we? As they learned the names of plants and birds, learned to recite the capital cities of the world, learned about all those religions, did they ever think we should have done the same? That we should have done more, learned a trade, completed courses, and finished diplomas? Did they ever notice how envious Bajram and I were that they had the opportunity to do something decent with their lives, something worthwhile and respected? That they picked everything up so quickly?

I wondered why Bajram was so keen to sign all the forms they brought home, why he was always happy to tick all the boxes. How could he possibly have thought that his children would work, pay taxes, then return to him and help make his dreams come true instead of their own?

These thoughts plagued me for a long time. When I was walking home from the supermarket, I sometimes burst into tears in the middle of the street. When I was in the shower, I sometimes slumped to the floor. I held my stomach. Every inch of my body ached. And as, out of force of habit, I prepared far too much food and sat down at my little table, I looked in turn at the oven dish and at the empty chair opposite me until I stood up, put the dish back in the oven, and moved the chair out of sight.

The phone calls to my siblings and parents became more sporadic, and I began to fade from their minds. I sent my children text messages asking them to visit me, but they didn't seem all that interested in coming. When my younger son visited me he didn't ask anything about me, he asked only about his father though I was still here and his father was not.

20

He called me out of the blue and asked if he could come over. In his life six months wasn't very long at all. It had gone so quickly that we barely noticed it. *We can still do things together, see each other and go for dinner together.*

"Hi," I said at the door. "Good to see you."

I greeted him and showed him into the flat.

"How are you doing?" he asked, took off his yellow sneakers in the hallway, and stepped into the living room to shake his legs, which were crammed into tight running shorts. His thigh muscles looked like enormous slabs of meat, somehow separate from the rest of his body.

I didn't know what to say. Should I tell him the truth or should I answer his question in such a way that I could then turn it round and ask him the same thing?

"I'm doing fine," I said and looked at him. "How about you?"

He had taken off his damp gray cap and propped his left leg on the sofa to stretch the back of his thighs. "Yes, all good," he said.

"Are you hungry?" I asked because I knew how hungry he always was when he came home after exercising.

"Have you cooked?" he asked.

"No, but I was just going to make something for myself," I said and instantly felt inadequate: I should have had something ready, I thought; making Bolognese sauce will take too long, he hates fast food, he never eats anything frozen, and processed food is something he simply cannot understand. He would push it to one side and demand something better.

"You don't have to do that for me. I can have something small. A piece of fruit, maybe?" he said and sat on the floor.

I opened the fridge in desperation. If we'd still been together he wouldn't have been this polite. He would have hurt me in the way that only a lover can.

"You can have an apple," I said after noticing a single apple at the bottom of the fruit bowl on the kitchen table.

"That would be great," he said, picked up the apple, thanked me and stepped over to the sink to rinse it, took a knife out of the top drawer, and began eating in that way he had of cutting off chunks and popping them into his mouth using the knife and his thumb.

He leaned against the wall behind him, pulled his leg up against the wall to stretch his thigh some more, and stood there munching his apple until he'd had enough of that position, put the apple and knife on the table and left them there, the way he always did, and peered beneath the sofa.

"That's odd . . . ," he began hesitantly. "It must be behind the sofa. It would barely move if you didn't lift it out every now and then. How come it doesn't get bored?"

"It's always there," I said. "You know that. It's very sensitive and well behaved."

"I know, but why don't you lift it into the terrarium you bought? It'll dry out over there," he said bluntly and picked up the apple and knife again.

"It doesn't like the terrarium," I said and began wondering what I could say or do so that he wouldn't start the conversation about what he thought I should and shouldn't do with the snake, where I should put it or where I should keep it, how it was living at too low a temperature.

"I've redecorated," I stammered and walked toward the bedroom.

I showed him the new look in my bedroom: a black-rimmed mirror leaning against the wall, new black sheets, and curtains that didn't let in the small amount of daylight coming from the windows that looked out onto the street.

"Nice," he said, catching his breath.

"Thanks," I said and watched him sit on the edge of the bed and start bobbing up and down as though he had too much energy.

I wanted to walk up to him, grab him from behind, wrap my arms around him, smell him. I had remained standing in the doorway, and it felt as though my shoulders were glued to the frame.

He stood up and turned to face me, raised his hand to the zipper on his jacket, and pulled it down.

"You know . . . I was lying when I said I'd cheated on you."

"I know that," he said and began stepping toward me.

"Right," I managed to say before he was right in front of me and placing his hands on my hips.

"Right," he repeated.

We looked at each other for a long time, he and I, without saying a word; I touched his naked chest and he rubbed my lower back and said it the same way he'd said it the first time: I love you. That's what he said. *I want to be with you. I've been thinking about things a lot, and I'm sorry I walked out and left you.*

And he said he'd missed me, said how right it felt to hold my hand, how well he slept when he was with me, and how different life was without me. I raised a hand to his cheek but he pulled it down again. For a while I didn't say a word to him, then I said yes, I love you too—and I let him lift me into the air, I swung my legs round his hips, let him throw me on the bed, and we sat there opposite each other, he looked at me and I looked at him and the light behind him, and his outline was as clear-cut as a sheet of folded paper and every bit as white.

And when he went home, he asked if he could come the following evening and spend the night. *I'll bring some things with me,* said his text message.

Come on round, I replied, my hands trembling. I wiped my sweaty brow on my shirt and threw my phone at the wall.

The day he returned darkened into a black, sudden night. The snake had slithered behind the sofa, its skin smelled rancid, in dim lighting its color turned from brown to black, and it moved slowly but surely across the floor like a pile of rolling pebbles. Only the dust that caught on its skin made a noise, the sound of silent whispers, of Blu Tack being peeled off the wall or the faint gasp escaping from the mouth of one out of breath, a wheezing that was at once silent and fast as a bullet.

Then the snake arrived, closer than ever before. It pulled its tail up next to its head and began hissing like fragile porcelain, and I could hear from its rough throat and tongue how dry its mouth was.

I lay on my bed, one hand on my brow and my head turned toward the snake. It was coiled up on the floor, its tail was quivering now, and its tongue flickered back and forth out of its mouth. I sat up on the bed and the snake leaned backward as though I should have warned it about my sudden movement. This was a familiar game of ours.

But it wouldn't let me touch it. It resisted and bit my arm three times. Its powerful jaws tightened, bruising my skin, and its teeth sank beneath my skin. But its mouth still felt warm.

I finally got hold of it. Not caring about the bites I grabbed it with both hands. And at that very moment it started thrashing, its tail beat against the floor like a hammer and wrapped round my legs as though it were about to fall off the edge of a cliff.

I pressed it against the wall with my knee and elbows. There it was, trapped. It might be able to bite me again, maybe even try to escape, but it finally gave up and realized it couldn't get away.

Eventually it relaxed. Its tongue disappeared into its mouth and its body went limp and straightened out. I let it go and it fell to the floor, piling on top of itself like a crumpled garment. Then I grabbed it again, sank my nails into its skin, lifted it onto the bed, and placed it next to me like a licorice-caramel-patterned pillow. *Good night.*

I'd never seen it behave like that before, and I'd never handled it like that before—I'd always relented. Now I made the decisions. In this situation resistance was futile.

Before we fell asleep the snake adjusted its position, and as it quickly wriggled past me the sheets rustled beneath it as though someone had run his nails across them. A moment later it was right in front of my face. It craned its head forward and looked at me the way a pet looks at its owner. Its faint breath puffed in my face, and its tongue flickered round its mouth like wet hands.

When I awoke, it was a gray morning outside.

The snake had wrapped itself round me three times: once round my upper thighs, a second time round my stomach, while the thickest and strongest part of its body formed a third coil round my chest and lungs.

I'd been giving it hints and feeding its hunter instinct, and now my being asleep had given the snake the opportunity to react to my breathing, the swelling and relaxing of my chest. There's only one thing you need to know about boa constrictors: they react to motion by tightening their grip on their prey.

I tried to remain as calm as possible and held my breath as I looked at the snake's head, which it held right next to my face.

I looked at the coils it had wrapped round me. I tried to slip a finger beneath them and forbid it from continuing, to punch it all over and scratch its skin, but this made it tighten all the more.

With the snake still around me I ran into the kitchen. Each step was heavier and shorter than the previous one. It was holding me so tightly that at one point I wasn't sure I would make it. Then I gripped the fruit knife and stuck it into the snake's head.

There was soon a long gash in the snake's body, and it was now almost half the size it had been only a moment earlier. Blood was pouring out of it like a broken pipe. Its organs, guts, its elongated white lungs, its brown liver and pink kidneys spilled out in such a bloody mass that it was hard to imagine they had once all belonged inside its body.

I sat amid the gore and cut the snake open more and more, because I started to fear it might miraculously put itself back together and cure itself, that the gashes in its side would somehow heal and it would come back to life in the time it took me to stuff it into a black garbage bag, that it would stand up on end like a sturdy coat stand. That it would be immortal and say, *Don't tell anyone about this. I'll kill you if you tell anyone about this.*

A PHONE CALL

Hello, Emine," came the voice at the end of the phone. I would recognize that voice in the middle of a crowd, anywhere at all. Lowered by tobacco and old age, the voice was deep and coarse. There was no mistaking my father's voice.

He was one of the hundreds of thousands whose life had fallen apart after the war. Only one of his three sons had remained with him, brought his wife into the family, and finished building the house. The rest of us had fled, promising to come back one day, but none of us had done so. The war had changed everything. It laughed at things that had once been sacred and didn't care about people's faces.

"How are you?" I asked, though I knew he never called me unless he wanted something, to ask about any planned trips to Kosovo or to speak to Bajram. We treated each other like distant relatives who have nothing in common but the blood flowing through their veins.

"I want to apologize, and I want you to apologize. I want us to bury the past."

He paused for a moment, and in that time I began weeping silently.

"I'm sorry—for everything," I said, and the air that had

built up in my mouth burst out in a single gasp and I didn't know whether I was crying with joy or because I'd finally said something I had wanted to say for so very long.

"I'm sorry too. If only this had turned out somehow . . . ," he began and started to gasp for breath, ". . . differently." For a moment all I could hear was rushing at the other end, the sound of my father wiping his beard.

"Your son Bekim," he began and blew his nose.

Again he paused and took a deep breath.

"He was here," he spluttered. "Did you know that? Did you know he came to visit?" he repeated insistently when I was unable to pull myself together to answer him.

"I didn't know that," I said. "I didn't know he had visited you."

"I have to tell you what happened."

"Why did he visit?"

"That's why I'm calling you. I don't know why he was here. I thought you might be able to tell me that."

"I can't tell you that."

Then my father told me how my son had turned up at Mehmet's shop and how he had climbed up the boulder.

"Straight off Lula saw a ginger-and-white cat sitting happily next to him. The boy was stroking it. Imagine, he was stroking a cat. After a while he left the boulder and came back to the village. When he arrived, I saw him out of the window. You can recognize a person in so many different ways, Emine, from the way he holds his head, the way he wipes sweat from his brow, the way he gestures with his hands—even though it's someone you haven't seen for a very, very long time."

He took a breath.

"And the closer he came, the more clearly I saw it."

"Saw what?"

For a moment he was silent.

"The cat. He had a cat with him."

Again he was silent.

"A cat? You already told me he was stroking a cat on the boulder."

"Yes, he had a cat on his shoulder, a ginger-and-white cat dangling round his neck. Have you ever heard anything like it?"

I furrowed my brow.

"He turned up at the gate, knocked on the door, and waited outside. Your niece Arta opened the gate and asked him inside. Of course, Arta didn't recognize him. She wanted to play with the cat and tried to pick it up, but your son didn't pay her the slightest attention."

My father took a breath.

"He walked across the yard and stopped outside the front door. I held out my hand, but he wouldn't look at me. Instead he stared at the ground, gripped the plastic bag in his hand tighter, and spun it round. Then he stepped inside. Lula asked if he would like some coffee or tea or something to eat, but he didn't answer. He just peered round the room."

Again he took a breath.

"The boy sat down on the living-room sofa and fixed his eyes on me the minute I sat down opposite him. He placed the plastic bag next to him on the sofa."

"You're not lying to me, are you?" I asked.

"I swear this is God's honest truth."

He answered me agitatedly, almost offended. I knew that when he swore something, he was telling me the truth from start to finish.

"I asked how he was but he wouldn't answer. I decided to give him a friendly smile and say something to break the awkward atmosphere. I mentioned how much he had grown."

He explained that the boy had asked about Bajram, told him he'd heard that his father had died recently.

There was a moment of silence at the other end of the phone. Then he said he had told the boy about his father's funeral and his grave.

"When I asked whether he'd like to visit Bajram's grave, the boy suddenly stood up. The cat was still sitting proudly on his shoulder as though it were glued into place. *No,* he said. The hairs on my neck stood on end as though I'd had an electric shock. I didn't know what else I could say to him. The whole situation was unreal."

I said I was sorry.

"Then the boy said, *I was outside just now and caught this.* At that he held the plastic bag in the air. I could see something curved inside it, but the bag was so thick that I couldn't quite make out what it was."

I made a sound to encourage him to continue.

"When the boy picked up the bag, something started thrashing around inside it. At first all I could hear was a frantic hissing, but a moment later a hole appeared in the bottom of the bag, and out of the hole slithered a snake."

"A snake? Did you say he had a snake in the plastic bag?"

"Yes, it was a snake. A black-and-gray poisonous viper. There are plenty of them round here. I was rigid with fear and I didn't dare move as he dropped the bag over the snake. His hands were sure and strong, as if he had known precisely how to take hold of the thing. The snake's whole body was thrashing as the boy held it beneath the head. The cat on his shoulder hissed at first, climbed on the boy's head, even tried to hit the snake, and paced restlessly along the boy's shoulders until the snake had stopped writhing."

Again he blew his nose and waited a moment, trying to find the right words.

"Then he held the snake behind him and threw it at me. The snake. My legs almost buckled beneath me, my knees were trembling, and a feeling of horror welled up in my stomach."

He fell silent.

"Did you hear me, Emine?"

"Yes, I heard you."

"He threw the snake at me. It came hurtling toward me, headfirst, and the cat leaped after it. The boy snatched the cat in midair and ran out of the room. The snake struck my right thigh. It tried to bite me but didn't succeed. I was afraid, Emine. I've never been so afraid in my life."

"I'm sorry," I said.

"The snake started uncoiling itself and headed for the front door, and eventually it slithered into the garden and down into the field."

The call was cut off, and when I saw he was trying to call me again I didn't answer.

21

The following evening, he handed me a plastic bag and kissed me just the way he had before, as though six months hadn't changed a thing. He slipped his hand under my shirt, his thick, curved fingers gripped my bare skin, his teeth nibbled my lower lip, and he stood in front of me smiling.

I turned his last kiss into an embrace. As he placed his open bag on the hallway floor I noticed he'd brought clothes and shoes with him, and I noticed they'd been thrown into his bag willy-nilly, that the shoes were dirty. I pulled him into the living room and put the plastic bag on the table. In addition to a DVD and a carton of juice there was a book in the bag.

He'd asked me to lend him a book that would tell him about my homeland. I told him there weren't many stories written about my homeland and gave him György Dragomán's *The White King,* told him to read it slowly and think about its story, but he hadn't even opened it.

He knelt down and looked under the sofa.

"Where is it?" he asked.

I fiddled with the book on the table as if I hadn't heard his question. I was annoyed that he hadn't bothered to read the book, because I was convinced that when he realized the child narrator's father had been abducted and taken to a labor camp and would never return to the story, which the protagonist spends waiting for his return, when he was forced to question whether the young Djata really loves his father or whether he simply loves the idea of his father's absence, he would never be the same again. He would understand that endings in stories are never as interesting as the details of the beginning in which the fate of a ruined man drifting through life is revealed in the fact that he goes fishing every day though he doesn't eat fish or that he takes his partner for dinner at an expensive restaurant though he doesn't have any money.

After a moment I snap back to reality, turn to him, and tell him. "I took it back."

"Really?"

"Yes."

I told him I'd realized I didn't have the means to look after it, that I'd have to take it back. That he'd been right all along.

That evening we went to sleep as soon as the film ended. He thought the action thriller he'd picked was gripping; I said I agreed, though to me it was altogether uninteresting. We tumbled into bed and the evening quickly darkened as we lay there next to each other. He loves sleeping like that, I thought, otherwise he wouldn't breathe so lightly and wouldn't sniff my fresh sheets with such satisfaction.

"I'm happy," he began and closed his eyes. "Are you happy?"

"Yes," I replied and waited for him to place his hand on my shoulder and slide his fingers along my arm to show me quite how much he wanted to say what he'd just said, and how much he wanted me to respond the way I responded.

And that's exactly what he did. I listened to his calm breathing until at some point he placed his hand beneath his pillow and turned to face the wall. I looked at how deep set his spine was between the extensor muscles on his back, and I thought about his words. When he said he was happy, did he really mean it or was he merely happy at his own imagination, at the illusion in which he loved me in a way he would never be able to love me in reality?

I tried to go to sleep, but as I lay thinking about his words I began thinking about my mother, thinking I should call her and meet her more often. And once I'd resolved to call her the very next day I began thinking about my father. About that afternoon when I told my father I'd been pushed around in town, called names and punched in the nose, my eyeballs pressed into their sockets and my clothes pulled so hard that my sleeve had ripped. *Look, my sleeve is torn at the shoulder.*

Why have you got such a crooked nose? they asked. Why is your hair so black, your eyebrows so thick? Why are you wearing worn-out shoes? Can't you afford to buy new ones? You wear that same jacket every day—are you poor, are you a refugee? They shoved me between them, hit me, and laughed, one of them spat on my forehead, and the spittle trickled down my face and I didn't dare wipe it away. Wipe it away and you're dead, they said, wipe it and you're dead, you fucking parasite refugee.

I got out of bed in the middle of the night, picked up Sami's bag, and laid out his clothes. I sorted them out and wondered why, when I returned home that afternoon, I'd told my father I wanted to die. *I do, I really do. I'd rather die than go back there ever again.* As I fetched the iron I remembered how I'd regretted turning to him.

Now you listen here. First of all, you don't know a thing about death, and second, I'll tell you, he began. *I'll tell you what to do. Don't ever tell them your name, and don't say where you come from.* He drew his hand along my face and I felt his meager fingers on my cheek. *Don't ever tell them who your parents are, who your siblings are, don't get in people's way, and don't talk, and if they come and ask you something, you know what to do.*

"I'll lie."

"That's right. You lie. And if someone still gets in your face, you hit them harder than they hit you. Is that clear?"

Once I'd ironed and folded all his clothes I fetched the shoe brush from the hallway. I brushed the loose mud from his shoes and took them with me as I slipped outside, sprayed them with protective lacquer, and when I came back inside I polished them and watched them dry until I placed them on the shoe rack and went back to bed, lay next to him, and fell asleep in an instant.

THE CAT

I finally managed to get a job in a grocery store. At first I was so nervous that I almost decided not to turn up at all. I hadn't realized that working would be such a difficult and significant step. In the days leading up to my first shift I was afraid that I wouldn't be able to give people the right change, that they would come back to my register and accuse me of shortchanging them. I'd lose my job, they would call the police and add my name to a register so I'd never get another job.

On my first day at work I sweated like an obese man on a hot day. I had to go to the toilet so many times that I told people I wasn't feeling very well. I ran ice-cold water from the tap, soaked my hands in the sink, and took a series of deep breaths.

I wanted people to like me but I didn't know what kind of things to talk about with them in order for that to happen. I didn't know what the other employees talked about to one another, so I kept quiet and didn't talk about myself to anyone. I simply did what my boss told me to do.

It took a few months before I learned the names of the products and where they were kept. Thankfully the shop is so small that only on a few occasions have I ended up in a situation where I don't know how to answer the customer. Nowadays there's a sense of routine about my job and I don't need to think about it so much. Sometimes I find new favorite foods among the discounted items and I try out lots of Finnish recipes.

I like the fact that people have started coming to this country from around the world. Sometimes I find myself staring at them and feel like asking them where they come from. I wonder what circumstances they have left behind and what their lives are like now. But the Finns might not like that, they might roll their eyes and even swear at having to wait in line longer.

On Wednesday evenings I go to the sauna in our building. Such warmth amid such breathtaking cold always feels unreal, supernatural. It dives beneath the skin, and the boards are so hot they almost burn you.

On Saturdays I stroll round the town, walk through parks covered in glinting snow. I love that the winter is so cold here. The freezing temperatures make everything stop. The trees covered in snow stand still like statues, the snow hardens on the streets as thick as asphalt and tightens round the streetlamps like a hood.

I have become friends with one of my coworkers. She is in her fifties, a single woman with a lovely sense of humor who never had any children. She told me her husband had died of a heart attack. She lives with her three cats and two dogs. And when she asked me the same questions, I told her my husband had died too. After hearing her story, my own story no longer felt so dysfunctional. In this country, living by yourself isn't at all out of the ordinary.

We held each other's hand as we told our stories. She wiped the corner of her eye with a finger and I blew my nose, then she gave a deep sigh and looked up at the bright sky and the bare branches of the trees. Then we laughed, two women sitting on a park bench in the middle of winter.

In the spring she told me one of her cats had had kittens. *Just normal, mongrel kittens.* When she showed me a photograph of the three gray kittens and one black one sleeping next to one another in a basket, I asked her almost by accident what she was planning to do with them. *Could I have the black one?* I asked straightaway, and she smiled and said there was no one she would rather give it to.

The cat and I spend most evenings watching television or simply being close to each other. I scratch it, and it likes that. It has deep yellow eyes, and when it spends hours sitting on the windowsill and looking outside I feel strange, as though I don't know it at all, but when I put food on its plate I know it will always eat and that it is grateful.

For the most part the cat and I enjoy watching talent shows. I always cry when someone gets up onstage and starts to sing, someone whose life has been full of sorrow. When they speak of the loves they have lost, I instinctively think of Bajram.

I think of my siblings more rarely these days. They are all in new houses, in new countries, living new lives. They call me on special occasions and we exchange a few words, for formality's sake more than anything. But we never speak of how terrible our lives once were, and we never speak of the war.

I have started speaking to my children more often, even meeting up with them. Sometimes we go for long walks and visit cafés, and sometimes I go shopping with them. Our conversations are often stiff because I don't always understand their work problems and I don't know how much it is appropriate to ask them about things. I'm not sure whether I should perhaps ask for their forgiveness. But I don't want them to feel they have to explain their business to me because they shouldn't have to explain anything to me. We have started planning a trip to Kosovo because we would like to visit his grave.

My daughters have Finnish husbands with whom they plan to have children. My elder son and eldest daughter have good jobs, and my youngest children are studying hard. I am so proud of them that I am always eager to answer if someone asks about their lives.

At some point everyone should experience what it feels like to run out of options. That's what I think. Because in a situation like that you think you're losing your mind. Only now I know it's not the least bit dangerous. When I received the letter Bajram had sent me I sat at the kitchen table because I thought I might lose my mind at the very contents of that letter. But when I opened it and read the few lines he had written to me and the children, I slid the letter back into its envelope, turned it in my hands for a moment, and put it away in the cupboard, because he had addressed it to people who no longer existed.

22

I got out of bed and walked into the living room. Sami was looking out of the window at the weighty snowflakes falling to the ground. He said he'd been thinking about things all night, turned his head, and looked me in the eyes.

I wasn't angry about my father's death. I was relieved, relieved that he had finally found a way to turn to the only option still open to him. The only thing that made me angry was Sami's tone when he had asked me, because my father hadn't been a father to me, not the same way as his had been a father to him.

"I think it's high time you told me," he began and glanced at his clothes, neatly folded on the sofa.

When I didn't answer immediately, he shot out a volley of questions, as if it would be easier for me to start from a single detail. *What was he like? What did he look like? When was the last time you saw him? Tell me, please, say something, trust me.*

I picked up the pile of clothes and said that my father had left this country long ago. As I walked into the bedroom, I told him it had taken months before I even heard he had left. I placed his clothes in the wardrobe, and once I returned to the living room I said it had taken even longer before I heard he had died.

I put a hand on my hip, shifted my weight from one leg

to the other, and hoped that Sami had more clothes than I did. Then I pressed my hands to my face as I realized I had never told anyone about my father's death; I had always said we weren't on good terms or that he'd left us when I was young.

Sami gripped my shoulder and turned back to face the window, and the snowfall was lighter now, more drifting. He was silent, but his questions weren't over; they were there in the way he moved his head, in the trajectory of his coffee cup as he drew it closer, in the grip with which he tried to hold me still, and they were in his mouth, in the delicate rhythm in which his lips tried to form words.

For a long time I hadn't understood my father because he didn't view life the same way as others. Whereas other people asked each other what they wished for in life, my father asked people what they wished for in death. He couldn't understand why people didn't spend time wondering about the way in which their lives would one day come to an end. It would happen to every one of us; it was the only thing that united us. *How on earth can they bring themselves not to think about it, not to discuss it?* he would ask, shake his head, and eventually burst into laughter.

Then he would start to list ways of dying: cancer, a car accident, suffocation, falling to the pavement, drowning, burning, being shot. *Do me a favor,* he said. *Close your eyes and imagine what it would be like if you accidentally leaned against a circular saw and your arm was sliced off and you'd never be able to get it back again. Instead of fingers, there would be nothingness. Or what would it be like to fall from the deck of a ship into the freezing water? The motors would swallow you up in a millisecond no matter how strongly you tried to swim away.*

I wasn't sure whether he really wanted to die or whether all he wanted from death was what it would mean for his loved ones.

A heart attack, a plane crash, a stroke, tuberculosis, cirrhosis, being crushed, being starved, freezing to death. *What would you choose? If you could?*

Then he would start battering his fists against his head, go into the bathroom, fill the bath, and lower himself into the tub, as though he imagined he could end his life through the force of sheer willpower, or he would tighten a belt around his neck, press a sharp knife against his throat, and threaten to cut himself. Once, he ran into the bedroom, fetched a pile of blankets from the cupboard, buried himself beneath them, and said, *Sorry, Daddy's very scared right now.*

And I listened and watched, I listened to his stifled voice and I watched as the blankets shuddered to the rhythm of his flinches, I watched until he began to gasp for breath, and I went to him and stroked his damp back and said I was sorry, and when he vomited at the side of the bed I mopped everything up even before he stood, and as I stroked him, as I cleaned up the mess he had made, I felt nothing for him but disgust, his viscid sweat oozing between my fingers like egg white.

"That's what my father did," I said.

I stepped behind Sami to see him more closely, to watch his reaction. Then he turned to look at me, took my arm, and wrapped it around him.

"Thank you," he said and slid his fingers between my own.

His hand was warm and strong and squeezed my hand, and I thought of the warmth that existed between our hands, the rustle that occurs as he pulls on an item of clothing I have washed for him, the soft hiss from his nostrils as he breathes against my forehead. Did my father ever experience anything like this?

All those years I'd hoped he would die, though I didn't understand what death truly meant. And as I wished for his death, I didn't realize that one day my wish would come true, nor did I realize that, when it finally happened, I would think of him so often: what clothes had he worn or what pieces of furniture had he acquired, who had cooked for him every day and what kind of crockery did he eat from, who tidied his apartment, did he have anyone to change the sheets or simply to check that he didn't lose too much weight?

And I wonder what my father thought about when he woke up in the morning and remembered he was alone, or on the morning he died. What was my father thinking about when he fetched his revolver from the glass cabinet on that early morning? Had he had enough of searching for answers or asking questions as he slipped the bullets into the cylinder and cocked the gun? Was he thinking of what he had left behind? I wonder as I picture him placing the barrel into his mouth, his dry lips closing around it, as I catch the taste of metal when my tongue runs along my teeth, as I hear the faint sound of the trigger or imagine how hard he must have had to pull it, and the cold metal stings my limbs, makes my bones ache, pinches them.

A light bursting from the window splits his head in two as I see him there, sitting at the table, and he looks at me, askew, over his shoulder and I wonder, Was he thinking about me, was my father thinking about me at the moment he finally refused to carry on living, in such violent fashion?

I never got an answer, but I'm sure that's what my father was thinking.

And from time to time, when I hear his voice, I go for a long walk in the forest or down by the shore, and when I come back I take my significant other by the arm, he is a beautiful, decent man, and I embrace him and ask what he would like to eat, because I know how happy this makes him—and I go shopping with him and sit in the passenger seat of his car and he grips the upper half of the steering wheel with his bare hand, his skin taut with the cold. He is wearing a pair of sunglasses, and I look at his hand, his concave knuckles and his fingers, straight as bullets, and his white skin where the frosted light thickens like brilliant ice.

Acknowledgments

Thank you to everyone who has commented on this manuscript. My dear friends Merdiana Beqiri, Marisha Rasi-Koskinen, Virva Lehmusvaara, Krista Lehtonen, and Aura Pursiainen—thank you all for your insightful comments and suggestions. This novel would not have been the same without you.

Thank you to my family for their support, understanding, and love. Thank you for believing in me all these years. Thank you to my mother and father, especially for checking so many details on my behalf. Thank you to my sister and brothers for listening and commenting. *Ju dua.*

Thank you to everyone at Otava, particularly Antti Kasper and Silka Raatikainen. And to my editor Lotta Sonninen, the greatest thanks of all goes to you.

Pushkin Press

Pushkin Press was founded in 1997, and publishes novels, essays, memoirs, children's books—everything from timeless classics to the urgent and contemporary.

Our books represent exciting, high-quality writing from around the world: we publish some of the twentieth century's most widely acclaimed, brilliant authors such as Stefan Zweig, Marcel Aymé, Teffi, Antal Szerb, Gaito Gazdanov and Yasushi Inoue, as well as compelling and award-winning contemporary writers, including Andrés Neuman, Edith Pearlman, Eka Kurniawan, Ayelet Gundar-Goshen and Chigozie Obioma.

Pushkin Press publishes the world's best stories, to be read and read again. To discover more, visit www.pushkinpress.com.

—————

THE SPECTRE OF ALEXANDER WOLF
GAITO GAZDANOV

'A mesmerising work of literature' Antony Beevor

SUMMER BEFORE THE DARK
VOLKER WEIDERMANN

'For such a slim book to convey with such poignancy the extinction of a generation of "Great Europeans" is a triumph' *Sunday Telegraph*

MESSAGES FROM A LOST WORLD
STEFAN ZWEIG

'At a time of monetary crisis and political disorder… Zweig's celebration of the brotherhood of peoples reminds us that there is another way' *The Nation*

THE EVENINGS
GERARD REVE

'Not only a masterpiece but a cornerstone manqué of modern European literature' Tim Parks, *Guardian*

BINOCULAR VISION
EDITH PEARLMAN

'A genius of the short story' Mark Lawson, *Guardian*

IN THE BEGINNING WAS THE SEA
TOMÁS GONZÁLEZ

'Smoothly intriguing narrative, with its touches of sinister,
Patricia Highsmith-like menace' *Irish Times*

BEWARE OF PITY
STEFAN ZWEIG

'Zweig's fictional masterpiece' *Guardian*

THE ENCOUNTER
PETRU POPESCU

'A book that suggests new ways of looking at the world
and our place within it' *Sunday Telegraph*

WAKE UP, SIR!
JONATHAN AMES

'The novel is extremely funny but it is also sad and
poignant, and almost incredibly clever' *Guardian*

THE WORLD OF YESTERDAY
STEFAN ZWEIG

'*The World of Yesterday* is one of the greatest memoirs of the twentieth
century, as perfect in its evocation of the world Zweig loved, as it is
in its portrayal of how that world was destroyed' David Hare

WAKING LIONS
AYELET GUNDAR-GOSHEN

'A literary thriller that is used as a vehicle to explore big
moral issues. I loved everything about it' *Daily Mail*

FOR A LITTLE WHILE
RICK BASS

'Bass is, hands down, a master of the short form, creating in a few pages
a natural world of mythic proportions' *New York Times Book Review*

JOURNEY BY MOONLIGHT

ANTAL SZERB

'Just divine… makes you imagine the author has had private access to your own soul' Nicholas Lezard, *Guardian*

BEFORE THE FEAST

SAŠA STANIŠIĆ

'Exceptional… cleverly done, and so mesmerising from the off… thought-provoking and energetic' *Big Issue*

A SIMPLE STORY

LEILA GUERRIERO

'An epic of noble proportions… [Guerriero] is a mistress of the telling phrase or the revealing detail' *Spectator*

FORTUNES OF FRANCE

ROBERT MERLE

1 *The Brethren*

2 *City of Wisdom and Blood*

3 *Heretic Dawn*

'Swashbuckling historical fiction' *Guardian*

TRAVELLER OF THE CENTURY

ANDRÉS NEUMAN

'A beautiful, accomplished novel: as ambitious as it is generous, as moving as it is smart' Juan Gabriel Vásquez, *Guardian*

A WORLD GONE MAD

ASTRID LINDGREN

'A remarkable portrait of domestic life in a country maintaining a fragile peace while war raged all around' *New Statesman*

MIRROR, SHOULDER, SIGNAL

DORTHE NORS

'Dorthe Nors is fantastic!' Junot Díaz

RED LOVE: THE STORY OF AN EAST GERMAN FAMILY

MAXIM LEO

'Beautiful and supremely touching… an unbearably poignant description of a world that no longer exists' *Sunday Telegraph*

THE BEAUTIFUL BUREAUCRAT

HELEN PHILLIPS

'Funny, sad, scary and beautiful. I love it' Ursula K. Le Guin

THE RABBIT BACK LITERATURE SOCIETY

PASI ILMARI JÄÄSKELÄINEN

'Wonderfully knotty… a very grown-up fantasy masquerading as quirky fable. Unexpected, thrilling and absurd' *Sunday Telegraph*

BEAUTY IS A WOUND

EKA KURNIAWAN

'An unforgettable all-encompassing epic' *Publishers Weekly*

BARCELONA SHADOWS

MARC PASTOR

'As gruesome as it is gripping… the writing is extraordinarily vivid… Highly recommended' *Independent*

MEMORIES—FROM MOSCOW TO THE BLACK SEA

TEFFI

'Wonderfully idiosyncratic, coolly heartfelt and memorable' William Boyd, *Sunday Times*

WHILE THE GODS WERE SLEEPING

ERWIN MORTIER

'A monumental, phenomenal book' *De Morgen*

BUTTERFLIES IN NOVEMBER

AUÐUR AVA ÓLAFSDÓTTIR

'A funny, moving and occasionally bizarre exploration of life's upheavals and reversals' *Financial Times*

BY BLOOD

ELLEN ULLMAN

'Delicious and intriguing' *Daily Telegraph*

THE LAST DAYS

LAURENT SEKSIK

'Mesmerising… Seksik's portrait of Zweig's final months is dignified and tender' *Financial Times*